"So what makes you restless, Cole?"

He opened his mouth to deny the claim, then gritted his teeth.

"You once said you were looking to settle down, but you haven't yet. And send for your mother, but you haven't. And now you're dragging a pregnant mare across country—looking for the perfect spot?" She shook her head. "There is no such place."

Her perception stunned him. Just seven months ago, his ma had asked him how many criminals he needed to put behind bars before he was satisfied. Twenty? Fifty? A hundred?

Just one more. That had been his justification. But after arresting one outlaw, Cole would hear of another that needed to be stopped. And another.

With parted lips, she watched him. For the first time in his life, someone out-silenced him.

"Way past my bedtime." He was off the porch and halfway to the barn before he realized he hadn't said good-night.

However, it was the wisest thing to do. If he turned around and went back, he'd tell her things best kept secret. For now anyway.

Anna Zogg has long been fascinated by the West—ranch life, horses and the tough men and women who tamed it. Ever drawn to her Native American roots, she and her husband, John, reside in the heart of the West. Visit annazogg.com to learn more about her love of music, her eclectic taste in fiction and some very special children.

Books by Anna Zogg

Love Inspired Historical

The Marshal's Mission

ANNA ZOGG

The Marshal's Mission

HARLEQUIN® LOVE INSPIRED® HISTORICAL

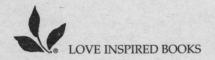

LOVE INSPIRED BOOKS

ISBN-13: 978-0-373-42525-9

The Marshal's Mission

www.Harlequin.com

Printed in U.S.A.

I will both lay me down in peace, and sleep: for Thou, Lord, only makest me dwell in safety.
—*Psalms* 4:8

To my dear friend and sister in the Lord,
Marilynn Rockelman.
Without you, this story might never have been told.

Chapter One

Wyoming Territory, 1882

Who is that?

Hand poised over a scoop of dried beans, Lenora Pritchard peered out her kitchen window. Across the ranch yard, a form ducked out of sight. Was that Toby? Her son had left an hour ago to look for his missing dog. Why was he skulking around the barn?

Wiping her hands on her apron, she stepped onto the porch and stared. Nothing. She was certain she saw someone slink around the building not two minutes before.

A sudden gust of chill wind whipped her long skirts. She shivered as she gripped the porch's column. Was rain coming? All afternoon the sky had been clear and beautiful.

As she looked upward, she gasped. A bank of ominous clouds rolled in from the north. Marching like an army, the mass devoured the warmth and light of the mid-April day. Many an unprepared traveler had died of exposure because of weather changes this time of year. Though her son wore his coat and hat, would they be enough to protect him in freezing temperatures?

"Toby!" The roaring wind swallowed her call. She ran down the steps and into the yard. It was then she spied a half-dozen chickens, pecking in the long grass alongside the house. They were supposed to be locked in the fenced-in area attached to the coop. How…?

Darting between the shed and barn, Lenora yelled for her son again. When she saw the mangled enclosure, she gulped. The small, wooden building leaned at a crazy angle, held somewhat upright by the attached lightweight fencing. Had the wind blown it over?

As though in answer, a blast of air snatched the combs from her hair and spun it like a tornado. A single splat of icy rain hit her skin. She had to get the chickens inside. *Now.*

"Toby," she called again. Her ten-year-old was nowhere in sight.

With the coop useless, the barn would have to do.

"Shoo. Shoo!" With arms spread, Lenora tried to herd the hens toward the open door. Cackling in alarm, they scattered in every direction other than the one she wanted. Her frustration rose to an impossible level. Why was her husband dead when she needed him most? Nothing like this ever happened while Amos lived.

After she managed to get a few chickens into the barn, she peered around the empty building. Had she imagined that lurking form?

"Ma!" Toby loped uphill from the direction of the stream, his green eyes wide. "I found Blister, but he—"

"Help me get the chickens inside," she panted.

"But, Ma…"

"Hurry." She bolted to find the rest.

The wind built, catching the birds' feathers and nearly toppling them. Dirt stung Lenora's face. A distant rumble of thunder warned of the impending downpour. Together she and Toby ushered the stragglers into the barn.

Out of breath, she counted those corralled in a corner stall. Thirteen. While the hens settled in one corner of the shadowy barn, the rooster strutted around his flock.

"Okay, Toby. Shut the door."

Leaning out, he yelled, "Blister! Come on, boy. Come on."

Lenora gnawed her lip. Would their dog pester the chickens? Blister usually ignored them. However, this arrangement would have to do. For now.

As the dog slunk inside, her mouth gaped. A tight rope wrapped around his neck and torso. Dirt caked him. And he looked skinny, like he hadn't eaten in the four days he'd been missing. Where had he been? Though he usually wandered, he never stayed out more than two.

"Bring him closer." She fumbled to light the lantern.

Amos had always kept one handy in the barn. And a shotgun. Out of sight from the entrance, the weapon rested on a crossbeam's pegs.

As her son pulled his dog into the circle of light, she hung the lantern on a nail.

"What in the world?" With her back to the barn's wall, she squatted to examine the dog. It appeared as if someone had lassoed Blister with a fine length of rope. A three-foot piece dangled, frayed in the middle as though he had tried to gnaw his way loose. But clearly someone had cut the end.

"This is what I was trying to tell ya, Ma." With his hand resting on his dog's head, Toby's gaze met hers. "Who did this?"

"I don't know." But even as she spoke, she knew Jeb Hackett could have. He hated their dog. "Let's get that rope off." The noose had rubbed Blister's skin raw in one spot. For several minutes, she worked at the knot in vain. The dog began to pant.

"I'll have to cut it." She was reaching for her knife when the sudden rattle of the barn door startled her. With a squeak of alarm, Lenora shot to her feet.

A man's silhouette filled the doorway. Arm gripping Blister, Toby swiveled his head.

Too frightened to move, she glanced at the gun hanging out of reach, then back at the faceless form.

"Didn't mean to scare you, ma'am." The man's deep voice sounded low, even apologetic. He stepped forward, sweeping off his hat in one fluid motion. "Wondering if I could spend the night here. Got a mare with foal. Bad storm's a'coming. Freezing rain."

As though punctuating his words, sleet clattered on the roof for several seconds. A rumble of thunder shook the barn.

She shivered from more than just the chill in the air. "I—I'd have to ask my husband. Up at the house."

"But, Ma," Toby protested. "He ain't—"

"Hush." She hardened her voice. "Don't interrupt."

Blister's panting filled her ears. She glanced at him. Why wasn't he barking at the stranger?

"I'd be much obliged, ma'am." The tall man nodded as he took a step closer.

"Go to the house, Toby." Lenora hoped her stern tone masked fear. Was this the man she had seen earlier? Prowling by the barn?

Obviously, he was in with Jeb Hackett. Was he trying to play on her sympathies? She saw right through his lame story of traveling with a pregnant mare. No fool did that in Wyoming Territory. Leastways not this time of year.

She tightened the muscles of her leg, assuring herself that her hidden knife was still strapped to her calf.

Because her son hadn't moved, Lenora grabbed the end of the dog's rope and spoke in a no-nonsense voice. "Tobias Joseph, do as I say."

"Yes'm." Toby sidled past the man and ducked out the door. Not until she heard the fading patter of his feet did she relax a fraction.

The stranger indicated Blister with a tilt of his head. "Looks like you've quite the task." Before she could respond, he tossed aside his hat and shrugged out of his slicker. A gun hung low on his hip. "Mind if I help?"

She raised her chin a notch. "What about your horses?"

"They can wait a few minutes."

As he strode toward her, she backed behind Blister. She glanced at her shotgun, now farther out of reach.

After turning up the lantern's flame, he knelt before Blister.

"Easy, boy," the stranger crooned as the dog growled low in his throat. "What's his name?" When Lenora didn't answer, he met her gaze.

In the lamp's light, the deep blue of his eyes gleamed. Sandy hair curled over a smooth, tanned forehead. Two or three days' growth of whiskers shadowed his face.

"B-Blister."

"Hey, Blister. Take it easy." The man held out a tentative hand. Panting, the dog turned his head away. "That's it. I won't hurt ya." Still on one knee, the man scooted nearer. "Appears as though someone lassoed him."

Her grip tightened on the rope. "I suppose."

If Jeb was responsible, she needed to play dumb. Blister always bristled and barked when he showed up. Since Amos's death, the dog had become more aggressive. Because of that, Jeb no longer dismounted. If he rode too close to the house, the dog would nip at his horse's heels.

Even if this man had no connection to Jeb, she planned to stick to her story. The sooner she barricaded herself in the house with Toby, the better.

Thunder boomed. A torrent of rain began to beat the roof like a pounding drum.

The stranger's eyes narrowed as though considering her. "Whoever did this likely dragged Blister in the middle of nowhere."

How could he know that?

"Tied him up and left him to die." Anger inflamed his rising voice. "Convenient way to get rid of a dog. You the one responsible?"

Lenora twitched. "What?"

"I asked if you did this." Pointing, he rose. "And are you hiding the truth from your son?"

"Get away from my ma." Toby's young voice rang as he stood by the barn door.

The man spun. When Lenora saw her husband's six-shooter in her son's hands, she gasped. She didn't realize he knew about the hidden pistol, tucked behind the mantel clock in the house.

With both thumbs, Toby struggled to cock the gun. "Did ya hear me?"

The stranger spread his hands. "Take it easy, son."

"Leave my ma alone."

Lenora's grip on the rope tightened. "Toby—"

"I mean no harm." The stranger took a step toward her son. "Either put the gun down. Or shoot me."

"Don't—don't hurt him." She panted the words, not sure whom she addressed. If her son injured this man, Jeb Hackett would accuse Toby of attempted murder and string him up in the nearest tree.

Was this what Jeb hoped? Have an excuse for him and his men to descend on her ranch? Ever since her arrival in Amos's buckboard twelve years ago, Jeb had never hid the fact that he had his eye on her.

The tall man blocked the way, standing between her and Toby. Arms still spread, he moved closer to her boy. "You pull a gun on someone, you best be prepared to use it."

"I'll kill you." Toby's voice rose as he aimed at the stranger's chest.

"I'm prepared to die," the man said in a maddening, unperturbed tone. "But are you prepared to be a killer?"

Face contorted, Toby's hands shook so much that Lenora feared he would accidentally pull the trigger.

Dear Lord, please don't let him.

Outside another thunderous rumble reverberated. The sound matched the frantic hammering of her heart.

"What's it to be, son?"

When Toby stiffened, the stranger swooped forward and grabbed the six-shooter. Before Lenora could blink, he released the hammer and emptied the bullets into his hand. Chest heaving, her son appeared more relieved than frightened.

Now what? The tall man fingered the shells. Measuring the distance to her shotgun, she commanded her paralyzed muscles to unlock.

"You did right." The stranger nodded to her boy. "It's a terrible burden to live with a man's death on your soul."

She stumbled forward and seized her gun. As soon as she released the rope, Blister sidled to Toby, positioning himself between the man and boy. She stared. The dog never acted like this. Why wasn't he bristling or growling?

The stranger barely glanced her way before tucking

the six-shooter into his belt. To Toby, he said, "I want you to bring my mare inside. She's gotta get out of the rain. Can you do that?"

Hesitating, her son shot a look her way.

Lenora gave one sharp nod.

His green eyes squinted up at the stranger. "Yessir."

"After that, see to my geldings. They'll be fine under the lean-to."

After another glance her way, Toby disappeared out the door. He secured it so his dog wouldn't follow.

Still wary, Lenora clenched her shotgun while the man pocketed the bullets.

He snapped his fingers at the dog. "Come here, Blister. Let's get that rope off you."

Head low, the dog slunk beside the man.

"Good boy." After the stranger pulled out a huge knife, he looked up and spoke to Lenora. "I'd feel a lot better if you quit pointing that barrel at me and helped."

Squelching her fear, she set aside her shotgun. After she crouched next to Blister, the man took her fingers and placed them on the dog. "Keep him quiet." His rough hand guided hers as together they stroked the dog. He spoke in a calm, mesmerizing voice. "That's it. You're doing good."

Something amazing happened to the dog. His drooping eyelids seemed to freeze into place. He stopped panting as though listening. Did he understand this stranger was there to help?

Lenora shifted her gaze from the dog to the man.

Though weathered by the sun, his face appeared to be kind. His smooth brow reflected the absence of worry or anger. Contemplative. Smile lines settled in gentle creases by his eyes and mouth. But clearly he wouldn't shirk from the tough things in life.

Not like her. Amos had always taken care of the bone setting, the chicken killing and the bloodletting while she hid in the house. Lenora had grown up a city girl with a gentlewoman's ways. Before her husband carried her to the untamed West, the most ghastly event she'd witnessed was the birthing of kittens.

Now that he was gone, an avalanche of needs pressed on her. She had to hang on a few more months until she could sell the ranch.

The stranger adjusted the dangling rope as though ascertaining the best place to cut. She held her breath as the gleaming knife poised over the dog's throat. With care, he sawed through the tough fibers. All of a sudden, they gave way.

"There." He pulled the remaining pieces off Blister before sheathing his blade. "Good boy." He patted the dog's head, then examined the fur. "T'appears he lost a little skin, but he should heal just fine." He felt along the torso while the dog licked his hand.

What had come over Blister? And herself? Ten minutes of her life had disappeared without her knowing. Unsteadily, she climbed to her feet and smoothed down her rumpled skirt.

In the corner of the barn, a blood bay mare waited. The horse nickered, the sound tender, welcoming. The barn door flew open.

A wet Toby came in, shaking off rain. "I'm all done, mister."

"You unsaddle my horse? And untie the other?"

"Yessir. Put your gear under the lean-to, so's it won't get any wetter."

"Many thanks." The tall man turned back to her. "If you wouldn't mind, I'll see to my horses now. And I'll pay for feed." A hint of a dimple appeared in one cheek. "Assuming that's okay with your husband."

Did he suspect no man was around to ask? She opened her mouth, but nothing came out. All she could manage was a nod.

After a two-fingered salute, he walked toward his mare.

"Blister!" Toby dived to his knees and hugged him. "He's going to be okay now, right, Ma?"

Her throat tightened. "I reckon so."

She studied the man across the barn as he wiped down his horse with an empty feed sack. Lowering her head, the mare rubbed against him in obvious affection. He certainly had a way with animals. And with her son. As Lenora recalled the feeling of his fingers on her hand, her skin tingled.

Amos had been dead only five months, and she was flustered by a stranger's kindness? What was wrong with her?

Loneliness. The long winter months with just her and Toby had affected her more than she wanted to admit.

Then she hardened her heart. No longer was she an impressionable sixteen-year-old who could be ensnared by a man's charisma. After she married Amos, she discovered he offered little else. She would never again fall for good looks or flattering speech.

As she watched the stranger tend to his horse, she determined that he had better not try charm on her or she would fill his hide with buckshot.

Chapter Two

"So are we friends now?" As US Marshal Jesse Cole settled his saddle in one corner of the barn, he spoke to the yellow dog.

With a grunt, Blister rested his head on his front paws like he was apologizing for his earlier hostility.

"'Bout time, after all I did for you."

Earlier that day, he had come across a howling and frantic animal, tangled in scrub pine in the middle of nowhere. The moment Cole cut him free, the dog took off in a dead run. That should have been the end of the story. But what if the rope snagged on something else? He had followed to make certain Blister reached safety. Foolish decision. In his worry for the dog, he had not stopped when his mare stumbled. Had she stepped in a hole?

Running his hands over Sheba's fetlock, Cole decided it felt a little swollen. Nothing broken, though.

He straightened as footsteps splashed toward the barn. The woman's son? The earlier torrent had died down. Now rain tapped the roof in a gentle staccato.

The door creaked open. "Hey, mister. Y'hungry?" Dark hair plastering his forehead, Toby stood just inside. He carried something wrapped in a towel, held close to his chest. Food?

Cole smoothed his hand over the mare's still-damp rump. "Tobias Joseph, right?"

"Yessir." The youngster's chest puffed up. "Named after my ma's pa."

When his gaze shot to Blister, he seemed to forget Cole. "Hey, boy. How're you doing?"

The dog's tail thumped on the dirt floor as the youngster loosened the cloth and dropped a meaty bone.

Cole grinned. His assumption that the towel-wrapped item was his meal proved unfounded. Or was it? Either way, he was glad he hadn't agreed to supper. The sooner he sacked out, the earlier he could get started in the morning. This ranch held too many a mystery—starting with the lassoed dog. Although Cole admired his gun-toting hostess, he had already spent too much time dwelling on the endearing way her hair fell across her cheek. And her lips, pursing in fabricated determination.

Did he believe her comment about her husband? Not in the least.

"There ya go, boy." Toby backed away. After grabbing the bone, the dog retreated to a corner. Despite the sleepy purr of the chickens, Blister kept a wary eye on them.

Cole studied the youngster who looked to be somewhere between nine and twelve. His lean frame took after his mother's. She appeared to have dark eyes whereas Toby's were light. Green? Difficult to tell in the shadowy barn. Likely the boy would sprout up and pass her in height, but his shoulders would never be broad. His pensive forehead mirrored the woman's gentle nature.

Cole cleared his throat. "I was named after my grandpa too."

Mouth puckering, the boy toed the straw at his feet.

"Ma said he died before I was born. Same time as my grandma. Back east a'ways."

"Sorry to hear that."

Stepping closer, he pointed at the mare. "D'ya mind my asking what kind of horse she is? Never seen a blood bay like her before."

"You got a sharp eye. Sheba's a Morgan. I'm hoping she's the beginning of a great line of horses."

"Wow." Without fear, the youngster approached the mare. He let her nose him before stroking her neck. "And she's pregnant?"

"Yes, but she's not far along. I expect she'll foal late August." Cole again questioned his decision to bring her with him. However, his mare was the perfect cover for his Wyoming Territory mission.

"She sure is a beaut." Toby studied her with a critical eye.

"What's different about her?"

The boy stepped back and scratched the top of his head. "Her muscles seem kinda bunched. And the arch in her neck is unlike others I've seen."

"Good. What else?"

He planted fists on his hips. "Her eyes have a look about 'em. I could almost tell what she's thinking." He stepped closer to rub her soft nose. "And she's good-natured. Not like Chuck and Midge's horse. She was always mean."

"Who're Chuck and Midge?"

"Our hired help. Well, not anymore. One day, they just up and left." The youngster ran his hand over the mare's shoulder. "I love her dark mane and tail."

Cole grinned at the boy's horse sense. Reminded him of his brother, for some reason.

"Sheba," Toby repeated, smoothing his hand across

her. He threw a glance over his shoulder. "So what's your name, mister?"

"You can call me Cole."

"Thanks, Mr. Cole."

"Nah, just Cole. Been that ever since I was your age." He tilted his head and studied the boy. Something seemed to be weighing him down. Cole knew he didn't have to pry. Folks volunteered all sorts of information if he remained quiet.

He didn't have long to wait.

"Thanks for helping Blister. He means the world to me."

"Glad to." He paused, yielding to his curiosity about the dog. "You give him that name?"

"Yep." The boy grinned. "A man in town didn't want him no more. 'Bout three years ago. Pa said I could have him, if I wanted. I had a blister on my hand that looked the same color as his fur. Seemed only natural to call him that."

"It's a good name." Cole leaned against the stall's column and crossed his arms. "Tell me, do you know how he ended up with a rope around his neck?"

Had someone tried to hang the dog? Somehow Blister had escaped, only to get tangled up in scrub pine.

Toby's mouth compressed. "Nope."

"Y'sure? I can't abide cruelty to animals."

The boy wouldn't meet his gaze as he stroked Sheba. Because his mother had schooled him about what to say? He managed a tight shrug. "Blister's always roaming. Ma thinks he wandered too far." He turned. "She would've cut the rope off him if you hadn't come along."

Should Cole ask about the boy's father?

When he had first arrived and banged on the door to the house, no one answered. After seeing only the woman and Toby in the barn, he concluded the boy's father was drunk, dead or absent. Which was it?

Given the woman's overreaction earlier, he settled on her being a widow. One way to find out for certain.

As Cole spread his bedroll, he chose his words with care. "Wouldn't your pa have helped?"

The youngster's expression grew stony, fingers tangling in Sheba's long mane. "I reckon."

So, he and his mother are alone.

No sense pushing the boy for the truth. Besides, it was none of Cole's business. By morning he would be on his way. He wanted to reach Silver Peaks before noon. After he found a place to stable his horses, he would check into a hotel and call it home for a spell. Should he reveal he was a US marshal to the town's sheriff? Cole again weighed his options. Best to get to town first and check out the lay of the land.

"Are your geldings Morgans too?" Toby climbed a stall's lower rung to rest his arms and chin on the stall's top board. "I couldn't tell for sure in the dark."

"Nope. They're not."

"They're pretty gentle too. Except one tried to bite me."

Cole chuckled as he settled against his saddle. "That would be Nips. Sorry I didn't warn you about him. I haven't been able to break that bad habit."

"And the other?"

"The sorrel's Rowdy. He can get his dander up pretty quick, but overall he's steady."

"Toby." The woman's voice called over the gentle patter of rain. "Toby, where are you?"

He ran to the door. "Coming, Ma." The youngster swiveled. "So are you coming up for supper, Cole? Ma saved over some stew from dinner."

"Nah, I'm more tired than hungry." Besides, he didn't like being beholden to them any more than he already was. A worry pebble had lodged in his gut. What about them troubled him?

Toby grinned, his expression betraying wisdom that exceeded his age. "Too bad. Ma's the best cook in Laramie County. And she makes a fearsome pie." He took off across the sodden yard.

When Cole's stomach growled in protest, he looked down at his concave abdomen. "Oh, hush." Jerky and hardtack would suit him just fine.

Before first light, he would hit the road and distance himself from this place. Nothing and no one would distract him from his mission.

"What?" Aghast, Lenora's grip tightened around the large serving spoon. "You *invited* him for supper?"

"I thought that's what you said."

"I told you to ask if he was hungry." If so, she would have sent Toby to the barn with a bowl of stew. She wasn't quite ready to have a stranger come into her house, no matter how friendly he had been.

"Don't matter." Her son rested an elbow on the table. "He said he was tired."

"*Doesn't* matter." She finished serving leftovers into his bowl. "Please don't use slang. You know I can't abide it."

"Yes'm." He leaned his head against his fist as he slumped in the chair. "Cole sure has some nice horses. Especially Sheba."

"Mr. Cole." She finished laying out the remainder of the meal.

"He said to call him Cole. Without the *mister*."

Lenora frowned.

"I'm sure, Ma."

"Very well. Since he insisted." She slid into the seat next to him. "Please don't slouch."

As her son straightened, he grimaced—displaying his thinking face. "Do you like Cole, Ma?"

The direct question took her aback. How much could she say to her ten-year-old? Though he sometimes acted grown up, she couldn't forget he was still a child.

"I like him just fine. But we can't forget he's a stranger." She stared at her hands, clenched in her lap. "And now that your pa's gone, we have to be cautious. That's all. Remember what we talked about?"

Toby fingered the spoon beside the bowl. "I s'pose."

The nearest town was located several hours away. No doubt her son was lonely. But she didn't want him to latch on to the first stranger who had ridden onto their ranch since Amos's death. Though something about Cole tugged at her to trust him, she resisted.

"Let's pray." After they clasped hands, Lenora bowed her head. "Thank You, Lord, for Your provision. May we truly be grateful." She paused, suppressing a barrage of anxiety-riddled requests. "Thank You for returning Blister. In Your Son's name. Amen."

"Amen." Toby scooped a large spoonful of food into his mouth.

Before she took three bites, he finished one bowlful. She served him more while he wolfed down a hunk of bread.

"I declare, you eat more than your pa…ever did." She smoothed his dark, damp hair, hoping he didn't notice her slip of the tongue.

Grinning, Toby ate two bites in quick succession. "After I'm done, can I go check on Blister?"

"I'd rather you didn't disturb our guest. He's probably sleeping by now."

Scraping the spoon across the bottom of the bowl, Toby frowned. "Think he'll stay, Ma?"

"Cole?"

"Yeah." Eyes hopeful, her son looked up.

Her cheeks warmed as she considered that possibility. "I expect he's on his way somewhere important. Probably be gone first light."

"Where?"

"I don't know. Maybe Oregon Territory. Or California. People are still crazy with gold fever."

"Couldn't you ask him to stay? Maybe hire him? Seein' as how Chuck and Midge are gone."

She took care answering, not wanting to raise his hopes. "I'd have to think on that some."

Should she confide to her son that she planned to sell the ranch? Frank Hopper, their nearest neighbor, had not yet responded to her proposition.

Toby scratched the top of his head with his knuckles. "Why do you think Chuck and Midge left? They didn't even say goodbye."

Debating how much to speculate about their sudden and secretive departure, Lenora chewed her lip. "I'm sure they had a good reason."

Last fall, Amos had begun building a small place for the couple. The frame of a building stood across the corral that was in the center of the yard. He'd even carved Midge one of his rocking chairs for which he was famous. Had Jeb Hackett bribed or threatened them? With them gone, she and Toby couldn't manage the ranch by themselves.

In silence, she and Toby finished their meal. The fire popped and crackled, the damp logs hissing. The sound reminded her she'd have to chop more wood soon. Their winter stacks were almost gone. As soon as Lenora entertained that worry, a dam broke of all their other needs. They not only had the garden to tend to, but the cow to milk, pig to slop and chickens to feed.

The weight of each concern grew heavier.

New seedlings were just poking their heads up through the rough soil. Had she planted too early? The freezing rain may have damaged them. Then their cow was drying up. Could they hold out until their other one calved? The pig was getting so big, he would have to be slaughtered soon. But which neighbor could she call on to help?

Staples were running low as well as their smoked pork and venison. She pushed aside the unpleasant thoughts of shooting, then gutting a deer. How could she process all the meat by herself? Toby, of course, would be a great help, but the two of them didn't have time to do everything.

She wouldn't even begin to consider the bigger needs of the ranch—the calves that had yet to be branded and castrated, the fences that needed mending and a host of other chores. After Chuck and Midge had disappeared, she reconciled herself to selling out while she could. Though she hated the thought of taking Toby away from his home, he would eventually adjust to city life. At least he would no longer be lonely.

Appetite gone, Lenora rose and scraped the remainder of her stew into the slop bowl. Her shoulders hunched as she sighed. "You can take this to Blister in the morning. And don't forget the pig."

Toby slipped his arm about her waist and leaned his cheek against her shoulder. My, but he was getting tall!

"It'll be okay, Ma. You'll see."

"I know." Her chest heaved as she considered moving away.

"I been praying every night that God would send help. Do you think He sent Cole?"

Had He?

"That'd be nice." When her voice cracked, she cleared her throat. "But let's not make plans until we find out what Cole intends to do."

Her son squeezed her waist before turning away to clear the table.

Later as she lay in bed, staring at the dark ceiling, she dared to whisper, "God...?" Her plea stuck in her throat.

How many times over the years had she begun a prayer, then stopped? Because she asked the same things over and over?

The nights Amos didn't return home, she fervently prayed it wasn't because he was thieving or gambling. When she smelled whiskey on his breath or cheap perfume on his clothes, she refused to let him kiss her. But no matter how hard she prayed, he never turned from his wicked path. He still rode with the outlaw gang.

As tears slipped down her temple, Lenora brushed them away. With a rueful heart, she thought of her husband buried in the backyard, a simple tombstone marking the spot. Under his coffin rested a satchel of stolen money.

That terrible and dark secret would remain entombed—not only with Amos, but in her heart.

As Lenora pulled the blanket higher, the same plaintive questions whispered in her mind. Why did *he* get shot robbing that bank? Why hadn't Jeb Hackett been killed instead?

Chapter Three

In the early-morning hours, the tramping of horse hooves sent a shaft of fear down Lenora's spine. She threw a towel over her biscuit dough and yanked open the door. A quick swipe of her fingers across her apron removed the dusting of flour. One hand fumbled for the barrel of her rifle, standing just inside the doorjamb.

Where was her son? She hoped he was still abed in the loft. When she saw who came up the road, she gulped. *Please let Toby stay asleep.*

No telling what her son would do when he saw Jeb Hackett.

He and two of his men thundered into the yard, their horses kicking clods of mud high into the air. Though the sun had not yet crested the horizon, rosy light painted the mountains to the west and the grassy plains in the south. Someone had let the chickens out already. Cole? The hens that had wandered to the rutted road scattered and squawked as the riders approached. Somewhere in the distance, Blister began to bark.

"Halloo." Jeb reined his dappled gray beside the corral in the middle of the yard.

"Morning." She wove a thread of politeness into her

tone as she remained in the open doorway. No sense irritating him unnecessarily. Another reason she kept the rifle out of sight.

"Well, ain't you a sight to behold." Jeb smirked. "Your hair is done up real purdy. Like you was expecting me."

Tightening her lips, she hoped it resembled a smile.

He pushed back his hat. "Looks to be a fine day, 'Nora. How about you come a'riding with me and the boys?"

Her jaw clenched. Over the last five years, he'd used that horrid nickname. Every time she'd bristled, Amos had told her it meant nothing. Jeb was merely teasing.

That only proved her husband had no backbone. Not only was he a thief and a liar, he fraternized with thieves and liars. Jeb Hackett was the biggest one of all.

No doubt many a woman had fallen for his handsome face, curly blond locks and icy blue eyes. His handlebar mustache might disguise the cruelty of his mouth, but nothing could hide the wickedness of his heart.

"You know I can't, Jeb. I've work to do."

"Well, now, we can solve that today." After swinging one leg over his horse's neck, he hooked his bent knee on the saddle horn. He leaned forward, resting an elbow on his leg. Like he had all the time in the world. "Since we're neighbors an' all. We could join our property and have a nice-sized ranch."

His friends guffawed, one punching the other in the arm.

"Frank Hopper is thinking of buying me out." She kept her tone level. "You paying more than him?"

"F'sure." Jeb grinned as he twisted the end of his mustache. "What I'm offering is better than money."

Her cheeks flamed. "Why you low-down—"

"Ma," Toby's voice called. "Ma!"

Lenora tensed as her son ran across the yard. How

much of the conversation had he heard? From inside the barn, Blister continued to bark up a storm.

With clenched fists, Toby stationed himself in front of her. She wrapped her arms over his shoulders and pulled him closer. If need be, she could yank her son into the house and slam the crossbar into place. There they would be safe.

For a little while at least.

"Well, well. If it isn't the little man himself." Jeb sneered. "I was wondering when the itty-bitty cockerel would show up. That your mangy dog I hear? Thought he'd be dead by now."

Toby stiffened. Jeb's buddies chortled.

Her mouth went dry. Was Jeb confirming that he'd lassoed Blister?

Her son spoke first. "What'd you want, Hackett?"

"Hain't you learned to speak respectful to your elders, boy? If you were mine, I'd teach you to hobble your tongue."

"Well, I *ain't* yours."

Jeb's scowl deepened.

"That's for certain," snickered one of his men. The two laughed. The instant their leader glared at them, they quieted.

Lenora took an unsteady breath. "I appreciate you all coming by. I'm sure you have to be on your way now."

Jeb squinted. "Not going to invite us in? Or feed us? We rode all this way to discuss some business."

Business? A chill nipped her bones. "I—I'm sorry. I don't have anything prepared."

"We can wait, can't we, boys? Y'see, I'm thinking you've been without a husband long enough, 'Nora. How 'bout you and me getting hitched?"

Marry Jeb? Her heart chugged to a stop as the sun burst over the horizon, spotlighting his handsome face.

"If I don't suit ya—and I don't see why not—you could always pick Charlie here. Or Dandyman. They'd do you right fine."

Identical leers passed over the faces of all three men.

Dear Lord... Lenora didn't know what to pray.

Instead of warming, the sunlight grew brittle, spearing the air with shards of yellow crystal. She could hear nothing but the whistling wind and the horses as they stamped and blew. Even the morning birds stopped their happy chirping. Her chest tightened until she feared she would faint.

The barn door slammed, drawing her attention.

Cole walked across the yard with studied nonchalance. Like he lived there.

Is he in with them? Lenora choked down the panic that rose in her throat as she shoved her son behind her.

Cole pulled up short as though surprised by the men on the other side of the corral. Thumbing back his hat's brim, he glanced between them. "G'morning."

Jeb's eyes squeezed to slits. "Who're you?"

He smiled as though oblivious to the man's rudeness. "The name's Cole."

Jeb shot Lenora a glance. "You didn't tell me about him."

"I…" She coughed and tried again. "I didn't have a chance."

As Cole rested a boot on the fence's lowest rung, the polished gun at his hip flashed in the morning light. "The lady's been kind enough to let me rest up my horses."

"Is that so?"

"My mare stepped in a hole yesterday. Hopin' she won't be lame long."

Irritation erupted on Jeb's face as though he had no idea how to respond to small talk.

Lenora piped up. "You can stay as long as you like, Mr. Cole."

Jaw jutting, Jeb glared at the stranger. "If you know what's good for you, you'll pack up the minute your horse recovers and move on."

Grinning, Cole leaned his left elbow on the fence. He casually hooked a right thumb in his belt, directly above the butt of his revolver. "Actually, I'm thinking of settling down around here. Maybe you could recommend a good location. I plan to breed horses. Fine stock."

Cole couldn't be in with the Hackett gang. Not with Jeb's open hostility.

Convulsively swallowing, Lenora glanced between the men. How would Cole fare if it came down to shooting? The sun at his back would be no advantage with one man against three. Besides, no one ever stood up to Jeb. His father, Eli Hackett, was rumored to own half of Laramie County. Time and again, his outlaw son had weaseled out of trouble. Regardless of how heinous his crimes, Jeb had not spent one night in jail.

He scowled at Cole. After swinging his leg back over his horse's head, he thrust his boot through the stirrup. "I ain't done with you yet, 'Nora." He jerked the reins and kicked his horse into a gallop.

Not until the men were out of sight did she sigh in relief.

With narrowed eyes, Cole stared after them, mouth flattened into a grim slash. Only when he looked in Lenora's direction did his expression relax. After a nod, he turned on his heel and headed back to the barn.

"I'll send Toby when breakfast is ready," she called.

Cole turned. "Sounds real good. I'll clean up." He squeezed the brim of his hat.

Still shaking, Lenora breathed a prayer of thanksgiving aloud. "Thank You, Lord."

Perhaps God *had* sent him.

Toby came from behind her. "Jeb Hackett won't come back, will he, Ma? Leastways not while Cole is here, right?"

"I hope not." She passed the palm of one hand across her heated neck.

What if Cole stayed for more than a couple of days? Would Jeb take that as a personal insult? He would think nothing of having ten of his cronies thrash any man who dared challenge him.

Perhaps it would be best if Cole left as soon as his horse recovered.

But what would happen the next time Jeb dropped by when she and Toby were alone?

"Meal was excellent. Thanks." Cole leaned back in his chair. When had he last eaten that well? He vowed to split a cord of wood in payment. The stack leaning against the house seemed low. It might last a mere week or two.

"Another biscuit? They're best fresh." The woman Hackett called Nora extended a plateful.

He declined with one hand as he patted his stomach with his other. "No, ma'am."

After Toby wiped his mouth with a napkin, he grinned. "Told ya Ma is the best cook in the county."

"Sorry I doubted it." Cole regretted skipping supper. Determined to be on his way, he had arisen long before sunup. However, his mare had limped just enough to warn him they shouldn't travel another mile until she rested a spell. In the predawn, Toby had surprised him by showing up at the barn. Together they had led the three horses into the back pasture. Sheba had rolled in the grass, apparently happy to stay put. The geldings had bucked and played.

If Cole had left at first light as planned, he would have missed the arrival of the three visitors. When Toby had whispered Jeb Hackett's name as they peered through the barn's slats, Cole couldn't believe his ears.

Hackett was the very man he sought.

And had Cole left, he would have forfeited this incredible meal. Fried potatoes, eggs, bacon, beans, fresh coffee and hot, flaky biscuits—what more could a man want?

Sighing again in pleasure, he contemplated a nap. Nah, he had wood splitting to do.

"Can I take this to Blister, Ma?" Toby scraped leftovers into the slop bowl.

"Certainly. But you keep feeding him like that, he'll get fat and lazy."

When Toby laughed, his adolescent voice cracked. She glanced at Cole, hand pressed to her chest as a soft smile graced her lips. Because her motherly heart swelled at the proof that her boy was growing into a man?

Grinning, Cole watched the youngster hasten out the door.

Once they were alone, he met Nora's dark eyes. A slow blush crept up her cheeks. Light coming from the window glanced off her honey-brown hair, braided and pinned up. She smoothed a stray strand into place.

Realizing he'd been staring, he cleared his throat. "Where'd you learn to cook like that?"

"Minneapolis. My aunt ran…well, *used* to run a restaurant. Before she moved back east. After my parents died. But that was a long time ago."

He considered the obvious discomfort in her tone.

"She's one…*incredible* teacher." He took care to mind his words. It had been a long while since he had spent time in the presence of a lady. This woman's gentle ways and modulated speech left no doubts about that.

How had she ended up in the wilds of Wyoming Territory without a husband? And why hadn't she yet remarried? Any man would count himself blessed to have a wife who was not only talented, but beautiful.

Truly modest, Nora inclined her head. Another mark of one gentle born.

He glanced around as he sipped his coffee. Nice house—not the usual soddy other homesteaders lived in. They sat in a large open room with two windows that faced north and west—so she could see who was coming up the road? Pegs lined a space by the door where he had hung his hat and coat. A pump poised above a large basin—another extravagance in a frontier home. Two chairs clustered by a fireplace. A built-in ladder lined the back wall, leading to a loft. Where Toby slept? The only other door likely led to a bedroom.

Dragging his gaze away, Cole focused on the blue and white dishes that lined the mantel. "My mother has bone china similar to yours. Where'd you get them?"

"My great-grandmother. She brought them from England."

He finished his coffee. "Nice to see so many in one piece." A few had chips, but most were intact.

"I used a scandalous amount of straw to pack them." She nodded to his plate. "Are you sure you've had enough to eat?"

"Yes, thanks again." When she rose, he jumped to his feet and grabbed some dishes. "If you don't mind, Nora, I'd like to repay your kindness by doing some chores."

White petticoats flashed as she spun to face him. He

didn't understand the sudden hostility that flared across her face. Before he could react, she grabbed her rifle and shoved it in his chest.

"Whoa." Cole froze.

What had he said? Or done? This was nothing like the night before when she had held her shotgun like a shield.

Knuckles white and mouth set, she looked every bit like she would use the rifle. "What did you call me?"

"I…" His mind went blank. "Nora, I believe."

"You're in with Jeb." Her teeth clenched. "Is he out-side now? Laughing?"

"Lady, I've no idea what you're talking about." Arms still extended, he clutched the dishes between tightening fingers and thumbs.

Fury seared her face. He sucked a sharp breath when she cocked the rifle.

"He better not've touched a hair on Toby's head, or I'll shoot you dead right here as you stand."

A she-bear with cubs would be less intimidating.

"Just a minute." Understanding dawned. "I heard Hackett call you Nora. Remember? Isn't that your name?"

Her eyes narrowed. The tension in the room eased not one bit.

Sweat beaded on his upper lip. If Toby came running back into the house and startled his mother, her twitch-ing trigger finger would end Cole's life.

She seemed to take even more careful aim. Like she would make certain not to miss.

"I'm setting these down now. Slow like." He lowered the plates to the table. With two fingers, he lifted his Colt Single Army Action revolver from its holster and set it on the table within her reach. "I'm unarmed. Except for a knife in my boot. The one I used on Blister last night."

Her gaze darted to his gun and back.

He again raised his hands and leaned away from the rifle's muzzle. "I had no idea what your name was. We never quite got around to introducing ourselves."

Chest heaving, her fingers tightened on the barrel.

He tried a different tack. "I got that pistol from my father who fought in the war between the states. Because of his exemplary courage, he was awarded this gun. Before Pa passed away, he gave it to me. That'd be two years ago next month."

"What about your mother? And if you lie…"

"She lives in Dodge City, Kansas. I regret to say I haven't visited her in about seven months. But I hope to see her after…" He stopped before saying, *After I put Hackett behind bars. Or swinging from a rope.* This woman would assume he was lying—trying to get into her good graces considering her obvious abhorrence of the man. Instead, Cole amended, "After I settle and start my horse ranch. I plan to send for my mother. Now that it's only me and her."

At least that was the whole truth. The woman's shoulders relaxed a fraction.

"Like I told your son last night, m'name's Cole. Ma called me that because…" He paused, confounded at his desire to confess. "Well, it *is* my family name. But when my little brother got shot…" He stopped yet again. Would the guilt continue to burn for the rest of his life? "Andrew was about your son's age. I was fourteen. That's when Ma stopped using my first name. I think it hurt too much to call only one son to dinner. So that's when I became just plain ol' Cole."

Her mouth quivered ever so slightly. The rifle in her hands lowered an inch. "How'd your brother get shot?"

Surprised at the question, he took a moment to answer. "We were playing behind the mercantile when we heard a ruckus. Andrew ran out of the alley to find out what was going on. A man was robbing the store, saw my brother out of the corner of his eye and fired." The painful memory stuck in his throat. "He died in my arms."

He relived the memory of sand soaking up his little brother's blood. The sickening smell of copper. The whole street, a river of red, still drowned Cole in nightmares.

That was the day he decided to become a lawman. He'd never looked back.

Until today, he had withheld the details from everyone. How had this woman so easily lulled him into sharing?

Mind apparently made up, she returned the gun to its spot by the door. She licked dry lips and spoke in a stilted voice. "My name is Lenora Pritchard." She lifted her chin. "As you've probably guessed, I don't have a husband. He died last year. Buried out back. Along with two of our babies that…" She tilted her head in the direction behind the house.

Cole clamped his jaw shut when he realized it hung open.

Lenora *Pritchard*?

It couldn't be…

Before he could stop himself, he asked, "Amos Pritchard was your husband?"

Her gaze snapped to his. "What if it was? What do you know about him?"

He slowly sank into a chair. "I heard tell of an Amos Pritchard in Cheyenne. At the Inter-Ocean Hotel. Quite a gambler if memory serves."

All true, although Cole only knew about him secondhand. Rumors abounded about the six-member gang—and Amos Pritchard was Hackett's right-hand man. Their leader was a gambler, cheat, liar and womanizer among other things.

Amos's widow had gone white. "He didn't cheat you, did he?"

"What?" Cole momentarily forgot what he'd told her. "No, ma'am. I don't gamble."

She frowned, clearly uncertain about what to do with his tale. Though Cole disliked hiding the truth, he decided to keep his US marshal status secret. For now. Perhaps remaining undercover while he ferreted out the secrets of the Hackett gang was the best plan.

If so, he might to live to tell the tale.

Two other lawmen had come to Wyoming Territory on the same mission. Neither had been heard from again. Cole had no intention of disappearing like them.

But Lenora…

He stared up at her. How had a lady like her gotten hooked up with a spineless flash in the pan like Amos Pritchard?

Before Cole got stupid and said too much, he rose, the heavy chair screeching on the smooth wooden floor. "If you'll excuse me." He brushed by her.

"Mr. Cole."

He turned.

His revolver rested in her open hand. Their eyes met. Obviously, she not only believed him, but trusted him enough to return his gun. Acknowledging her courage with a nod, he slid the weapon back into its holster.

"Much obliged." He grabbed his coat and hat before heading outside.

Of all God's green earth, how had Cole ended up in the camp of the very men he sought to bring to justice?

God had led him there. Had God also caused him to run across Blister in the middle of nowhere? And made his horse go lame? Cole wrestled with the uncomfortable possibility that God superintended his life.

The woodpile rested between the house and shed. Despite the nip in the April air, he peeled off his vest, and tossed hat and coat aside. After rolling up his sleeves, he grabbed the ax's handle.

So Amos Pritchard was dead—that fact unknown until today. From where Cole stood, he could see a tombstone rising from the spindly, brown grass behind the house. Two smaller markers rested nearby. What did Jeb Hackett want with his friend's widow? Did he seriously propose marriage? He didn't seem the marrying type. Lenora was a beautiful woman, to be sure, but she made it clear she wanted nothing to do with the likes of him.

After positioning a good-sized log on the chopping stump, Cole swung down and split it clean in two. He pulled his gloves from his waistband before chopping the wood into smaller pieces. No sense blistering up his hands.

What if God *had* led him there? If so, why not stay put on the ranch? Because of that morning's exchange, Hackett would believe Cole was looking for a place to settle—the perfect cover while he conducted his investigation into the gang. He had six months to put together his case before reporting in.

While at Lenora's ranch, he could pump her for information. If she proved reticent, Toby promised a wealth of knowledge—as long as Cole handled the youngster with care. The boy and his mother were tight. Which was good. Real good.

Cole split another log and a third, his muscles warming to the task. After being in the saddle for so many days, the activity felt great.

With Lenora and Toby alone on the ranch, they likely had an unending list of chores. After helping them with some critical tasks, Cole would move on. Ten days should be more than enough time to discharge his debt and gather the information he needed.

Not for one moment would he rest until he proved Jeb Hackett had robbed that Cheyenne bank five months ago.

Chapter Four

Later that afternoon, Lenora grabbed her sunbonnet and went to see what could be done about the chicken coop. The raised building still leaned at a crazy angle with only the attached framed wire fencing keeping it upright. Had the wind really blown it over? Amos had always promised to shore up the base but had never gotten around to it. Perhaps the flimsy wood had finally given way. The contorted fencing left gaps that would allow in predators.

But how to make it usable again? First things first—she needed to push the small coop upright. Then she could determine what else needed to be fixed.

"Toby?" Where had that son of hers got to? Earlier she'd heard him chatting with Cole while he chopped wood.

She shoved one corner of the building. It moved a little. She pushed harder, but it wouldn't budge any farther. Lenora yanked open the wobbly door and went inside the fenced enclosure.

The reason she couldn't right the building became obvious in a moment. One of the foundational posts was cracked. In the soft dirt under the coop, the partial outline of a boot print showed.

Lenora sucked in a breath.

The memory of the lurking form rushed at her. No doubt a cowboy boot made this print. And it had to have been before the torrent. Did Cole damage the coop?

Her breathing slowed as she wrestled with herself. What about that morning? The stories about his father, mother and brother? He looked like a gunfighter with the way he toted a gun on his hip, not a rancher.

"Was he lying?" She tightened the chin strap of her bonnet.

Their conversation after breakfast came back to her. Cole had referred to Jeb by his last name. She distinctly remembered calling the outlaw by his first. How had Cole known?

"You didn't tell me about him." Jeb's words came back to her. Not because he didn't know Cole, but because he hadn't expected to see him? If so, they had put on a good act for her.

What did Cole want?

Pressing her hand to her forehead, she determined to keep him at a distance. Be polite, but uninvolved. Make sure he understood she tolerated his presence, but not welcomed it. As soon as he figured out she wasn't an easy mark, he'd move on.

With that resolved, her gaze rested on the chicken coop. This had to be fixed, but how?

"Toby? Can you hear me?" she again called. Perhaps they could right it. Then she could secure the fencing and the coop would again be usable.

"Coming, Ma. Where are you?"

"By the coop."

Her son soon joined her. Alone.

"We need to push this upright."

Toby squinted at her in the bright sunlight. "Want me to get Cole to help?"

"No, we don't need him." Her sharp words cut the air.

Though he made a face, he said nothing more.

Together, they shoved against the building. It budged a little.

"Let's rock it. Maybe that'll do the trick."

The two of them pushed rhythmically. Slowly they gained more ground. The fractured board suddenly gave way with a loud *craack*, and the building shuddered into an upright position.

Lenora stepped back. Even with one post broken, the coop appeared stable. "Let's get some stakes to anchor the fencing."

Toby looked at her as if she were crazy. However, he said, "Yes'm," before heading to the shed. He soon returned with two hammers and an armful of stakes.

Thankfully Amos stored an abundance of tools and woodworking supplies.

She and Toby began the tedious task of pounding stakes into the ground. Soon perspiration trickled down her temples. Through her sunbonnet, the sun seared the back of her neck.

"Need some help?" Cole's voice interrupted the thumping of the hammers on wood.

"No, thank you." Lenora didn't bother to look up as she spoke.

"But, Ma…" Toby piped up.

She shot her son a warning glance. "We are perfectly able to take care of this ourselves." Rising, she faced Cole, aware of her heat-bruised cheeks and damp clothing. She spoke in a cool tone. "I appreciate your chopping wood. You've done more than enough."

His eyes narrowed.

A trickle of sweat ran down her throat. When his glance strayed that way, she swiped it with the back of her hand. She forced her breathing to slow. And not be the first to break the silence.

"Suit yourself." Cole turned on his heel.

"Ma," Toby's soft voice protested. "He ain't—"

"Isn't." She whacked the stake with extra force. Before continuing, she glanced around to make certain Cole wasn't nearby. "Tobias Joseph, we are not discussing Mr. Cole again. And I don't want to hear you asking him for help. Do you understand?"

He took a long time to respond. Too long. "Yes'm."

She caught her breath when he added, "But I'm still going to pray."

For a moment, she gaped at Toby's open defiance— the first time in his almost eleven years. He really was growing up fast.

Her eyes stung a little as she bent to her task. And it wasn't just because of perspiration.

"I brought your supper, Cole."

He looked up from his occupation to see Toby loitering by the barn door. Behind him hovered his faithful sidekick, Blister.

Was that how it was going to be? Though Cole had no idea what had come over Lenora earlier, he would oblige by staying out of her way. Her obvious dismissal—not only when he'd offered to help with the coop and now the glaring lack of a supper invitation—left him to conclude he was no longer wanted.

Had she rescinded that offer to stay as long as he liked?

"You want it?" Toby gripped the towel-covered tin pan. For a moment, he nearly declined. But that would be stupid. "Much obliged." He set aside the six-shooter he'd been cleaning. After Toby handed him the dish, he leaned against his saddle. "Want to join me?"

Now why had he said that? No doubt the boy's supper awaited him at the house.

However, Toby's face lit up. "Sure." He sat nearby. A crooked grin tugged at one corner of his mouth. "If we run out, I know where to get more."

Cole found himself grinning, as well. "Good. I'm hungrier than a hibernating bear." Chopping wood had fired his appetite. Or perhaps his temper because Lenora had been so cold?

Blister sat on his haunches nearby. Tongue lolling, he was already salivating for handouts.

Lenora had sent her son with a generous portion of beans. With the pan between them, they used the accompanying biscuits to scoop up the juices. Blister whimpered and pawed the air when Toby ignored him too long.

"Sorry, boy." He broke off a morsel and dabbed it in the mix before feeding his dog. "But that's it."

He gulped down the offering, then panted for more.

"No, go lay down." The boy frowned at his pet. "That's all you're getting."

After one grumble, the dog slumped onto his belly. However, his eyes continued to follow the boy's every move.

Cole grinned, glad that the dog was well loved. And trained.

Worry lines marking his forehead, Toby ate slowly. "Cole?" When he looked up, the boy continued. "You mad at Ma?"

His frankness took him aback. "Nope."

The boy licked his lips before continuing. "You say something to make *her* mad?"

His and Lenora's showdown in the morning flashed through his mind. That was done and settled, right? "Not that I know of."

Toby scrubbed a fist across the top of his head, a habit when he seemed puzzled. "I don't get why Ma is mad now." Food forgotten, he stared at nothing.

"Maybe she's just scared." The words surprised Cole.

A long-forgotten memory of his parents arguing came back to him. It had been late, and Cole was supposed to be asleep. Was he nine? Ten? He had crept partway down the stairs and listened to his mother accuse his father of uprooting their family because he would never be satisfied with their location.

When Cole had later asked his father about it, that's how he had answered—Ma was scared. Now as Cole looked back, he understood why. Pa's kind of discontent unsettled a woman.

An inevitable and more recent recollection followed. The last time Cole had seen his mother, she had accused him of that very thing—restlessness. Only he wasn't looking for the perfect place to settle like his pa, but trying to right the world of all its problems when that was none of his business.

"What's Ma scared of?" Toby's green eyes met his steadily.

"Not rightly certain." Finished with his food, Cole brushed off his hands. "Your pa's gone now. Maybe she's worried about how she will take care of you and the ranch. All by herself."

"But I can help."

"Yes, and you do. But she's facing some adult-sized chores. I know your ma's tough, but I think she's scared about getting it all done."

Half-eaten biscuit still in his hands, the boy seemed to ponder. "Do you reckon that's why she cries?"

Cole scratched his chin.

"I heard her last night. She didn't cry much though. Not like before." Toby's frown deepened. "When Pa was alive, she used to cry a lot. I reckon she was really scared, huh?"

At a loss how to answer, Cole said nothing. How much did Toby know about his father? No doubt how the boy felt about Hackett. From inside the barn, Cole had witnessed hostility in Toby's stance and tone of voice. But why such animosity toward the outlaw? Especially if Amos Pritchard and Hackett were so close?

"Toby." Lenora's voice reached them inside the building.

He ran to the door. "Be there in a sec, Ma." Toby shoved the rest of his food into his mouth while Cole gathered the towel and empty dish.

"Oh, let me get your pa's gun too." Earlier, he had taken time to show Toby the proper way to disassemble it for cleaning. However, the work on the chicken coop had interrupted them. "Give me a second, and you can take it up to the house." He quickly put the pieces back together.

The boy took the gun. "Can I ask you something, Cole?"

He grinned. "Sure." Toby was an endless well of questions.

"You believe in God, right?"

"Of course."

The youngster took a deep breath, face twisted in thought—another habit Cole had begun to notice. "I prayed that God would send someone to help Ma." He squinted up at Cole. "Do you think God sent you?"

Cole straightened with a jerk. Hadn't he himself wondered about God moving mountains? Only that morning?

"Can anyone know for certain the way God works?" He answered slowly, reluctant to agree but not willing to deflate the boy's faith.

Toby hung his head, but it wasn't in defeat. "If it ain't you, I guess I need to keep praying." Without another word, he turned on his heel.

For many minutes, Cole remained rooted in one spot. A dislike—of being dismissed—grated on him. Especially since Toby had unwittingly done it. The meaning seemed clear—if Cole wasn't the answer to the boy's prayer, then someone else would be.

Dismissed.

Toby wasn't the only one. Earlier, Lenora had done that very thing. And Cole had no doubts which way she leaned. She wanted him to clear out. The sooner, the better.

Because she was hiding something?

His gut told him no. Over his career, not many fooled him. He saw no deceit in Lenora Pritchard's deep brown eyes and clear forehead. How had she remained untainted by her outlaw husband? She was a delicate rose in a weed patch.

Maybe he should leave her in peace. She had enough to worry about. He didn't need to add to it.

"Maybe she's scared." His own words pounded against him as dusk descended on the land. It didn't take all his book learning to see that she had fallen behind with ranch work. Likely that would continue until she ended up clearing out. Then what would happen to her and Toby?

"It's not my business." The argument rose and escaped his lips as he stretched himself on his bedroll. But even as he spoke, the callousness grated on his soul. She was a woman in need. And he couldn't call himself a man if he tucked his tail and slunk off just because she was slightly hostile.

Very well, he'd stay. Whether Lenora liked it or not. The only way she would force him to leave was if she stuck the rifle's barrel in his chest and demanded he get off her land.

Chapter Five

Why was Cole still there? Lenora leaned forward to peer out the window as the sun peaked in the afternoon sky. With the barn door open, he leaned a hand on the doorjamb chatting with her son. Hadn't she made it clear that she did not want him around?

She had purposed to not invite him for breakfast— and hadn't allowed Toby to either. However, she later saw Cole down by the corral, fixing a wobbly fence post. When he replaced the broken post on the chicken coop, she waffled between being annoyed and grateful.

Why hadn't the man gotten the message?

Clearly ecstatic, Toby bubbled with enthusiasm as he explained how Cole had replaced the board without disturbing the chickens. That morning, the hens had laid two extra eggs, proof that their visitor had sweet-talked them.

Lenora tended to believe it had more to do with all the extra bugs they'd eaten when they'd run around the yard. And reveling in their temporary freedom.

Guilt had finally caused her to invite Cole for their noon meal with Toby the happy message bearer. Through-out dinner, she listened while they chatted about fishing. Her son promised to show Cole the best spot in the nearby stream.

After the meal and his solemn thanks, she sighed in relief. Maybe he would leave right after? Nope. She heard him chopping more wood. No doubt Toby kept him company.

Why wouldn't Cole go?

Later that afternoon as Lenora checked on her pie in the oven, she half listened to the staccato of feet, running across the yard. Toby called her name, sounding out of breath.

"Ma!"

Catching the note of panic in his voice, she straightened.

In another moment, his boots pounded up the porch stairs. He burst into the house.

One look at his face told her he was scared.

"What is it?"

"You gotta…" He paused, gulping air. "Something's wrong with Porky. You gotta come quick."

Their pregnant heifer?

After Porky's mother had died giving birth, Toby had adopted the skinny calf and hand raised her. Lenora couldn't remember exactly why he named her Porky, except he likely misunderstood Amos's explanation about the orphan. Had their son thought they were discussing a piglet? Somehow the name had stuck, a family joke. Now Porky was pregnant with her first calf.

Without waiting, Toby spun on his heel and disappeared out the door.

Lenora pulled the unfinished pie from the oven and moved pots from the stovetop. With her son already several yards ahead of her, she lifted her skirts and ran.

Behind the barn, a splotch of black and white huddled

in the middle of the pasture. Why was Porky lying down? Had Amos erred by breeding her last fall to their great big beast of a bull? She was not yet due.

When Lenora reached her, one look proved something was seriously wrong. Head extended, the heifer strained as though to push out her baby. One of its hooves briefly made an appearance before sliding out of sight. It was obvious she'd been trying to calve for hours. Most alarming was the sunken look in her eyes. She appeared exhausted.

We can't let her die. Toby's heart would break.

"Let's get her up." Lenora grabbed the rope halter, one Toby had braided.

While she tugged, her son pushed on Porky's rump and yelled. Nothing. After several halfhearted tries, she slumped back into the soft grass. Again, she strained to push out her calf. Again, her ribcage heaved as she failed.

For several minutes, Lenora paced, at a loss about what to do.

"Is she gonna die, Ma?" Toby's young face screwed up with fright.

"I don't know, son." Another moment passed until she made up her mind.

Tamping down revulsion, she unbuttoned and pushed up her sleeves. She had witnessed a cat giving birth—this situation couldn't be much different. And she herself had brought three babies into the world, although Toby was the only one who had lived. After getting to her knees, she felt inside the birth canal, trying to determine why the calf couldn't arrive on its own.

Hands slick with birthing fluid, she touched a small foot and leg inside its mother. Calves were supposed to come hooves first, followed by the head. She should be able to feel the soft flesh of the muzzle. Why not?

No matter. Lenora grasped the hoof and pulled while

Porky strained. The leg made it out a little farther but, as soon as the contraction passed, it disappeared back into its mother. For countless minutes, she pulled. Porky strained with each contraction but failed to deliver her calf. Confounded, Lenora rose. Shoulders cramping, she wiped her hands on her apron.

The nearest ranch was Jeb Hackett's. No way would she ask him for help. Frank Hopper's homestead was six miles distant, but the afternoon waned. Besides, by the time Toby rode there and back—assuming he could even find Mr. Hopper on his acreage—Porky could be dead. The next closest neighbor was too far away.

"Do you think Cole could help?" Toby's lips pressed together, as though he feared how she would respond.

Would Cole even want to? After the way she'd treated him?

She had heard him chopping more wood, but after a couple hours he disappeared. How could she even ask him for a favor?

She stared again at Porky, the last shreds of pride fluttering away. This situation was beyond her. Again. But anything was better than Toby's pet dying.

"Go see if you can find him. Ask him…" She paused to reword her request. "Tell him that *I'm* asking for his help. Please."

Toby took off like a shot.

While she waited, she patted Porky's neck. "It'll be okay, girl."

Head sinking lower, the animal appeared to have given up.

It seemed a week passed before Lenora saw two forms appear around the side of the barn. Cole broke into a trot with Toby hard on his heels.

"Thank you for coming." She sounded out of breath

though she had done nothing but wait. While Cole watched the heifer succumb to another contraction, she explained what she knew. When she heard herself babbling about how important Porky was to them, she bit her lip. Cole appeared to pay no attention.

Would he deride her for caring so much for an animal? Or tell them this was their problem and walk away?

Without a word, he knelt to slide his palm across Porky's bulging belly. His frown deepened as he muttered, "This isn't good."

Like Lenora, he rolled up one sleeve and reached inside the birth canal.

Less than a minute later, he rose. "Calf's the wrong direction."

"A breech?" A wave of terror washed over her. She pressed a hand against her throat as she fought the sudden faintness that gripped her. Almost three years before, she had lost a baby because he was breech. And nearly her own life.

The memory of her tiny boy, skin ashen, still brought tears to her eyes. He had looked like a miniature of Toby with fine, dark hair. After Amos had put the baby in her arms, she had wept uncontrollably. Lenora remembered little of the passing days while she had mourned the loss of Baby Amos. A tiny marker in the backyard stood as a silent sentinel for the infant who never had a chance to live.

Cole's gaze met hers steadily—the first time since he had joined her in the pasture. With the late-afternoon sun beating down on them, the blue of his eyes appeared all the more intense.

"I could try to shift the calf." He glanced up into the fading light. "But we don't have a lot of time."

"Couldn't we take her to the barn?" Toby asked.

"She's pretty weak." Cole shook his head. "Doubt we could get her to her feet at this point. But out here, she'd be helpless with the…" He broke off when Lenora began to twist the apron between her hands.

Because of coyotes? Or a mountain lion?

Please, please*, do something.*

As though she had pleaded aloud, he stripped off his vest and shirt. He tossed them aside. At first he was kneeling, then lying flat on the ground, toes digging into the grass for leverage. Was he trying to swivel the calf? Porky didn't help as she labored against him.

After several minutes, Cole was panting hard. "Just a little…" He grunted as his hold apparently slipped. Finally, he sat back on his heels. Chest heaving, he seemed to consider the options. He peered at Lenora. "Are you up for helping?"

"Anything. Just tell me what to do."

He turned to her son. "Go fetch rope, the finest you have. Several lengths. Check my gear for some if you don't have any."

"Yessir." Toby again raced across the pasture.

Cole ran his knuckles under his chin. "I'm going to try to slip a rope around the front hoof. Both, if possible. Then I'll push against the calf while you pull the rope. Can you do that?"

She nodded.

"I gotta warn ya—this may not work. Could tear up her insides. Or break the calf's neck."

"We have to do *some*thing. I can't just…" She waved toward Porky.

"Worst case, we'll lose 'em both." His cheek muscle flexed as he rose. "But there is another option."

She waited.

"I could cut her open. Save the calf. Maybe."

Lenora squeezed her eyes shut at the thought.

"That'd be the last resort. I'd wait until you were up at the house. Toby and I'd handle everything."

"Mr. Cole. *Cole*," she amended, injecting firmness into her voice. "I trust you'll do what you can. And I thank you for your help. No matter what happens."

He seemed to size up her words. After a single nod, he squatted by Porky. "She's looking mighty tired. I hope…" He rested a hand on the animal's rump.

Her son soon returned with a length of rope.

"Toby, you're up front. Lenora, stand behind me."

The youngster grabbed Porky's halter while she positioned herself. She wrapped one end of the rope around her wrist while Cole reached inside the birth canal with the other, a small loop tied in place. After some maneuvering, he panted for Lenora to gently pull.

"I got one hoof." He felt around inside the heifer. "Pull a little harder. Head feels like it's coming around. Gently. Yes, that's it."

After a few moments, he reached in the birth canal with the other end of the rope. This one gave him more trouble, but finally he grunted in relief. "Got it." As he lay flat on his stomach, Cole twisted his head to look back at her. "Keep steady pressure on both lines. Don't pull too hard. Don't jerk."

"I'm ready." Positioned inside the circle of rope, Lenora kept it taut.

"Toby, you're doing great."

Her son took a firmer grip on the halter.

"Lenora, lean your weight on those lines a little more. Perfect." Digging his boots into the soil, he rasped as Porky strained against him. "More pressure."

With the rope around her waist, she was nearly leaning backward. Cole seemed to be pushing as hard as he could to shift the calf. Porky strained while Toby stood spread-eagled at her head.

"That's it, Lenora." Cole grappled with the slick line. "Harder."

Rope cutting into her, she groaned. One moment she was leaning back with nearly her full weight, the next toppling head over heels as Porky gave a huge bellow. With a gush of birthing fluid, a small form slid from its mother.

Lenora staggered to her feet as Cole untied the calf's hooves.

"A heifer." He met Lenora's gaze, mouth tight. The little baby lay unmoving, a small heap of slick, black hair.

Before she could entreat him to do something, he was already on one knee, clearing the mouth and blowing into her nostrils. He thumped the calf's rib cage and rolled her to her chest several times. After endless moments, the baby coughed and shook her head.

Cole grinned at Lenora. "Looks like she's gonna make it."

Throat tight, she merely nodded.

"What about Porky?" Toby piped up.

The new mama appeared exhausted, head hanging low, nose nearly touching the ground.

Without answering, Cole dragged the newborn under Porky's nose. She seemed not to care. Struggling to hold up her wobbly head, the calf gave a sharp bawl. As though awakened in an instant, Porky snuffed at the twitching form. In minutes, she was making low sounds in her throat as she cleaned her baby with a long tongue.

Clutching her hands to her chest, Lenora released several pent-up breaths as she watched the miracle of a new mother with her calf. Embarrassed when she caught Cole staring at her, she brushed a tear off her cheek.

Dusk had begun to settle on the landscape, but enough daylight remained for her to see Cole's mud-streaked chest. She knew she, too, must look a fright, but she didn't care. When their gazes met, she smiled.

"You did good. Real good." The warmth of his approval beamed from his nod and crooked grin.

"Thank you." She could barely get the words out.

When the calf fought to stand on unsteady legs, Porky staggered upward. As she licked the stiff black hair, she knocked the calf over several times. Lenora made a sympathetic sound when the newborn toppled yet again.

"Glad we got her out in time." Cole pointed to the darkening horizon. "Daylight'll be gone sooner than we think."

Purple streaked the sky. The deep color reminded her of…

"My pie," she blurted. Had she left it in the oven? She couldn't recall. By now it would be burned to a crisp.

"Go on to the house." Cole indicated the direction with his head. "Toby and I'll make sure these two get settled in the barn."

Lenora bolted. When she reached the porch, she tossed aside her filthy apron before going inside.

All her cooking was as she had left it. She blew out a breath of relief. Now she recalled taking the pie out and the pans off the stove. After washing her hands, she stoked the fire. A glance in her bedroom's mirror confirmed she looked a sight. Dirt smeared her face while her hair streamed across her shoulders.

Before Cole and Toby arrived, she changed out of her dress and washed herself with cold water. She didn't bother trying to fix her hair beyond raking fingers through the tangles and tying it with a loose ribbon.

Was her partially baked pie still edible? Back in the

kitchen, she assessed the gooey crust, soaked with the juices of the wild berries. Perhaps if she heated the oven hotter than usual and rebaked it, the pie could be rescued.

Two sets of footsteps on the porch alerted her the men had arrived. Toby entered first, grinning while Cole remained by the door.

"Porky and calf are safe in the barn. I'll keep an eye on them tonight." Cole stood just inside, fingers gripping the handle. His shirt and vest were back on, but she could see a streak of filth across his neck that disappeared under one button. "Thought I'd let you know before I bed down for the night."

"You're staying for supper, aren't you?" She bit her lip at how eager she sounded.

He hesitated a moment. "Don't want to be any trouble."

"You aren't. Just cold beans and bread."

Still, he appeared to vacillate.

Toby glanced between them. "I'll go wash up, Ma."

After her son went to the outside basin, Lenora spoke. "Cole, I—"

"You don't need to—"

They both stopped.

He tilted his head. "Ladies first."

After taking a deep breath, she again started. "I wanted to thank you."

"I believe you already did that in the pasture."

"Yes, but…" She paused, aware of the heat that singed her cheeks. "But I needed to repeat it. You didn't owe us…*me* any favors. Not after the way I—"

"Say no more." He held up a hand.

"Please, allow me to apologize." She took a deep breath. "I'm sorry. Truly."

Though she still didn't know how the coop had been

damaged, she hoped it wasn't because of him. She didn't want it to be.

Lord, please don't let me be wrong about Cole.

She took a quick breath. "And my earlier offer still stands. Feel free to stay as long as you like."

Head tilted, he seemed to contemplate her words. "I'd be pleased to accept, Lenora. As long as you don't mind my doing some chores in exchange." He turned, but stopped and again faced her. "I'll be back after I wash up."

He disappeared into the dusk. Heavy boots tromped across the porch and down the steps. She pressed cool hands against her cheeks. When Toby burst into the room once more, she swiveled so he wouldn't see her face.

He began setting the table. For three.

"Come up with a name for the calf yet?" She strove to keep her tone light.

"I was thinking Coal. On account of her having no white markings at all."

Pondering how to voice her concern, Lenora chewed her lip. "Shouldn't you check with Cole first? He might not like having a calf named after him."

"Already did." Toby smiled up in her eyes. "He laughed, Ma. Told me it was a grand name."

Lenora smoothed her son's hair. "Then I guess it's settled. Coal is perfect."

Long after their guest continued on his way to his destination, they would have something by which to remember him.

Then the thought of Cole's leaving struck her. It would be hard to see him go. And not just because he was useful around the ranch.

Then she shook herself. In a few short months she

planned to leave Wyoming Territory. What about Cole? He seemed to be traveling west. Perhaps she needed to consider going that direction too.

Chapter Six

As he relaxed in his chair after the meal, Cole watched Lenora and Toby. With supper bedded down, he felt no hurry to follow suit.

"Okay, young man." She smiled at her son. "You are done with arithmetic for the night."

"Hurray." Toby stood up to gather his slate.

"But not with your spelling."

With a groan, he slumped.

Trying to squelch his amusement, Cole slouched in a chair, one foot extended in front of him. Lenora gave her son a list of words. Jamming the heel of his hand against his forehead, Toby sighed. He bent over his work, mouth puckered in frustration.

Just like me when I was his age.

"That is misspelled." She pointed to his slate. "What is the rule about *I* and *E*?"

"I don't know." Her son's tone betrayed his exasperation.

Lenora's eyebrows rose as she waited.

"Is that the '*I* before *E*, except after *C*' rule?" Cole volunteered.

She threw him a mock glare. "Shh. No helping."

"You did. A couple times already."

"That's because I'm the teacher." She turned back to Toby. "A few more words and we'll have dessert."

"Are we having *p-e-i*?" Cole inserted.

Lenora swiveled, jaw thrust in mock irritation. "Keep that up, mister, and you won't get any."

Grinning, Toby's eyes met Cole's.

"Good, because I'd rather have *p-i-e*." He rose to pour himself another cup of coffee. That also gave him an excuse to look at the pastry, cooling on the sideboard. Though Lenora had fussed that the dessert was practically ruined, it still looked good enough to eat. What had Toby said about her pies? They were fearsome?

Cole would soon find out. Turning, he leaned against the sideboard as he watched mother and son. What a pair they made.

A memory—of his ma and Andrew—flashed through his mind. His brother had been working on spelling too. Because they had relocated so much, Ma always had them do their book learning at home. And she was a strict teacher. This one time, Andrew had squawked about how unfair it was that Cole didn't have to do spelling anymore. Their mother explained that was because he was three years older. And soon enough he would be doing his own work.

Then Cole remembered. That was the night before Andrew died.

Lenora's eyes met his. "Having second thoughts?"

"S'cuse me?" He straightened with a jerk. It wasn't often he allowed himself the luxury of losing himself in memories.

"About the pie." She nodded at the pastry. "I know it looks terrible, but I'm hoping it tastes better than it appears."

He shoved away his recollections. "So far, I haven't been disappointed by anything you've made. See no reason to start now."

Smiling, she turned to study her son's spelling.

"That one is right." She pointed to Toby's slate. "What about that one?"

Her son growled before erasing his work and trying again. "Can this be the last word, Ma? Please?"

"Of course." She kissed the top of his head before approaching the sideboard.

As she pulled the pie closer to cut it, Cole scooted out of the way.

"No, I meant can this be my last spelling word *forever*?" Toby glanced at Cole, then his mother. "I don't need any more spelling or arithmetic. I'm almost eleven."

"Age has nothing to do with learning," she answered in a serene voice as she dished up generous portions.

When Toby still didn't appear convinced, Cole added his two bits. "Almost eleven? When does this happen?"

"Next month."

"I mean how many days?"

"It'll be in…" The youngster's forehead wrinkled, and his lips moved as he calculated.

Cole again took his seat as Lenora set a hunk of pie in front of him. Glancing up, he caught her grin before she smoothed it out of existence. Because she knew why he was asking Toby the date?

Her son finally resorted to counting on his fingers. "Seventeen—no, eighteen days."

"See there." Cole grabbed his fork. "Your arithmetic skills just came in handy."

The youngster glanced their way with narrowed eyes. Like he knew his mother and Cole were ganging up on him?

"Okay, put your homework away and let's have pie." She set his piece down.

It didn't take long for Toby to do as he was told. They both dived into the tart dessert. After the first bite, Cole gave Lenora a thumbs-up as it simultaneously melted in his mouth and made it pucker. She smiled and took a delicate forkful. Mindful of his manners, he forced himself to eat slowly. Somehow, he got the feeling that she preferred good deportment.

Again, just like his ma. Once upon a time, he recalled her threatening the three men in her family with no dinner if they acted like pigs diving into their slop.

He considered. Why so many memories of Andrew lately? For sixteen years Cole had been successful in suppressing them. With the remembrances came the uncomfortable feeling that he was shirking his duty—the whole reason he had come to Wyoming Territory. Because he hadn't been more aggressive about pursuing the Jeb Hackett gang?

Truth was, Cole liked it there. It would be easy to set down the burden of his life's mission for a spell.

"Hey, Cole." In the warm glow of the lantern light, Toby's mouth was stained red from the pie's berries. "I was thinking about Sheba."

"Oh?" He smacked his lips.

"If she has a filly, you should name her Queen." The youngster grinned at him. "You know, the Queen of Sheba?"

Lenora and Cole both chuckled.

"I'll keep that in mind." The youngster certainly had a knack for naming critters.

In no time, Toby finished his pie. More than once, he rubbed his eyes, his dark, tousled hair falling over his forehead. Cole noticed that the boy had failed to get all the grime from behind his ears.

Had Andrew once been like that? In Toby, Cole felt like he was seeing a portion of his little brother's life that he had missed. An odd longing to see the boy grow up echoed through him.

But Lenora…

The comely brunette reminded him of a path that he had chosen not to pursue so that he could become a lawman. When she laid a gentle hand on her son's shoulder, Cole couldn't help his thoughts. What would it feel like to have her caress his shoulder? Or impulsively hug him? When she looked at Cole, her soft smile did something funny to his heart.

He abruptly rose. "Thanks for the pie."

Two sets of round eyes gazed at him.

Before Lenora asked, he volunteered, "Been a long day. I want to get an early start tomorrow."

She blinked as though she'd not heard him correctly.

I need to leave.

Forget the ten days he'd promised himself to stay. He should pack up and move on. Regardless of his reasoning though, that would be wrong. Especially since Lenora needed help. But what about the investigation? The accusation pounded him. He should find another spot—less entangling—from which to investigate the Hackett gang.

How could staying *and* going both be the right thing to do?

"We usually finish the evening off with Bible reading and prayer." Lenora's lovely voice soothed his rising tension. "You're welcome to stay. If you like."

"Some other time perhaps." He edged to the door.

"Oh. Cole?"

He was already halfway out when her words stopped him.

"Thank you again for saving Porky." She smiled as she added, "And Coal."

He gripped the door so hard his fingers stung. "You're welcome." He dragged his gaze away from the endearing scene.

"Good night, Cole," Toby called. "See ya in the morning."

With more force than he intended, he shut the door.

As he strode toward the barn, his mission kept pounding in his head. He was there to solve the mystery of the Cheyenne bank robbery, prove Jeb Hackett's guilt and arrest not only him, but his gang. They had absconded with nearly twenty-one thousand dollars. Not one bill had been recovered.

What would Lenora's reaction be when she found out who he was and why he was there? Cole slumped down on his bedroll and pulled off his boots. No doubt she would be pleased to see Hackett behind bars. But how would she feel about Cole not telling her he was a US marshal?

She'd think I was a liar. Just like her lying, thieving husband.

Cole pressed his forearm to his eyes as though to blot out his thoughts. Later, he could explain why he didn't come right out and tell her. The hurt on her face materialized in his imagination.

But why should he care how Lenora felt?

As he flopped to his side, he yanked a blanket over his body. He shouldn't be worried about her emotions.

Even so, he admitted that he did care. Perhaps a little too much.

He came back.

After Lenora had risen early, she saw from the open barn door that Cole had left. Yet a couple hours later, he rode back into the yard, a duck carcass in hand. He'd gone hunting? Or had that merely been an excuse for his return?

As she sat on the porch doing some mending, she watched him smack barbed wire with the side of the pliers. Cole moved to the next spot in the fence that needed repairing and repeated the procedure with quick ease.

Like he'd been doing it his whole life. Well, perhaps he had.

Many times she was tempted to ask him if he had been skulking around the barn several days back. He couldn't have been the one who broke the chicken coop. But what did she really know about him? He could be an outlaw, hiding out on her ranch.

But better him than Jeb Hackett.

Since Cole had ensconced himself there, Jeb hadn't returned. And she wanted to keep it that way. Every day, she expected the outlaw to show up and do some unspeakable evil. Or force her to marry him or one of his buddies.

She recalled the last time Amos had invited Jeb for dinner, her protests unheeded. The way he had addressed her with that despicable nickname in a sneering, condescending way made her stomach clench even now. When she had caught him openly staring, he had not bothered to avert his gaze. Like he owned her. She shivered as her imagination summoned a man-sized reptile, paralyzing her with a chilling stare.

Pushing unpleasant memories away, she concentrated on the man across the yard while she rocked and sewed. Cole had repaired several wobbly fence posts, fixed the chicken coop's mesh, replaced several boards in the stalls, and who knew what else. Earlier he'd told her that he planned to repair the house's roof before it sprung a leak during the next heavy rainfall. He pointed out several shingles that appeared loose.

But first, he wanted to finish the barbed-wire fencing around part of the yard to keep roaming cattle from trampling her garden. He asked her if she planned to fence off all her land. Last year, Amos had mentioned that as well, but had never gotten around to it. A lot of ranchers and farmers were doing that since the open ranges were becoming more and more overgrazed.

Perhaps she should buy more fencing materials.

Then she drew herself up short yet again. In a month or two, she hoped that fencing wouldn't be her problem, but Frank Hopper's, her neighbor. He said he would give her an answer by May about whether or not he would buy her ranch. Well, it was pert near May, and she had heard nothing. Had he decided against it, but neglected to tell her?

Her gaze strayed again to Cole. What if he stayed? The three of them could handle the ranch's workload at least until the fall when she could sell off cattle. With the money, she could hire some reliable help. Did she dare ask?

I want him to stay. Lord help me, I don't want him to go.

When he approached the porch, she bent over her darning, pretending that she hadn't spent near an hour staring at his strong back and broad shoulders. When he cleared his throat to get her attention, heat climbed into her cheeks.

"How're you doing?" She looked everywhere but into his deep blue eyes. Or at the dimple that creased one cheek when he smiled.

"Good." He tossed his hat onto the straight-back chair

on the other end of the porch. "I got a good start on re-pairing the fences."

"Sweet of you to help out. Are you nearly finished?"

"Yep. Only about ten thousand miles or so to go."

"That—that sounds great." She stared past his head and rubbed her ear, nearly jabbing herself with her darning needle.

His grin deepened, as though aware of the reason for her consternation.

Ducking her head, she drew her mending more closely to her face. This repair would require a longer needle than the one she'd been using. She wove the shorter one through her shirt's collar to keep it handy.

"I was wondering," Cole began.

"Hmm?" She squinted at the hole in Toby's sock. Land sakes, that boy could wear them out faster than she could fix them.

"My glove. Got a bit of a tear. Mind sewing it? Would make the fence fixing a little gentler on my hand."

Tempted to chide him, the teasing died in her throat when she saw blood by the jagged hole. "Oh." She bolted up, dropping the sock and dumping her sewing basket. Her spool of thread bounded away, unraveling at the speed of lightning. Scissors clattered and other items scattered. Cole bent about the same time, barely avoiding hitting her head with his.

When Lenora overcompensated, she staggered and ended up falling against him. "I beg your—"

"My fault. Sorry." He grabbed her arms until she stood upright.

For a moment, their faces were mere inches apart.

Cole straightened and stepped back. After scratching his chin, he pointed. "You sit. I'll get this."

"But your hand…"

"I'm sorry. I should've known you don't like the sight of blood."

"It's not so much that, it's just that *you're* bleeding." As soon as she spoke, she clenched her hands and pressed them against her skirt. "What I meant to say—" she spoke with care "—is that you were injured doing me a favor."

He grinned and held up his palm. "This is hardly an injury."

Her disquiet grew. No matter what she said, it was wrong.

Finally she gathered her wits. "Well, you should have made a bigger deal of it. When Toby gets hurt, he hollers until I promise him an extra piece of pie."

Cole threw back his head and laughed. "I'll have to remember that."

"In the meantime…" She hastened into the house. "I have some salve that'll help."

He pulled on a sandy-colored curl above his forehead as though he were using that instead of his missing hat to salute her. "Much obliged."

Where was that salve? She grabbed a jar off a shelf in the kitchen area. "It'd heal faster if you wash your hands before I put this on."

He did as she bade, using a rough rectangle of soap and wiping his hands on a small towel.

After scooping out the creamy ointment with one finger, she cradled his hand and pulled it to her chest. Barbed wire had caught and torn the flesh in the meaty part of his thumb. It had to hurt. She got a better grip, preparing to apply the salve.

Suddenly realizing this wasn't Toby, she jerked back. Cole didn't comment about her abrupt movement. With his strong hand resting on hers, she rubbed the healing concoction deep into his skin.

They stood so close, she could feel his warm breath on her cheek. Her heart began to hammer. Did she imagine it or did his breath quicken too?

"There." She coughed to clear her throat. Somehow she managed to turn and tighten the lid on the jar without meeting his gaze. Or breaking anything.

"Ow!" His sudden yell made her jump.

She spun. "What's wrong?"

Grinning, he held up his hand. "You said I might get an extra piece of pie if I hollered. Better late than never?"

Lenora grabbed the towel he'd used and flung the balled-up material at him.

Catching it, he merely laughed, the sound somehow making his blue eyes deepen in color. She lost the war to keep from grinning back at him.

It felt like forever to say something. Finally she found her tongue. "Break time's over. Get back to work, mister."

"Anything you say, Lenora."

She sucked in a slow breath, pleased to hear him call her by name. The way he drawled out the second syllable, like he was caressing the word...

She was the first to look away.

"Thanks for fixing me up."

After he stepped onto the porch, she called, "Leave your glove, and I'll tend to it directly."

By the time she put the salve away, he'd repacked all the contents of her sewing basket. It sat by her rocking chair. Cole's glove rested on the arm.

He was nowhere to be seen.

Fanning herself, she perched on the seat's edge. Land sakes, the day seemed too warm for April.

After examining the tear, she determined regular thread wouldn't do a proper repair. She needed sinew, along with a thimble and her strongest needle to jab through the thick leather. In no time, she bent over her task, promising herself she'd do the best possible job. By the time she finished, her neck felt stiff. Ignoring the discomfort, Lenora examined her work with a critical eye. The repair seemed bulky. Next time he wore this, it'd likely be uncomfortable.

Wasn't a pair of Amos's gloves lying around somewhere? No use their wasting in a trunk, waiting for Toby to grow into them. As she thought about giving the gloves away, a sense of relief washed over her. Like letting go of Amos's things was releasing bad memories about him.

She would hunt for the item once dinner was finished. Which reminded her…

After checking on the duck stew, she adjusted the flues so that it wouldn't overcook.

Footsteps sounded above. Two sets?

"Tobias Joseph, be careful," she called out the open door. As an afterthought she added, "You too, Cole. My salve won't mend a broken neck."

Overpowering Toby's giggle, Cole's laugh sounded deep and rich. It was the sweetest music she'd heard in a long while.

Chapter Seven

"Here, hold this." Cole gave the hammer to Toby. "Watch your step."

Some of the wooden shingles were loose. Despite the rope he'd tied about the boy's waist and thighs, he didn't want to scare Lenora half to death if she saw her son dangling by her kitchen window.

The grim thought followed that perhaps she might like to see Jeb Hackett with the rope around his neck.

They'd not seen the outlaw in many days. Perhaps he wouldn't be back. Leastways, not while Cole was there. Even with two men guarding his flank, Hackett had galloped off like a frightened schoolgirl. Because his veiled threats didn't scare off Cole? Perhaps a man who didn't cower before the almighty Hackett name intimidated him.

Cole tucked the speculation away in his mind.

"Appreciate your help," he said to Toby as he secured the shingles. Like the boy, he was barefoot even though they'd probably end up with a passel of slivers. Boots up there increased the chances of injury. Or an early death. Cole was no fool. A sturdy rope secured him as well. The roof had quite a pitch and, according to Lenora, Amos intended it that way so that snow wouldn't have a chance to build up on it.

Another unusual thing Cole noticed was how far off the ground her husband had constructed the house. At least five steps led from the ground to the porch. Lenora claimed it was because of possible flooding, but that seemed unlikely. The nearby stream, downslope from the ranch, glistened in the sunlight. Seemed no threat.

Did that mean Amos built a hidey-hole in the flooring?

As he and Toby moved across the roof, securing shingles, he stepped on a soft spot.

"What in the world?" Cole squatted to feel the wood, puzzling over the unevenness. After studying it, he lifted an odd shingle that didn't quite lie smoothly. However, it appeared attached to a row of them. Digging his fingers under the wood, he raised a whole section—nearly three feet square. Something caught after he lifted the panel an inch.

"That's just the trapdoor," Toby explained.

"What?" Cole had never seen anything like it. Upon closer inspection, he realized the ridge hid the hinge. Amos had been clever in stacking the shingles so they looked no different on the trapdoor than on the rest of the roof.

"Pa was a master craftsman." Toby grinned, clearly in pride. "He made rocking chairs too, like the one on the porch. And he built this whole ranch, pert near by himself."

"So what's this all about?" Cole pointed to the trapdoor.

"I'll show you. Gimme a moment." Before clambering down the ladder, the boy untied himself.

A few minutes later, Cole heard something ease—like

a thick latch being moved. When the trapdoor opened a few inches, he helped lift the heavy wood.

"Well, I'll be a mule's fool." He stared at a grinning Toby, who looked up from below. After poking his head into the gap, he saw the boy's bed in the loft.

"It even has a rope with knots, tucked here on this shelf. I guess if the ladder isn't handy."

"For what?"

The youngster shrugged. "Dunno. Maybe if there was a fire?"

Perhaps. Or for quick getaways?

Cole studied the roof, noting how anyone sneaking out this way would be invisible to any riders coming up the road. Unless someone waited at the blindside of the house, they wouldn't see the escapee sneak off toward the back corral, grab a horse and be gone before they knew it.

The next thought slammed into Cole's mind. What kind of man would leave his wife and son to deal with the trouble at the front door while he slunk off?

Coward.

Perhaps it was time to start questioning Lenora about her husband.

Cole stretched his tired back. After settling his boot sole on the porch rail, he sipped his coffee. With supper finished, he lingered with deliberate nonchalance.

Twilight gripped the land with a firm hand. Crickets chirped a persistent cadence, lulling the world into slumber. In the mild evening, the fragrance of wild grasses vied with the pungent scent of cattle manure. Stifling his yawn, Cole waited.

Behind him through the open door, he heard Lenora's melodic tones and Toby's high-pitched responses. Their voices lowered as they prayed together—asking God to watch over them and the ranch, to preserve their country and to help them love their neighbors as themselves.

"And please protect Porky and Coal," Toby prayed. "Watch over Sheba and Rowdy. And help Nips stop biting."

Cole clapped his hand over his mouth to keep from chuckling aloud.

The boy continued. "Most of all, God, thank You for sending Cole to help us. And please keep him safe."

Sober in an instant, Cole straightened. A sense of humility washed over him. He recalled his own mother praying for him the last time he'd seen her. Since her begging had not dissuaded him from his mission, she had asked God to watch over him. To help him give up the fool notion of trying to make up for Andrew's death by hunting outlaws for the rest of his life. To settle his heart.

Behind Cole came a quiet "Amen." A chair scraped, and Toby mumbled something in a sleepy voice followed by a long yawn. Lenora murmured her love and kissed her son before he clambered up the ladder to his loft. Silence again settled in the house.

Hearing her soft step, Cole pretended he didn't notice her pausing in the open doorway.

"Seems like a fine night." Her gentle voice washed over him.

He let the sounds of crickets fill the quiet before he finally responded. "That it is." He glanced over his shoulder.

The light from the lamps behind her molded her shapely form and tiny waist. Would she retreat? Or join him on the shadowy, covered porch? He couldn't see her expression but sensed her hesitation. Perhaps she needed a little prodding.

"By the way, the gloves you gave me fit perfectly.

Came in real handy today." Earlier, he and Toby had dug holes in the hard ground to place new fence posts.

"Glad to hear it."

"I hope I didn't work your son too hard."

A small chuckle escaped her. "He's exhausted. Could hardly keep his eyes open during our Bible reading. Likely he's asleep by now." Still she remained in the doorway.

"He's quite a boy. Growing up to be a fine man."

Her sigh and smile testified his words were balm to her motherly heart.

He turned to study the way the waning moon spilled light over the landscape. Black dots of grazing cattle littered the rolling hills. The snowy mountain peaks in the far distance glowed in the fading light.

"Would you care to join me?" Cole mentally kicked himself, hoping his forthrightness wouldn't scare her off.

Her breath caught a little before she answered. "Don't mind if I do." She took the rocker that was a mere three feet from where he stood. Head leaning against the high back, she stared across the yard.

They settled into companionable silence as he sipped his coffee.

In the many days since his arrival, they'd established a routine. Every morning when he arose, he'd find that she was already up, scraping out the ashes from the stove or collecting eggs. By the time he took care of livestock and Toby had milked the cow, she had prepared a simple breakfast. Afterward, he and the youngster would head out for the bulk of the day, doing repairs around the ranch or the never-ending job of mending fences. When they returned in the early afternoon, Lenora had a big dinner prepared for them. Several more hours of work awaited after that, and then it was supper time.

Hard to believe a week had flown by. In that time, he had accomplished a load of work.

So why haven't I asked her the hard questions yet?

He mentally squirmed. Because he didn't want to disrupt the cordiality between them? His intrusive queries would disquiet her, no matter how delicately he asked them. So where to start?

Gripping his coffee cup, he gazed at the grassy plains to the east. "How'd you and your husband meet?"

If the question surprised her, it shocked Cole. He hadn't meant to be so direct.

Though he kept his face pointed straight ahead, he could see her staring at him out of the corner of his eye. A full minute ticked by. Would she answer?

"He came to Minneapolis," she began slowly. "Remember my telling you about my aunt's restaurant? Well, it was attached to a hotel that my parents owned. Ma waited on customers while Pa handled the hotel end of it. My aunt cooked and ran the kitchen. Sometimes I served tables or did odds and ends. Mostly assisted in keeping the operations running smoothly—besides my book learning." She paused. "One day, Amos took a room at the hotel."

She fell silent. Because the memories pained?

"Right off, Pa disliked him. 'Course, I was only fifteen." The chair creaked softly as she began to rock. "Pa wanted me to grow up a little more. Then marry a banker. Or lawyer. Not some cowboy with wild dreams about owning a thousand head of cattle. But Amos kept hanging around. Stayed a couple months while working at the lumber mill."

So Lenora's father hadn't approved of Pritchard. *Figures.* He had probably seen right through the shallow cowboy.

"Is your father still alive?" Though Toby had already said his grandpa had passed away, Cole pretended he didn't know to keep Lenora talking.

"No. He and Ma died from typhoid within a day of each other. Caught it when they were traveling—seeing about getting a contract with a new supplier. Only reason my aunt and I were spared was because we remained in Minneapolis."

"So after they passed, you two continued to run everything?"

Lenora nodded. "For a few weeks. But it was too much for my aunt. Even though Minneapolis was a real city, she didn't like how rough and tumble it was. She preferred the more sedate East Coast. After settling with creditors and selling the businesses, she split the money with me. When she asked if I wanted to go with her, I..." Lenora stopped a moment. "I remained behind. Buried my folks one day and was married the next. I was barely sixteen."

Again, Cole stared out at the landscape. No question how she felt about her decision now. Regret laced her tone.

So Pritchard married her for money. Once Lenora was alone, he took advantage of her youth. And that was twelve or more years ago? Then Lenora wasn't yet thirty. A few years younger than he.

How had she maintained a youthful face and pretty smile, with all the grief she had experienced married to a man like Amos Pritchard? No doubt her faith sustained her. While Cole had run from God, she had apparently clung all the harder to Him.

A pang of regret gripped him. Not just for bringing up painful memories, but because he saw so clearly how they differed in handling the tragedies in their lives.

He didn't want to delve too deeply into that.

"This is a nice ranch. Your husband picked a fine location." After dumping the coffee grounds over the rail, he set his cup on the porch.

The moonlight, coming at an angle, shone on her face as she looked up at him. "Amos had claimed his hundred and sixty acres a few years before we met—he took advantage of the *Homestead Act* like tens of thousands of others. He'd constructed some of these buildings before we married. After we arrived, he invested in cattle."

So that's why Pritchard needed the money. Had he really tried to make a go of the ranch? What had happened?

Cole chose his words with care. "Amos was a top-notch craftsman. Your rocking chair is as fine as creamed gravy. The house and outbuildings are excellent too."

"If only he'd stayed content." The brightness of the moon highlighted her pinched brows and pursed mouth.

Prudence told him to politely excuse himself, but Cole's boots felt nailed to the wooden porch. He had a job to do, no matter how difficult.

With one hand resting on her chest, she continued. "I don't know why, but Amos always wanted more. A finer house, more cattle, more..." She bit her lip.

Cole dug his fingers into the hard wooden rail on which he leaned. "Some men seem to be restless from birth."

Like his own father? Always moving from place to place, looking for...what? Ma had finally declared that she was staying put in Dodge City. Though they had settled, Pa's gaze never turned from the horizon. Some days Cole would awaken in the morning to find his father had gone somewhere. They wouldn't see him for weeks at a time.

"Some men are born restless," he repeated.

"Or they're discontent because their friends teach them to be." Bitterness laced Lenora's tone.

Was Jeb Hackett the friend she was talking about?

Cole let silence consume the acrid memories that hung between them.

"How'd Amos die?" If he was going to get answers, perhaps bluntness was the best way.

She ducked her head and stared at her hands. "They found him a few miles northwest of here." She picked at a hangnail. "Some say he was waylaid by bandits. Or Indians."

"Shot?" When her head jerked up, he added, "By bullets? Or arrows?" That information could be vital. Especially since Cole had not known about Pritchard's death before his arrival.

Lenora chewed her lip and again looked away, this time to the moonlight-splashed yard. "Bullets. And in the back. Twice."

A thrill ran through Cole.

Robbery reports claimed that an outlaw had been shot. A bystander testified he'd seen one man get hit twice.

Was this proof that Pritchard had been one of the six robbers? If that placed him in Cheyenne, then perhaps it implicated Jeb Hackett, as well. Pritchard would never have acted on his own.

Cole's heart quickened as he anticipated not only solving the robbery mystery, but also retrieving the money.

When Lenora sighed deeply, he regretted asking so many questions. If her husband had been one of the Cheyenne robbers, then she had been widowed for just over five months. Cole imagined her sitting by the fireplace through the long winter months. Had she worried what her future held?

However, he again reminded himself of the reason

he had come to Wyoming Territory. No matter how he felt about Lenora, he still had a job to do. He turned his thoughts from her to the robbery.

If Pritchard had died a few miles from the ranch, that meant he had ridden at least six hours on a fast horse to get there. Certainly he knew his end was near. Was that why he had overshot the ranch and had ended up in the middle of nowhere? Because his mind was already failing? Or had he focused on a particular destination?

Cole clamped his lips together to keep from speculating aloud.

The creak of Lenora's chair pulled him from his thoughts. Sorrow etched her expression. Had she known what kind of man her husband was? Toby said she cried a lot while Amos lived. Because she abhorred his thieving? Despised every stolen penny used to support their lives? The Hackett gang went way back—almost eight years. Rumors abounded of cattle rustling and horse thefts, of waylaid travelers and held-up stagecoaches. No evidence could ever pin the Hackett gang. Only recently had they added bank robbery to their ever-expanding exploits. The outcry against them had finally caught the attention of the US Marshals Service.

Did Lenora know any of this? How soon after she married did she find out about Amos?

Now that Cole knew of her gentle heart, she had to grieve over her outlaw husband.

"Sorry I brought up such a painful subject." He crossed his feet as he leaned on the rail.

"I wish…" Her fingers dug into the armrests of the rocking chair. She stared down at the porch's rough flooring. "I wish Amos had never met Jeb."

With care, he crafted his sentence. "He stopped by the

first morning I was here, right? The blond-haired man who did all the talking?"

"Yes. Him." Her voice hardened. "I don't doubt he taught Amos to be discontent with his lot. To look for the easy way through life." Lenora suddenly roused herself. "I'm sorry. I don't often get to…"

To tell others what happened? To explain how she felt?

Besides Toby, she apparently had no one to talk to. Not one person had stopped by the ranch in the time Cole had been there. Because the neighbors considered her leprous? Marriage to a man like Amos Pritchard had tainted her reputation.

Or was something more sinister going on?

She stopped rocking, waiting to speak until he met her gaze. "So what makes *you* restless, Cole?"

The question caught him off guard. Why did she think that? He opened his mouth to deny the claim, then gritted his teeth.

"You once said you were looking to settle down, but you haven't yet. And send for your mother, but you haven't. And now you're dragging a pregnant mare across country—looking for the perfect spot?" She shook her head. "There is no such place."

Her perception stunned him. Was he indeed restless like his father? Though their motivations might be different, perhaps Cole had inherited more of that proclivity than he thought. Just seven months ago, his ma had asked him how many criminals he needed to put behind bars before he was satisfied that he'd finally avenged Andrew's death. Twenty? Fifty? A hundred?

Just one more. That had been his justification. But after arresting one outlaw, Cole would hear of another that needed to be stopped. And another. Nine years had passed and still more awaited.

But admitting he was a lawman to Lenora Pritchard—the wife of a known criminal—would be foolish.

With parted lips, she watched him. His speechlessness grew more unbearable, pressing down on him. For the first time in his life, someone out-silenced him.

"Way past my bedtime." He was off the porch and halfway to the barn before he realized he hadn't said good night.

However, it was the wisest thing to do. If he turned around and went back, he'd tell her things best kept secret. For now anyway.

No telling what she would do if he blurted that he was a US marshal, looking to fasten a host of crimes on Jeb Hackett. If nothing else, Cole would be content to tie the outlaw to the Cheyenne robbery. When things got ugly—and Cole had no doubt they would—he couldn't ask Lenora to choose sides. Especially when he up and disappeared some morning. As with every job he accepted, he had to consider it could be his last.

Knowing he could die on the morrow, he should not get attached to Lenora.

Fool. You already are.

The accusation rang in his heart.

After he settled in his sleeping spot, he tucked one arm under his head.

Was he as restless as both Ma and Lenora accused? Perhaps he'd been lying to himself for years about why he never let any woman get close. Why he never married.

And most important—why he could never forgive himself for not stopping Andrew from running into the street.

After he finished this job, maybe it was time to lay aside his badge. Buy property. Raise horses like he'd always wanted. Since his arrival, peace had wrapped around his soul and soothed the guilt that ever hounded him.

But would this peace last if he were to finally settle in one place? Could Lenora be the one to quiet his restless heart?

Chapter Eight

Over breakfast, Lenora announced, "I need to hitch up the buckboard and head to town." She watched Cole for his response. After last night's abrupt end to their conversation, she feared he'd taken off before dawn. What had caused her to be so bold as to talk to him like that?

His blue gaze met her steadily. "I'll go along if you like."

"Can Blister come too, Ma?" Toby piped up.

"I don't know if that'd be such a good idea." However, she didn't like the thought of leaving him behind. What if he wandered away from the ranch again for days at a time? Locking him in the barn while they were gone seemed a bad idea too.

"Please, Ma?" As though anticipating her response, her son added, "I'd tie him in the buckboard before we reached town. That way he wouldn't get into any fights with the dogs there."

Lenora considered her son's wistful expression. "Very well."

In no time, they sat in the wagon with Toby and his dog in the back. Lenora packed pickled and fresh eggs with which to barter, along with clarified butter. She counted her money and brought only what was needed. As was her custom, she slid her rifle in the scabbard next to the seat. Amos had always insisted they have it close whenever they traveled.

Cole also toted his rifle, wrapped in buckskin and resting in the back along with his saddlebags. "I couldn't leave them behind." He spoke with a grin. When she made a face, he added, "I need to pick up some ammo while I'm in town."

He had hitched up his pinto, claiming he wanted Nips to spend more time in the harness. They rode in silence for a while, but Toby couldn't abide that for long.

Kneeling, her son leaned on the seatback and poked his head between them. "Where did you grow up, Cole?"

"Here and there." A smile tugged one corner of his mouth.

Lenora hid her grin behind her bonnet, knowing his answer would tease Toby into pestering him more. Apparently Cole knew that too.

"Like Texas? Back east? Or Europe?"

"Spent some of my growing-up years in Missouri. Mostly in Kansas. Moved around a bit."

"Like where?"

"Places in the west. I even went as far as California once."

Toby's eyes grew round. "Wow. Did ya ever look for gold?"

"Nah. Saw too many folks crazy for wealth. I couldn't abide all that went with it."

"Like what?"

"Lying, stealing, cheating…" Cole's mouth tightened as he threw a glance over his shoulder. "All the fool things that ruin lives. And hurt their loved ones."

Lenora stared at him. Of his sincerity, she had no

doubt. Had he a relative who'd gone crazy for gold? He'd once mentioned that he and his ma were alone, after his younger brother got shot. Had Cole's father hunted for his fortune? She didn't have the heart to ask.

The desire for money, as she knew so well, could work a terrible evil in a person's heart. She shivered as she recalled how cold the leather of the satchel felt when she had buried it with Amos.

Toby's brow wrinkled as he stared at Cole's profile. A barrage of questions seemed poised on her son's lips.

"So what place did you like best?" She sought to redirect her son's thoughts. "And why?"

Cole's shoulders relaxed as his grip on the reins loosened. Because he too was glad of the subject's change?

"I always liked where I ended up the best." He threw her a sidelong glance. "And right now, it's your ranch."

Her face warmed and not merely because the sun sent out waves of heat that caressed her back.

"This is amazing country." He nodded in a couple directions. "Wide open spaces. Good grazing. Water a plenty. A man need look no further to find all he yearns for here."

Keeping her eyes on the dirt road ahead, Lenora sucked in a slow breath. Was he hinting he wanted to settle? Possibly nearby, on his own ranch? Her heart beat faster at the prospect.

"Pa used to say this territory would soon be part of the union." Toby's head bumped her arm as the wagon hit a dip.

"Likely that'll happen a'fore too long." Cole grinned. "Then everyone'll want land around here."

"Then you'd better get yours soon," Lenora stated. Aghast at her boldness, she turned away, using her bonnet to hide her expression. Though she didn't look at

Cole, she was certain he studied her. The bloom of heat on her cheeks spread across her face and down her neck.

Why had she spoken like that? As though she were inviting him to remain. Had she already settled on Frank Hopper's not buying the ranch? If so, she was prepared to pursue her other plan—of hanging on until fall.

What if Cole stayed on for a longer spell? The idea had worked on her mind since she first thought it. Not only would her ranch's value increase, but she might have time to find another buyer. Or would Cole be interested?

Or—the thought crystalized—perhaps he would take a share of her ranch in exchange for working it. He could raise his horses and she her cattle.

She tamped down her excitement, determining to speak to him when they were again alone. Perhaps after supper tonight?

After a brief stop, they reached town in a little over two hours. Silver Peaks boasted of a couple stores, bank, hotel and saloon, livery, telegraph station, church and other assorted buildings. Seemed like every year, more folks pulled up their roots and headed farther west. Very few horses were hitched to the posts that lined the street.

"Toby, don't go far," Lenora instructed. "We need to get home before dark. And I don't want to have to come looking for you."

"Yes'm." Leaving his dog tied in the buckboard bed, he leaped off the back and ran to a group of boys across the street.

Cole climbed down, but before Lenora could, he came around the other side to grip her hand. Her foot caught on her long skirts. If he hadn't grabbed her waist, she might have fallen into his arms. Or onto the street.

"You're in a mighty big rush," he chided after he'd set her down safely.

She lifted her chin. "I have a lot to accomplish in a short time."

"Anything I can help with?"

"Merely carry my purchases when I'm finished at the mercantile. But that'll be my last stop." She pointed to the one down the street.

"That I can do." He squeezed his hat brim before she hurried to the nearest store.

A glance back showed he absently patted Blister. Still tied, the dog strained the length of the rope to get closer. This was better than their dog barking after Toby who had disappeared around the corner of a house.

Lenora noticed the way Cole looked up and down the dusty streets. Wasn't much to see. He seemed to take great interest in the town. Almost as if he was making up his mind about something.

After getting her list from her pocket, she went into the nearest store to buy material and more thread. She needed to sew new pants for Toby, whose legs were growing so fast his clothing seemed to shrink while he wore them. Though the establishment offered store-bought items, she preferred to make her own. Besides, it was less expensive.

On a whim, she bought a fair-sized piece of soft, red cotton, smiling as she imagined what she could fashion from it. A scarf for herself, perhaps? Her face warmed as she considered making Cole a bandanna. The one he owned was beginning to show a little wear. It would be the perfect thank-you for all he'd done on the ranch.

She lingered over the calicos, longing for a new dress. However, she'd not brought enough money. Before midsummer, she would have to butcher the pig. Once the meat was smoked or dried, she could use it to barter.

The material she purchased put a bigger dent in her

coin purse than she'd planned. With that task done, she considered the next place she needed to stop.

As she reached for the door, it swung open. The minister and his wife stood in the doorway.

Lenora greeted them, unable to keep her gaze from straying to the woman's thickened middle. "Congratulations on your little one."

"Thank you." For once, the woman's smile displayed honest pleasure. "The baby's due any day now."

"How exciting." This child would be their first.

More chatty than usual, the woman went on. "A great benefit is Jeremiah gets a rest from his circuit. He will stay home until the baby's born."

"How wonderful for you both. I hope you enjoy your time together as a family."

"Thank you." Again the flash of a cordial smile. "Now if you'll excuse us…"

"Of course." Lenora moved out of their way so they could enter the shop.

Once again, she couldn't help but think they were kinder to her than ever before. Perhaps the taint of being Amos Pritchard's wife was wearing off? The double standard grated on her. They could secretly admire Amos's daring escapades while condemning his actions.

Excuse the man but blame the wife?

Pushing the unkind thoughts from her mind, Lenora headed to another store that carried a wide assortment of staples. She chose sacks of flour, sugar and coffee, along with some spices and assorted foodstuffs. A bale of wire and some feed completed her list.

When the bell on the door jangled, the proprietor looked up. "May I help you, sir?"

Cole drew closer. "Just helping Mrs. Pritchard with her supplies."

The man's eyebrows rose. "Is that so?"

Though Mr. Richards strove to keep his expression blank, Lenora detected something insulting in the way his glance darted between the two of them.

"Mr. Cole is…" What should she call him?

"Her hired help." Cole threw her a grin as he reached for the heavy flour sack.

"Hired help?" Eyes wide, the proprietor straightened. He glanced at a loafer who sat on a barrel, picking his teeth.

Not only did Mr. Richards seem surprised by her announcement, but several others who lingered in the large store did, as well. Conversation ground to a halt as people outright stared. Most folks she knew, but some were strangers.

"I'll put these in the wagon, Mrs. Pritchard." Cole slung the sacks of flour and sugar over his shoulder.

"Thank you, Mr. Cole. And please bring in the supplies we brought for bartering."

The proprietor bent over his pencil, brow pinched. "How long is your hired help planning to stay at your ranch?"

"We haven't yet settled that." Tamping down her irritation, Lenora spoke slowly. "Once I find out, I'll be sure to tell you next time I'm in town."

She hoped her frank stare and tone of voice conveyed her irritation. When had he become the self-appointed morality officer in this town? Or was he inquiring for another reason?

He leaned forward. "I merely ask because some folks around here don't favor strangers in the area."

Aghast, Lenora clamped her lips together. "Mr. Richards, I've lived here for over eleven years now. I would think I could hire whom I please."

His beefy cheeks expanded as he held his breath, then released it. Placing his hands on the counter, he leaned forward. "I'm just warning you for your own good. *Some folks* won't like it."

A chill ran down her back. Did he mean Jeb? Or his father, Eli?

Mr. Richards's next words confirmed her suspicion.

"Just saying it might be a good idea to get permission from Mr. Hackett."

"Permission?" She stared at him. Did Mr. Richards ask them every time he wanted to do something?

The proprietor used to be jovial and full of banter. Now, he seemed almost afraid to step out of line. As a matter of fact, Lenora noticed how people in Silver Peaks seemed subdued. Perhaps the reason so many left had less to do with the unexplored west and more to do with fear.

She reevaluated her assumption that Mr. Richards was rude. Perhaps he was warning her?

Jeb Hackett wasn't the only reason. His father, Eli, had grown in power and wealth over the years. Were the townsfolk frightened of him, as well? The cattle baron had hired a number of people to work his ranch—including gunfighters.

She managed a tight smile. "Thank you for your information, Mr. Richards."

"Anything else I can get you?"

"Perhaps. Give me another moment to look." She scanned all the delectable items she did without. Like the rose-scented toilet water in the slim, beautifully shaped vial. The delicate ivory lace on a spool. The hair pomade that boasted of thick, luxurious tresses after one use.

"Oh, how lovely." She caressed some delicate kid gloves.

"I recently acquired them." Mr. Richards laid them

out so she could examine the stitching and fine grain. "Reasonably priced."

"They wouldn't be practical. Thanks all the same." Sighing, she stroked the soft leather. Some days the coarse gloves she used hurt almost as much as the rough items she handled. "How much do I owe you?"

"Taking into consideration the items you brought…" The man bent over his numbers. His pencil scratched across a scrap of paper.

After he added the amounts and gave her the total, Lenora pulled out her coin purse and counted out the bills and coins. She hadn't enough? Again, she added up her money but was shy two dollars and seventy-five cents.

"I apparently didn't bring enough with me." She cleared her throat. "Could you put the remainder on my tab?"

Mr. Richard's expression grew stony. "I'm sorry. We had to close Amos's account."

Lenora's face flamed. "Well, then…can you put it on mine? You know I'm good for it, of course. This fall, when I sell—"

"I'm more'n sorry, Mrs. Lenora. That isn't possible. We no longer extend credit." He stared over her head, as though unable to look her in the eye.

"But Mr. Richards, I…" She pressed her lips together, aware of other customers in the store. Their whispers only kindled the fire that scorched her face.

In the time she'd been choosing supplies, three other customers had come and gone. Two of them had put items on their account. In all the time she'd lived in Wyoming Territory, he'd always extended the Pritchard family credit. What had changed?

Though she felt like abandoning the items she wanted to purchase, she had no doubt the other mercantile in town would refuse her credit, as well. Because the Hacketts controlled them?

Her mind raced to the items she needed. What could they do without?

"'Scuse me, Mrs. Pritchard." Cole's voice sounded beside her. "I was loading the items in the wagon and found this." He held out a five-dollar bill. "I'm sure it's yours."

"Oh. Thank you." Her hands shook as she took the money, then passed it to Mr. Richards. Was it hers? When Cole had joined her on the buckboard seat, she recalled dropping a couple coins when she had scooted over. Had a bill escaped at the same time?

Later, she would be sure to thank him for his honesty in returning the money. It couldn't have come at a better time.

The proprietor took the bill and gave her change.

"Did you get all the items you needed, Mr. Cole?" Anxiety pressed on Lenora. She wanted to get away from town as soon as possible.

"Yes."

"Then shall we go?"

"In a moment."

As she put away her coin purse, he grabbed some licorice from a bin and set five pieces on the counter.

Mr. Richards crossed his arms. "Sorry. They're not for sale."

What? Lenora turned back to the two men.

His jaw stuck out as he briefly met her gaze, then flicked to Cole. In fear or defiance?

"You saying they're free today?" Cole spoke in a pleasant tone.

The big man swallowed. "I'm saying I'm not selling."

To you. No need to finish the sentence.

Mouth agape, Lenora stared. A glance at the other patrons told her they should leave. Now.

But what could she say to Cole? Since he volunteered his help on the ranch, she couldn't order him around.

Her mouth worked, but no words came out. Besides, she got the distinct impression she should not interfere.

Mr. Richards had treated her with unfairness and now refused to serve a patron. Because he had chosen to kowtow to the Hacketts? Her earlier compassion melted into indignation.

Cole casually rested one hand on the counter. "You don't want to disappoint a boy by refusing to sell me licorice, do you?"

The proprietor's face colored a deep red. He began to sputter, then fell silent. Though Lenora couldn't see Cole's face, his body remained in a relaxed, friendly stance. No one could accuse him of threatening Mr. Richards.

The minutes dragged. A couple flies buzzed against the window while a clock on the wall clacked with growing intensity. One patron shifted her package, the brown paper crackling as loudly as Fourth of July fireworks. Lenora's heart pounded in her ears.

Who would back down first?

Mr. Richards grabbed the licorice and shoved them into a small paper bag. "On the house today."

"Much obliged." Cole touched his hat brim before grabbing the bag and sauntering toward her. "I'm ready now, ma'am."

She hurried from the store.

After they were outside, Cole's piercing whistle made her jump. It took her a moment before she realized he was getting Toby's attention.

Her son looked up, said something to his friends, then sprinted down the street. "Time to go?"

"Yup. Your ma's ready to get outta Dodge."

Toby made a face. "What?"

Cole grinned. "Just a phrase I picked up back home in Dodge City. Let's go." He helped Lenora up into the seat, got everyone settled and they were on their way.

Never was she more mindful of the ogling townsfolk they passed, the hands that hid mouths and the outright pointing.

Cole appeared oblivious, whistling some aimless tune under his breath as he kept his pinto to a steady, unhurried walk. Taking her cue from him, she adjusted her bonnet and pretended the stares didn't bother her. Toby waved to the group of boys he'd spent over an hour with, unaware of the subtle attitude changes in town. Which was just as well.

As before, they stopped in a wide spot in the road to give Nips a rest while they ate the simple lunch Lenora had packed.

"By the way, I got you something." Cole tossed the bag of licorice to Toby. "To thank you for all your help."

"For me?" His jaw dropped when he saw the candy. "Wow, thanks!" He popped two into his mouth.

Lenora nearly laughed out loud at his overly wide eyes and ecstatic expression.

"Want some, Ma?" His teeth and tongue blackened as he chewed.

"No, thank you." Besides it was too much fun watching him.

Cole also declined, giving her another reason to chuckle. Clearly her son thought adults were crazy to turn down such a delectable sweet.

After they were again on their way, her son talked

about the wonders of licorice. Then he prattled about one kid's new knife and another's slingshot. Next he told them he heard of a rabid dog two boys thought they had seen on the outskirts of town, the wild stallion someone captured and the man who claimed to have been tortured by Indians. Cole remained silent except to occasionally comment or answer one of Toby's questions.

Embroiled in her own thoughts, Lenora had little to say. Once she forced herself to put the town behind her, she began thinking about how much money she'd spent. As she recalculated the amount—several times—she realized that the five dollars Cole gave her could not have been hers.

Then his?

She must have been staring at him for several moments, because he threw her a glance. "Something bothering you, Mrs. Pritchard?"

"Yes. That five dollars."

His eyebrows rose in innocence as he turned his attention to the road.

"You said you found that money."

"Yep." He grinned. "Found it in my pocket."

She gripped the seat's rail. "So that *was* your money."

He took his time answering. "Actually, yours. I told you I'd pay you for feed. The night I arrived, remember?"

"But you gave me too much."

"Not for shelter and meals, along with the care for my horses. It would've cost me more if I'd stayed in town."

"Still…" When she thought of the amount of work he'd done on the ranch, *she* owed *him*. Besides, the way he'd given her the money in the mercantile had saved her embarrassment. And kept her from exploding at Mr. Richards.

And what about that matter of the licorice when he had

refused to sell? Cole had not grown angry or confrontational. Just waited. His very presence demanded respect. Mr. Richards could not help but yield to the better person.

Cole was like no man she had ever met before.

Chapter Nine

As they came up the hill, Cole sensed something was wrong long before he saw the house's open door. Fluffy white wisps rested on the porch like heaps of fresh-fallen snow. Were they feathers? The breeze lifted and scattered them.

In the buckboard, Blister began to growl, his yellow fur bristling.

Cole tugged on the reins, stopping the pinto. "Toby, tie up your dog again."

"Yessir." The boy's fingers shook as he hurried to obey.

Cole clucked at his horse to move on. Slowly.

With widening eyes, Lenora's fingers clutched his arm. "What…?" She never finished her sentence.

They had barely reached the yard when she leaped down from the buckboard and ran toward the house.

"Lenora, wait!"

She didn't heed his cry.

"Hold them." He tossed Toby the reins. "Don't come in until I say so. And don't untie Blister."

The dog yapped nonstop, the sound growing in intensity.

When Cole caught up to Lenora on the porch, he grabbed her arm. "Wait. It may not be safe."

After thrusting her behind him, he flattened himself against the exterior wall. He drew his pistol. Raising his voice, he called, "Whoever's in there, come out."

No answer.

He could hear nothing but Lenora's gulping breaths. When she tried to push past him, he grabbed her waist and pulled her back. "Let me check first. When it's clear, I'll let you know." He wouldn't let go of her until she nodded.

The first thing he did was duck his head around the corner to do a quick peek. No one appeared to be inside. However, it looked like a cannonball had passed through the large room. He peered above at Toby's loft. The small opening that served as a window to the interior was shut. Was someone up there? No telling.

"This is your last chance to come out." Cole cocked his gun, allowing the sound to reverberate in the room. Again, no answer. He entered, his boots crunching over broken china and pottery. A quick check of Lenora's bedroom revealed no one hid there. With caution, Cole climbed into the loft. The space was empty. But it had been ransacked also.

He put away his gun. "You can come in now, Lenora."

After one look at the room, she staggered back and gripped the door frame. For endless moments, she didn't move.

"Jeb." She spoke in a hard tone. "He did this."

That had been Cole's conclusion as well, but he asked, "Why do you suspect him?"

"Because he…" Again, she looked around as though unable to comprehend what had happened.

Cole followed her gaze. Pictures that had been on the

mantel now lay on the floor. Some of her bone china had been smashed, the pieces littering the handwoven rugs. Every shelf had been cleared, the contents of a couple tin cans emptied. Pillows had been slashed, their downy feathers scattered. Very little appeared intact.

"Lenora." He waited until her eyes met his. "What was Hackett looking for?"

A flash of emotion crossed her face so quickly, he nearly missed it. Fear? Guilt?

Did she know where the missing money was?

Cole's boots crunched over the debris. "What was he hoping to find?" His voice came out harsher than he intended.

Shock gave way to confusion as she ducked her head. "I don't… I…" Her mouth moved, but no sound came out. All of a sudden, she shuddered. She appeared unable to hold herself upright one second longer.

Was she crying? Her shoulders spasmed, but she made no sound.

He stood immobile, feeling helpless. Stupid. Only one thing to do.

With infinite care, he put his arms about her.

He had no idea how she would respond. Jerk away? Slap him? Nothing prepared Cole for the way she suddenly melted against him. Fingers against her mouth, she pressed her forehead against his chest. She succumbed to sorrow, crying so hard that her body shook.

Like a dam had broken. One that she had held in place for too long.

A strange emotion welled inside him. Empathy? He resisted the foreign feeling. Discomfort grated his heart. In all the years he'd chased down outlaws, he had always avoided the loved ones and friends of those victimized. He didn't want to see the depth of their suffering.

After all, he had enough of his own to last a lifetime.

If someone approached him, gushing their thanks because he had captured or killed an outlaw, he would usually mutter, "Just doing my job." Risking rudeness, he would hurry away.

But now, Lenora leaned against him, overcome by sorrow. Why didn't her grief repel him? Of its own accord, his hand slowly smoothed across her back. His fingertips brushed the soft skin of her neck.

This felt so right.

He wanted to tell her only plates had been smashed, not lives. But perhaps the dishes were a symbol of her broken life. One that no human could repair. He allowed himself to feel her pain, but for some reason it didn't hurt like he thought it would.

His hold tightened. Cole finally found the words to comfort, not only her, but himself. "We'll clean this up together. Put everything back in order. Then we'll get on with our lives. We'll not let the likes of Jeb Hackett destroy our peace of mind. Not now, not ever."

She nodded, ever so slightly.

Without circumspection, he yanked his bandanna from around his neck and handed it to her. It was dirty and sweat-stained, but she didn't seem to care as she dabbed her eyes. He continued to stroke her back.

"God sees. And He knows." Cole spoke softly, the words soothing the agony in his own soul. "You aren't alone. I'm here. You can count on me. No matter what."

Her tears abated. Still she nestled in his embrace. If possible, she relaxed against him even more. Her cheek nuzzled his shirt. A deep sigh escaped her.

"Ma! Cole?" Toby's voice reached them from outside. "What's going on?"

Blister's barking welled up in Cole's hearing as reality charged back at him.

After releasing Lenora, he stepped onto the porch. "Hitch Nips and come in here. But don't untie Blister yet. Your ma needs you right quick."

The youngster did as he was told and soon bounded inside. His young face registered shock. When Lenora saw him, she again broke down.

"It'll be okay, Ma. It'll be okay." Toby hugged her.

An outsider again, Cole merely watched. Clenching his fist, he resisted putting his arms around the two of them. This wasn't his family. And it wasn't his place to comfort. Not since Toby had come.

Cole cleared his throat. "I'll check the root cellar and barn to make sure no one's hiding out there. I'll be right back."

Lenora nodded, eyes red, cheeks blotched.

"Come on, Ma. I'll clean up." Toby took her hand and led her toward a chair. "You set and tell me what to do."

Cole headed out to check the outbuildings, but as he suspected, they were empty. It appeared as though someone had ransacked the root cellar, turning over bins and breaking things as they'd hunted behind jars. Someone had also searched the barn. Cole congratulated himself on hiding some of his things and taking along the rest. Wouldn't do for Hackett to find his badge.

Not until Cole was certain the three of them were alone on the ranch did he release Blister. The dog had barked almost nonstop since their return.

After Cole untied him from the buckboard, he ran around the yard, yelping and growling.

Yeah, Blister knew several someones had run roughshod over the place. After watching the dog follow the hidden trails, Cole grew confident that he would find no one lurking.

So what was Hackett looking for? It took no smarts to figure he was searching for the missing bankroll from the Cheyenne robbery. More than five months had passed, and not one dollar of the twenty-one thousand had appeared. That Cole knew of anyway.

Unbeknownst to them, the robbers had stolen newly minted five-dollar bills, not yet circulated. Find those bills, and Cole would track down the thieves.

Was Jeb Hackett convinced Lenora had the money?

Cole reevaluated his assumption that the outlaw had been in possession of it all along. Perhaps Amos Pritchard was the one to safeguard the bankroll? Lenora had claimed that her husband was found dead, miles from this ranch, but had he hidden the loot here first?

A chilling thought—one he fought to entertain—settled in his mind. One he couldn't shake. Had he misjudged Lenora and she knew where the money was? Perhaps she wasn't as innocent as she seemed. Why else would she refuse to answer his question about Hackett?

Cole's plans to eventually move to town changed. Besides, once the mercantile proprietor had discovered he was Lenora's "hired help," the man had made it clear he wasn't welcome. No doubt that information would spread until no one would take his money. Including the hotel. No, it would be better if Cole remained on the ranch and did his own quiet search. Perhaps he would find what Jeb Hackett had missed.

Though Lenora kept her gaze fixed on the dish she carried to the table, she could still see the gaps on the mantel where her bone china used to be. The long slash in the quilt her aunt had made fluttered as she walked by. The crack in the glass of her tambour clock—a gift from her father—seemed to lengthen. How long before her heart stopped hurting?

Likely never.

Though she, Toby and Cole had cleared the debris, the room still showed signs of violation in the pockmarked plaster walls and dented tin cans. Had Jeb and his men thrown things across the room? Not only that, but they had stolen Amos's six-shooter—one less gun to defend herself. She was glad they hadn't found her shotgun in the barn.

And good thing they hadn't discovered the small built-in trapdoor, under the rug in her bedroom. There she kept extra ammunition and some money. Despite how close her husband and Jeb had been, Amos had kept secrets. Because he knew his so-called friend could one day turn on him?

Lenora stepped to the door. "Toby."

Her son ran up from the barn with a promptness that soothed her heart.

"Yes, Ma?" His green eyes met hers steadily.

She ran her fingers through his dark hair and tilted back his head. "Could you tell Cole supper's ready?"

"He's already a'coming."

"Very well, then."

"I'll go wash up." He bolted out the door.

In no time, Cole and her son sat at the table. Normally they would have beans and bread, but this evening Lenora had one surprise—pudding, sitting in a covered dish. Now that Porky had calved, they had an abundance of milk. Soon Lenora would churn butter to put up. But where could she barter? Though the larger town of La Grange was farther away, likely their stores there would conduct business with her. Eli Hackett's influence couldn't have reached that far, could it?

Aware of how quiet Cole and Toby were, she slid into her seat. Her son's palm was extended, waiting for the blessing. Lenora caught her breath when Cole's open hand slid toward her. Warmth suffused her as their gazes met. He slowly lowered his head, as though allowing her to make the decision about holding his hand during prayer.

Slowly, she rested her fingers on his.

What should she pray? For once, she struggled with the simple words. After licking her lips—for the third time—she began. "Dear Lord, we thank...we thank You...for..." Her throat grew so tight, she couldn't continue. She *was* grateful—for so much—but fought an overwhelming urge to cry.

Silly woman, she chided herself, they were just *things*. So why did the invasion of her house upset her so?

As soon as she asked the question, she knew. After Amos had been laid to rest, she had assumed her troubles were buried too. That Jeb Hackett would leave her alone. How foolish to have assumed that.

Lenora sniffed, unable to stifle the sound.

Cole's fingers gently squeezed. "Lord, we thank You for Your many blessings, like the food we eat and even the air we breathe. And God, though I'm not much of a praying man, I ask that You comfort Lenora." His thumb caressed her knuckles. "Help her think on the many ways You watch over her every day. And that she is never out of Your hands. Amen."

"Amen." She thought the word came through her lips, but she couldn't be sure.

Toby's eyes widened when she lifted the dish's lid. "Pudding?"

She nodded.

"Thanks, Ma!" Her son smacked his lips as she filled his bowl.

"Been a long time since I had this." Cole's quiet voice contrasted with Toby's exuberance.

"I hope you enjoy it." She managed a tremulous smile in his direction.

"I know I will." He made a sound of appreciation after his first bite. "You know, I've been thinking…" He waited until she met his gaze. "I'm going to sack out on the porch. Just for tonight."

Toby's spoon paused midair. "How come?"

"'Cause I don't want to sleep in that big ol' scary barn." His voice quavered and eyes widened. "It's so far away from the house."

Ducking her head, Lenora hid her smile at the mock fear on Cole's face. Toby outright laughed. When he wasn't looking, Cole winked at her.

Truth be told, she would be glad to have him so close.

Later as she prepared to retire, she grabbed one of Amos's shirts to use in place of her destroyed pillow. Twice she checked to make certain the door was bolted and barred before going back to her room.

As soon as she lay her head on the wadded material, she caught the scent of the hair oil her husband used to use. He only applied it when he went into town. Likely to gamble. Or go a'thieving. Had he used it the last day of his life?

A painful memory invaded her thoughts.

"Take it," Amos rasped. He loosed the leather strap that bound the satchel to his saddle. In the dusk, his skin appeared ashen, a corner of his mouth crusted red with blood.

One look told Lenora he was dying. The terrifying truth strangled what she wanted to say.

*"Lord knows I've wronged you all these years. I prom-
ised myself I'd make up for it if I could." He coughed, the
sound rattling through his body. "You and Toby clear out
of here. You'll have more than enough money to live off of."*

*The satchel dropped heavily to the ground. His star-
tled horse tossed his head and began walking.*

*"Amos." The cry escaped her lips, but it was too late.
Her husband fixed his eyes on his destiny as he slowly
rode into the encroaching darkness.*

Clutching the shirt, Lenora sat up in bed. She wouldn't
touch that money. In the dead of night, she had buried it
where no one would think to look.

She jumped at the thumping footsteps on the porch.
Was that Jeb? Terror gripped her.

Then she heard Cole's low whistle at his call, "Blister. Good boy."

Relief swept over her. Taking a deep breath, she relaxed and pulled the covers high. Cole was close. He
would protect her.

Though she didn't hear him settle, she could imagine
him laying out his bedroll. Peace settled over her as she
closed her eyes.

He cares for me.

Not only did Cole prove it by staying close tonight—
when he knew she would be afraid, but earlier when
he had held her. Once again, she felt his strong arms
about her as she'd cried. His gentle touch on the skin
of her neck. His thumb caressing her knuckles while
they'd prayed.

Lenora sighed.

If she had her way, she'd keep Cole there forever.

Cold sweat poured off Cole's forehead as he sat up
with a gasp. His heart pounded against his chest and a

sickening feeling strangled his throat. Several moments passed before he realized that he'd had a nightmare. One that had recurred on occasion since he was fourteen.

Why now? Hackett's vandalism of the ranch had been several days before, so that couldn't be the reason. Upon Lenora's insistence, Cole had returned to sleeping in the barn. What disturbed his sleep?

"Andrew." Cole blew out a breath as he tilted back his head. Been a long time since he'd dreamed of his brother's death. The images and smells still haunted him.

"You've got to forgive yourself, Cole." His mother's words came back to him. If only he had kept his younger brother from running into the street. The moment he had discovered Andrew following him, he should have turned around and escorted him home. His ma had warned them both about taking that shortcut down the alley. And Cole hadn't listened.

He flung aside his blanket. After he yanked on his boots, he slipped on his shirt and vest. Out of habit, he grabbed his rifle. From experience, he knew he'd never get back to sleep. Not for a couple hours, anyway.

As he stalked toward the barn door, Coal the calf bawled. In the darkness, he heard Porky stagger to her feet. No doubt she lowered her horns, ready to protect her baby.

"Easy, girls," he said in a low voice. "Just gonna make the rounds."

Though he'd done that before he'd sacked out for the night, it wouldn't hurt to do it again. A routine he'd lately acquired, especially when he thought he saw a light on a nearby hill. From a campfire? The first time that had happened, he convinced himself he'd imagined it. The second time, he began making the rounds before settling down for the night.

Once burned, twice smart.

Perhaps making two a night would be a good idea, now that he knew Hackett or his men were on the prowl. Obviously, they kept an eye on the ranch. How else did they know everyone had left so they could ransack the place? Cole would ensure they didn't try something at night.

A quarter moon hung in the clear sky. Countless stars beamed down, washing the landscape with a gentle glow. Nothing appeared on the nearby hill tonight.

Sticking to the shadows, he listened to the night sounds. Undisturbed, a host of crickets chirped. In the distance, an owl hooted. No unusual sounds came from the chicken coop or the pigpen. Without moving, Cole merely watched the yard. On the porch, he could see Blister's head up, ears pricked forward.

He gave a short, sharp whistle. The dog immediately leaped up and loped his way.

"Good boy." Cole bent to pat his head. No doubt Hackett would be all the bolder if the dog were missing from the ranch. Was he the one who had lassoed Blister? Made sense now.

Maybe it was time for the dog to have a companion. A puppy so he could train up the newcomer. Cole would have to keep his ears open next time they were in town.

Staying in the shadows when he could, he prowled around the buildings. He paused by the back pasture when Sheba nickered and met him at the fence. "Heya, girl." He smoothed his hand over her neck, chuckling when the two geldings crowded her to get attention too. "If any of you see anything, you'd be sure to tell me, right?"

Rowdy tossed his head, almost in agreement. Watching the ears of all three horses, Cole decided they appeared calm. After a final pat to their necks, he moved on. He ended up on the porch steps, looking across the landscape.

Though Amos Pritchard had been a thief, he certainly had picked a nice piece of property. Cole himself couldn't have done a better job of positioning the ranch buildings. To the south wandered a friendly creek and to the north lay hills that would protect from the harsher winter winds. The buildings Amos had constructed were perfectly suited for the weather and his family.

For the first time in a long while, Cole felt he could breathe. The wide-open spaces gave him a sense of freedom. That was never the case in town. Here, no outlaw lurked in every building, ready to take his life. Despite the fact that Jeb Hackett was likely in the vicinity, peace washed through Cole.

It struck him that he felt right at home.

A creaking floorboard warned him that he was not the only one awake. The door squeaked as it opened.

Without turning on the step, he said in a low voice, "Why aren't you asleep, Lenora?"

"Oh, Cole." Her tight whisper greeted him from the darkness. "I heard something and…" A sigh revealed her relief.

"Just me, making the rounds." He glanced over his shoulder.

A large, fringed shawl draped across her shoulders and torso, covering her white nightgown to her knees. Bare toes peeped out from the hem.

Her movement revealed that she was putting her rifle back beside the doorjamb.

"Didn't mean to disturb you," he added.

She tucked the shawl more securely around herself. "Why are you up?"

"Couldn't sleep." His nightmare flashed through his mind. "So I'm making the rounds."

"Do you every night?"

"Usually before I bed down. Tonight, though, I…" He let out a frustrated breath, unable to explain. Yet.

Lenora didn't press him for details.

In the silence, the answer slowly came to him. He grew aware of his awakening emotions—they had been roused the moment he had stepped onto the ranch. Long before he had held Lenora Pritchard in his arms, he had begun to *feel* again. It both disturbed and beguiled him.

Would he run away from them? Or stay and allow himself the agony and pleasure of…? His mind stumbled over the word *love*.

No, *care*. That was it. He cared for Lenora like any decent human being should.

Behind him, the soft rustle of material interrupted his thoughts.

"Cole."

He turned to Lenora as she stood on a step above him.

Soft brown hair framed her face. Her dark eyes glittered in the pale light. "You've done so much for us already. Please, go get some rest."

He sucked in a slow breath as she rested her hand on his shoulder. Warmth penetrated his shirt and spread from her fingers across his chest. He reveled in her gentle touch.

If only…

When he glanced at her fingers, she pulled away with a small gasp. Brow pinched, she crossed her arms. Because she had been unaware of her gesture?

For endless moments, they stood silent. Cole fought the overwhelming yearning to take her into his arms again. Except this time, his embrace wouldn't be to comfort. Would she allow it?

I can't do that to her.

As soon as he put Jeb Hackett behind bars, he would move on to the next job. And the next.

Cole backed down one step and another until he was on solid ground. With deliberate effort, he spoke. "Good night, Mrs. Pritchard."

"Good night." Her words came out in a breathless rush.

He waited until she ducked into the house and put the crossbar in place. Only then did he allow himself to breathe.

Chapter Ten

"Not great, but good enough." Lenora surveyed the large room, satisfied with her wall patching. A week had passed since the break-in, and finally her home was again orderly.

If only she could get rid of the nagging fear that kept her awake at night. Though Jeb hadn't found anything—and she felt confident that he never would—his increasing boldness kept pace with her growing fright. The fact that he had invaded her home and ransacked her belongings proved that he had moved beyond the talking stage.

How could she convince him she had nothing he wanted?

She backed out of the room as though to distance herself from her thoughts. Since the break-in, she had become more jittery. More anxious. Poor Toby felt the brunt of her ill temper. Likely it was because she wasn't sleeping well. After she climbed into bed at night, she found it harder and harder to pray.

When she stepped onto the porch, she watched Cole lead their horse into the corral, her son trotting alongside. The day was yet young, the sun warm and bright.

A nice change from the last two days of gloom. It hadn't rained much, so the ground was still fairly dry.

Once they were inside the corral, he hiked her son onto the horse's back. Without a saddle or bridle? It was Amos's horse, one she didn't care much for since he was sometimes unpredictable.

While her oven heated, Lenora leaned against the porch rail to watch.

"Now remember what I said." Cole's voice reached her. "Take it nice and easy. Get used to his gait."

"Okay, Cole."

He unhooked the halter and stepped back. "Let's see whatcha got."

Nodding, Toby gave the horse a tentative kick. Nothing happened. Shrugging, he looked at Cole.

"First, you have to get seated properly." He helped Toby scoot forward a little. "There."

Again, her son nudged the gelding, who moved forward in a slow walk.

"That's it." Cole backed toward the split-rail fence. "Get a feel for his gait. Let him know who's boss."

Needing to check the oven's temperature, Lenora went back into the house. After placing her hand inside the space, she added more wood and adjusted the flues to make it hotter for bread baking.

By the time she returned to the porch, her son was bouncing on the back of the gelding, looking none too secure.

Tension coiled in her as she watched. When Toby had been a mere toddler, Jeb had placed their son on the back of a horse. Though she had begged her husband to intervene, he had only laughed, saying it was never too early for their son to learn to be a cowboy.

As the horse trotted around the perimeter of the fence,

Cole called out directions. "Make sure you have a tight grip of his mane. Push him into a canter. Don't let him be lazy."

Toby kicked the gelding's sides, but for some reason the horse shied. The next moment, Lenora screamed as her son plunged face first to the ground.

By the time she raced across the yard, Cole had lifted her son into a sitting position. In vain, her ten-year-old stifled his whimpers.

"What's the matter with you?" she shrieked at Cole. "Are you trying to kill him?" She helped Toby stand.

Covered with dust, her son wobbled. With his hand pressed to his forehead and tears streaking his dirty face, he seemed to have trouble breathing.

"Let me see." She pried his hand away where a large goose egg was forming. "Are you hurt anywhere else? Any broken bones?" She fought panic as she knelt in the dirt, assessing his body.

"No." Toby fought to sound brave.

If her son had been seriously injured…

She bolted to her feet and faced Cole. "What made you do such a crazy thing? How could you be so…?" She bit off the scathing things she was tempted to say. Grabbing Toby's arm, she marched him toward the house while he continued to sniffle. She pretended she didn't see him glance over his shoulder.

Once they got inside, she pumped water onto a cloth and made him hold it to his head. "That should take care of some of the swelling. Does anything else hurt?"

"No, Ma." Toby sat on a chair, head tilted back as he did what she bade.

"How could a man do such a fool thing?" She continued to mutter under her breath as she grabbed another cloth and brushed the dust from his skin. "Life is dangerous enough without…"

Without robbing banks? Or getting shot? All her fears welled up inside her.

I hate this place. I can't wait to leave.

Then why was she still there? Never in twelve years had she felt like the ranch was her home.

She bit her lip to stop the words, taking a deep breath to calm herself. For the sake of her son if nothing else.

After peeling the cloth from his forehead, Toby peered at her. "It was my fault, Ma. I asked Cole to show me how to ride without a bridle and saddle."

"Well, you're both fool-headed then."

Her son's mouth compressed. "It's not true. If I want to help round up our cattle, I gotta know how to ride better so's I won't fall off and get trampled. Pa never showed me."

Lenora sucked in a quick breath. Never before had Toby contradicted her.

He's growing up.

For several moments, she chewed the inside of her lip. But he was right. Amos had never given their son the skills to be a good rancher. Her son loved this place. How could she even think of taking him away?

"Let me cool that cloth." As she again pressed it to Toby's forehead, what he'd said nagged her.

She reasoned she was still upset over the vandalism. Her emotions were stoked to an impossible level. Only that morning, she had shrieked when a fat toad had jumped from under the chicken coop while she was collecting eggs.

What she'd said to Cole began to nag her. Her words were unkind. Unjust. And the way she had screamed at him…

"Stay here," she directed Toby. Before she chickened out, she strode from the room.

On the porch, she nearly ran into Cole as he carried the milk pail up from the barn.

"Oh, I…" She gulped.

He set the pail down. "How's Toby?"

"Fine. Fine." She pressed her lips together.

"No sprains?"

"No." She cleared her throat. *Just say it.* "About what I said earlier…"

"You were right. I could've at least—"

"No, I shouldn't have flown off the handle." She didn't add that her nerves were frazzled. That was no excuse.

"I should have asked permission first." He stepped closer until he was within a foot of her and spoke in a low voice. "You know I'd never do anything to hurt your son, Lenora. I care for that boy."

Eyes stinging, she nodded. "I had no call to speak to you like that."

Cole pursed his lips, but said nothing.

"Seems like I do that a lot with you. Apologize." She gazed up at him.

"I hear it's good for the soul." His twinkling eyes and dimpled cheek let her know he bore no hard feelings.

She managed a tremulous grin. "Guess my soul needs a lot of it."

"I'd say." Smiling down at her, his gaze flickered to her lips. She realized with a start that she had leaned toward him. Stepping back, she smoothed her hair.

He lifted the bucket of milk.

"Oh, I forgot about that. Let me—"

"I got it." He brushed by her and set it on the table. "Toby, how's your head?"

"Okay, I guess." His gaze flickered to Lenora. "Can I try again, Ma? Please?"

She caught her breath, tempted to tell him no.

However, Cole intervened. "I've been thinking that we picked the wrong horse for your first attempt." He turned to Lenora. "With your permission, I'd like him to ride my mare, Sheba. She won't spook like your horse."

She met her son's gaze. "Are you ready to try again?"

"Yes'm."

"Okay, then." She squeezed her eyes shut. "Please take care."

Toby leaped off his chair and flung aside the wet cloth. "Can we go now, Cole?"

"If that's all right with your ma."

She merely nodded.

The two were soon out the door. Though tempted to watch, she decided to stay inside and concentrate on baking. It gave her time to confront her emotions.

Fear had run her life from the moment she had found out Amos was a thief. She recalled flying off the handle many times when he did something reckless. But all her nagging had not changed him one speck.

Lenora slipped the bread into the oven, then leaned against the wall as thoughts barraged her.

I wish I'd prayed for him more often. And less against *him.*

The regret hummed in her soul. Though she had finally reached a place where she knew she wasn't responsible for her husband's actions, she realized she could have done more for their marriage. And for her own peace of mind.

She dabbed her damp eyes with her apron.

And now that her son was growing up, she had to learn

to bridle her tongue. Above all, she didn't want him to resent her trying to protect him from every possible risk.

A little later, when she heard Toby's laugh, she peeked out the door. He sat astride Cole's beautiful mare as she cantered around the corral's perimeter. As before, her son used no saddle or bridle. His legs gripped the mare's sides while his fingers clutched her dark, flowing mane.

Lenora's breath caught at the horse's fluid motion. Sheba's feet hit the ground in a magnificent waltz as she floated in the air. Her blood bay coat shimmered in the bright sunshine, mane and tail flying.

The most enthralling picture, though, was Toby. His face shone with joy.

"Look at me," he called to a grinning Cole. "I did it." He laughed again.

Pressing one hand to her neck, Lenora could not catch her breath. As tears wet her cheeks, she wiped them away. When was the last time she'd heard her son laugh like that? It had been years.

She clutched the porch's column. While she listened to Cole calling out encouragement, her chest spasmed. She felt she had eaten something too quickly and the food had trouble going down. Yet, the sensation caused more relief than pain. Her lungs expanded, giving her space to breathe. She felt free.

And all because of this man named Cole.

"We won't go far. We're just going to look over the lay of the land." Cole hoped he sounded convincing as he spoke to Lenora the next morning. Though they hadn't yet eaten breakfast, he wanted to get an early start. She surprised him when she agreed to let Toby go.

As they stood together on the porch, she shielded her eyes from the early-morning sun. Though dressed for the day, she had not yet pinned up her hair. It hung in long, burnished waves—because she'd just been brushing it? Light wove through the strands, the gentle curls cradling the liquid gold.

He dragged his gaze from its silkiness.

"How long will you be gone?"

"Couple hours." He scratched his chin with his knuckles. "Doesn't take me all day to herd cows till noon."

When she laughed at his father's saying, Cole's gaze lingered on her lips.

He brought himself up short. This was not the time to be distracted. "I'll let Toby ride one of my geldings. He's more predictable than your horse."

"I'd feel better about that. Thanks."

"If you want us back at the ranch—for any reason— fire your rifle into the air twice. We'll be here faster than you can say 'jackrabbit.'"

She chuckled, the sound easy on his ears. "Let me pack a breakfast before you go. Won't take long."

"And you're sure it's okay that Toby comes along?" Though Cole didn't expect any trouble, he wanted to assure Lenora he would protect the boy with his own life.

"He wants to learn about ranch operations. I think you'll be a grand teacher."

Educating Toby might be Cole's excuse to take off early, but he had another agenda, as well. He wanted to investigate the light he'd seen on the hill. It had been several nights since a campfire had twinkled in the distance. Time to check it out.

Toby leaped down from the ladder rungs that led to his loft. "I'm ready." When he brushed his hair back from his face, the goose egg he'd gotten the day before showed. Though it had reduced in size, a colorful bruise spread toward his eye.

"The weather can change in an instant," his mother warned. "So don't forget your hat and coat."

"I won't. Bye, Ma." He grabbed the items off the pegs by the door before vaulting off the porch.

With a bundle of food and filled canteens, they were on their way. After they crested one hill, Cole looked back to see Lenora still standing on the porch. He pulled up short and waved his hat before they traveled out of sight.

As they rode, Toby chatted about a deer he once shot over thataway. One time an antelope had startled his pa, appearing to leap out of the ground and going straight up in the air, like it had wings. Half listening, Cole kept one eye on the horizon and the other in their immediate vicinity as they followed a ridge.

Besides checking out the landscape, he also wanted to see how many cattle Lenora had. When asked, she had been unable to give him an accurate number. Because Amos never really cared? The way Cole figured it, the ranch was only a front for the gang's other, more lucrative business.

He and Toby had ridden about thirty minutes when they came to a stream. Sure enough, evidence existed that someone had camped out along the water. But this spot was too low to view from the ranch. Was there another location?

After cautioning the youngster to stay in the saddle, Cole dismounted. He dropped his gelding's reins to check the burned-out remains of the fire. All the while, he kept a sharp lookout. The coals were cold to the touch and crumbling. Probably not used in three days or more. Still squatting, he glanced around. It appeared as though two men had shared the camp. Loud buzzing rose over the sound of the trickling stream.

"Stay here, Toby. Be right back." After grabbing his rifle, he followed the noise. Peering through the brush, he saw the corpse of a bovine.

It obviously had been shot—the skull shattered by a bullet. No doubt the best portions of meat had been carved out and the rest left to rot. Coyotes and vultures had gotten their share. Now flies and ants swarmed over the bones and pieces of flesh.

Not only were Hackett's men watching Lenora's ranch, but they thought nothing of helping themselves to her beef.

"Did you find something, Cole?" Toby called from a distance.

He walked back. "Someone's been poaching. They're gone now." He stashed his rifle, and they moved on.

After traveling a little farther, he stopped atop a mound. More evidence remained of someone's camp, but they'd been more careful about covering their tracks. Small burned pieces of wood had been scattered. Apparently they'd used some scrub brush to sweep away the evidence of how many had camped there.

This had to be the source of the light Cole had seen a couple times. As he squinted at the ranch below, the buildings looked like toy blocks. But anyone with binoculars would be able to see all that was happening in the yard.

"Let's eat our breakfast here." He dismounted.

The ten-year-old frowned, perhaps sensing the tension.

"Just drop the reins. Rowdy won't wander far."

Toby did as instructed, watching the two horses begin to graze.

After sitting, he took the bread Cole offered. "Is someone stealing from my ma?"

He took a swig of water from his canteen. "Appears

so. Don't know who or how many cattle though. Best to not jump to conclusions."

The youngster's fist bunched. "It ain't right."

"I agree." Cole kept a lookout while they consumed bread and strips of dried beef. He'd be a fool to assume one of the gang wasn't watching them right now. Doubtful they would do anything in the light of day. Their cowardly sort always worked in the dark.

Toby studied the crust in his hand. "Do you think it was Jeb Hackett? The man who came over the other day?"

"No way to know for sure."

"I don't like him." His young face scrunched up. "Once when my pa was gone, he came over. I saw him touch Ma's cheek."

Stunned, Cole stopped chewing. "So what happened?"

"She slapped his hand away. But he just laughed." The bruise on the side of Toby's head pulsed to a deep red. "I think he wanted to steal her away from my pa."

Surprised at the youngster's perception, Cole said nothing.

Toby's chest heaved. "I don't like the way he treats my mother."

"I don't either." Cole's mind flashed to the day the three riders had shown up at the ranch. All of them had treated Lenora like she was a loose woman. But Jeb was the worst. "A man ought never to talk to a woman that way."

The youngster's face hardened. "When I grow up, I'm gonna kill him."

"Whoa. Now hold on." Cole inserted a stern note to his voice. "Defending a woman is one thing. Going out and picking a fight is another. You'd end up on the wrong side of the law." Since his words seemed to have little effect in softening Toby's inflexible jaw, Cole added, "And how would your ma feel about you swinging from a rope? Her son, the murderer?"

The boy's mouth worked as he apparently absorbed the warning. "So I should do nothing?" His voice cracked as it rose.

Cole leaned his forearms on his knees as he considered how to answer. "If Hackett brings the fight to you, then do something about it. However, be prepared to win or lose. Both will have consequences."

The boy's frown deepened as he appeared to think about it.

"Want more?" He offered Toby another piece of jerky.

"No, thanks."

Cole drank from his canteen, then rose. After he fished out his binoculars from the saddlebags, Toby's face brightened. "Is that a telescope?"

"Nope. Binoculars, because they have double lenses." He panned the area and studied the ranch below. "Here. Take a gander."

With eagerness, the boy put them up to his eyes. "Fearsome." He looked across the landscape, at the sky, the ground and even Cole, who couldn't stop grinning at the youngster's enthusiasm. While he packed up their things, the boy wandered to study rock formations and plants.

Not having the heart to tell him it was time to go, Cole let him explore. Out of habit, he checked the cinch straps of the geldings. As usual, Rowdy's needed to be tightened. His sorrel always held his breath when Cole saddled him. Consequently, the strap loosened as they rode. Nips's cinch was fine.

"Cole?"

The edge of panic in Toby's voice brought him up short. He immediately drew his pistol and crouched.

Several yards ahead, the boy stood facing away from him, frozen. It didn't take long for Cole to see why he had cried out. A huge rattlesnake rose up, head swaying and black tongue flicking. They were perhaps two feet from each other. Though Toby didn't move, the snake's tail began its ominous shake.

"Stay still." Cole crept closer. Normally he would tell the youngster to just back off, but apparently Toby hadn't seen the snake until he was right up on it. Likely the rattler was sunning himself on the boulder. "I'm going to shoot it. Don't move."

The boy whimpered.

"It'll be okay." Cole spoke with calm assurance.

After taking careful aim, he squeezed the trigger, then leaped toward Toby to yank him out of the way. The next moment Cole stomped hard on the snake. He cut the head off and grabbed the body by the tail.

Toby's eyes were huge saucers as he looked first at him, then the snake.

"Stay away from the head." Cole pointed to the spasming jaws. "You could still get bit." He led the boy away. By the time they got back to the horses, the boy still wasn't talking.

Cole lifted the lifeless three-foot body. Rowdy was the first to rear his head and snort in fear. Both geldings shied from the pale corpse.

"It's okay, boys. Deader'n a doornail." Since Toby still seemed in shock, he added, "Hey, what d'ya think of having this for dinner?"

The boy managed a tremulous grin. "I reckon that'd be okay."

"I'll cut the rattle off first. Would you like it?"

Toby gulped, but nodded.

"Your ma ever cook up a snake?"

"Oh, yeah. She knows. Pa brought home a few last year."

Cole retrieved a sack from his saddlebags and shoved the snake into it. Without a word, Toby handed him the binoculars.

The boy was too quiet. Because he had been more frightened than Cole first thought?

"Maybe we should get a couple jackrabbits for dinner in case your ma doesn't feel like fixing a rattler. What'd you think? I'll let you use my rifle if you want to shoot them."

"Okay." Color slowly returned to Toby's face.

Soon, they mounted their horses and headed back toward the ranch. On the way, Cole scratched his chin. "You know I was thinking. About the snake."

"Yeah?" Toby met his gaze.

"How about we don't tell your ma everything that happened, okay?"

"You mean lie?"

"No, no," Cole hastened to assure him. "If she asks for details, then by all means we'll tell her. But I recommend we don't volunteer the whole story."

"Because she might get scared?"

"Exactly. You remember what happened in the corral, right?" After the boy nodded, Cole continued. "Well, God made women delicate. Some get frightened more easily, especially when it comes to their children. I just don't want your ma to be upset about the snake."

Brow furrowing, the youngster seemed to think about that. After a moment, he nodded. "Okay, Cole."

He grinned, pleased that Toby believed him.

However, the boy surprised him by saying, "I'm glad you care how Ma feels."

Did he? The observation put a funny sensation in the pit of Cole's stomach.

Chapter Eleven

"They look…lovely." Lenora eyed the two jackrabbits Cole held by their back feet. Though she was pleased that he had already gutted and skinned them, they looked none too inviting. "You don't want these for supper, do you?"

Dinner was prepared and waiting. Since she had already cleaned the kitchen and stove, she didn't relish the idea of making another mess.

"Nah. Maybe tomorrow." Cole grinned. "Let them season a bit first."

She tried not to wrinkle her nose. One of Amos's favorite things to do was let meat "season." Once he had forgotten about a deer that he left hanging too long. Maggots had filled the carcass by the time he thought to check on it.

"So where are you going to put those?" Lenora pointed. "And for how long?"

"I'll string 'em up in the barn where I can keep an eye on them. And I think one day of seasoning will be plenty long."

Crossing her arms, she tried to hide her disgust. "Just

keep in mind that a bear might want to visit with those hanging inside."

He laughed as he patted his Colt. "I'll be ready. And if necessary, I have my Spencer repeating rifle. It's old, but reliable."

Her frown must have betrayed her skepticism, because he added, "It can fire up to twenty rounds per minute."

She tried to act impressed. "Let's hope that's enough to stop a bear."

"If one doesn't come a'calling, I'll hunt one. A bearskin rug in here would look nice."

"Mine are good enough." She pointed to her hand-braided ones. "Thanks all the same."

He dipped his head once, but seemed to want to say something else. When Toby stomped into the room, Cole added, "Also, we brought you a little something extra for tomorrow. Or dessert tonight." After he shot her son a look, Toby went back outside. In a moment, he brought a slightly bloody, burlap bag.

Lenora backed up a step. "What is that?"

"A little rattler."

She jumped. "Dead, I hope."

Toby giggled. "O'course."

"Is its head still attached?"

"No, Ma. Cole cut it clean off."

She glanced between the two of them, wondering at the mischievous grins they exchanged.

Cole stepped closer. "I skinned it already. If you'd prefer, I can fry it up. Outside."

"No. I know how to cook up a rattlesnake."

Again a look passed between them.

Before she could say anything more, Cole spoke. "I'd like to make Toby a hatband out of the skin and maybe a belt—should only take a few days. But I'll need a couple eggs to tan it. You won't mind, will you?"

"Of course not."

"Kind of a trophy."

She had the oddest feeling they withheld something.

"Ma," Toby said, now stepping forward to speak, "you shoulda seen Cole—shot its head pert near off."

She opened her mouth to reply, but again felt there was some hidden story.

Her son surprised her, though, when he turned to Cole. "Did you know Ma could've shot off the head faster'n you? And from twice as far?"

His eyebrows rose as he looked at her. "Is that so?"

"Toby," she chided, "don't brag."

"It ain't bragging if it's not about me, right, Ma?"

Her cheeks grew warmer.

Cole's eyes held a glint of challenge. "You can shoot?"

"Of course." She lifted her chin.

"Who taught you?"

"Amos. Thought I should know how to handle a gun."

"Based on Toby's assessment, Amos was either an in-credible teacher or you're a more than apt student." Cole tilted his head. "With your cooking skills as a guide, I'd settle on the latter."

She smoothed back her hair from her face. "It's noth-ing special."

"That remains to be seen."

Aware that Toby watched them both with a keenness that belied his age, she held out her hand for the bag. "Give it here. Let me see if I can whip up something edible." Soup would be the easiest after she marinated the meat.

She might as well make a mess of her kitchen again if it pleased them.

Cole nodded. "I'll go start the tanning process. Be back after a bit." He turned. "C'mon, Toby."

Together they went out the door.

On a whim, Lenora stepped to the porch and watched the two—one tall, sandy-haired and blue-eyed and the other with dark brown hair and green eyes. Cole patted her boy on the shoulder and said something that only Toby could hear. They both laughed.

What a pair they made. The thought drew her up short—*like father and son*.

Cole tucked in the shirt Lenora had given him the night before. Had it once belonged to Amos? Though he felt a little odd taking her husband's clothing, it solved the problem of his needing to wear something while she washed his things.

From the barn he watched as Lenora stood before a steaming cauldron, stirring the clothing in boiling water and soft soap with a large, wooden paddle. This was her second batch—the rest of the scrubbed items was already hanging on the line. Toby helped, staying close so she could direct him when she needed something.

Since they were busy, this would be the perfect time to scout around and see if he could find what Hackett missed. If Amos had dropped the money off at the ranch, Cole would be sure to find evidence.

He did a careful search of the barn. Keeping in mind that Amos was a master craftsman, Cole checked all surfaces in case of a false wall. He left Lenora's shotgun where it was, but noted nothing unusual about the building.

What about the unfinished cabin across the yard? The one Toby said was for hired help?

When Lenora and her son weren't looking, he sauntered to the building and stepped inside. Again, he took care to check the walls and floor. Nothing hidden there. Only the house remained. However, he couldn't just saunter inside with Lenora and Toby nearby. Not without some reason anyway. Perhaps the direct approach was best.

"I need more water," Lenora was saying to her son when Cole got within hearing range.

"I'll get it," he volunteered. Since the house was closer than the stream, it made sense to get water from inside.

"Thanks." She wiped her forehead with her arm before gripping the wooden paddle again. Then to Toby she said, "Please bring me more soft soap for the laundry."

Cole made a couple trips with the bucket, and while they were occupied, slipped into the house. A large pot sat on the stove with the two jackrabbits cooking. Good. He could always claim he was checking her stew. Without hesitation, he went into Lenora's bedroom first.

Straightaway, he found the small trapdoor in the floor under a braided rug. However, it led nowhere and contained only two dollars and some ammunition. With as much speed as possible, he restored the rug and was soon out of her room.

He quickly checked Toby's loft. Again, Cole found nothing except the opening in the ceiling. Amos had been clever in the way he constructed the panel and stashed a rope on a hidden shelf. A search of the rest of the house yielded no other finds.

With as much nonchalance as possible, Cole strolled out of the house. Lenora and Toby didn't seem to notice.

"I'm going to take a short ride," he announced.

Toby's head shot up. "Where? Can I come?"

"Nah, I'm just going to exercise Sheba. Nothing exciting."

The boy's face fell while Lenora appeared relieved.

In no time, Cole saddled up his mare and trotted her around the ranch yard. For a few minutes, he acted as though he was taking her through her paces, but soon he got back to his real reason—looking for any place Amos might have hidden the bank money.

Reports indicated the robbers had used a satchel. Had Amos buried it next to the biggest tree near the yard? How about beside that large boulder? Or at the corner of that fence?

Cole found several possible hiding places, but in the months that had passed since the robbery, the ground had hardened, obliterating any sign of newly turned dirt. Besides, he had to take into consideration that the man was dying. Would he really have had the strength to dig more than a shallow hole?

In that case, Cole would see a satchel poking up through the dirt. After riding around for over an hour, he turned back toward the ranch, no closer to solving the mystery of the money.

As he brushed Sheba, he concluded Hackett was wrong about the bankroll being there. In which case Cole needed to expand his investigation.

It's about time for my departure.

Toby had told him everything possible about his pa while Lenora had shared little else new in the several conversations they'd had. With the ranch being so far from town, Cole had learned all he could from this location. Besides the never-ending job of fixing fences, the ranch was in top-notch shape.

After finishing a couple more tasks, he really needed to go. No excuses. He would leave Sheba and Rowdy in Toby's capable care before riding off. But where?

The obvious answer came to him—he should offer himself out as a hired gun to either Jeb or his notorious father, Eli. However, Cole needed to be careful. If they suspected he was sympathetic toward Lenora in the least, he had no doubt they would shoot first, talk second.

However, if that move got him closer to answers, he was willing to take that chance.

Still dressed in his nightshirt, Toby peered through the mop of hair that fell over his eyes. "Are we riding again today, Cole?"

Lenora grinned at the eagerness in his voice as she brushed back his bangs. In the next few days, she needed to give him a haircut.

"If it's okay with your mother." Cole's gaze met hers as he sipped his coffee.

"Is it, Ma?" Toby turned wide eyes to her.

"I don't see why not." She had to smile at the way his face lit up when she answered. Truthfully, she liked the two of them spending time together. Her boy needed a man's example to follow—and what better person than Cole?

Not only had Toby begun to fill out because he was eating more, but he was beginning to put on some muscle from the hard work he and Cole had been doing. What made Lenora smile the most, though, was the way the youngster mimicked the man, even walking like him and picking up some of his mannerisms.

When guilt pricked her conscience—because he wasn't taking after his father—the emotion passed as quickly as it had come. She didn't want Toby to be like his pa. And she refused to feel bad about it one moment.

After he finished his breakfast, he seemed to fly up into the loft to change.

"I want your nightshirt, so I can fix that tear along

your sleeve," Lenora called after him. Had he been wrestling cattle in his dreams?

Instead of bringing it down, the clothing dropped through the loft's window that opened to the room below. Squelching a sigh, she shook her head. She hadn't rightly specified how he was to give her his nightshirt. After picking it up, she glanced to see Cole's response.

For some reason, he wasn't grinning. His brow wrinkled as he gripped his cup. "I plan to round up some cattle so we can get on with branding."

"Good." Lenora took a seat to finish her breakfast. "I know we're late taking care of that chore. But it's gotta be done."

"I plan for us to only be gone a few hours." His jaw flexed. "If we take Blister, we'll get more accomplished. Then be back quicker."

"I've got some mending and sewing to do, so I'll stay close to the house till you return." When his tight expression didn't relax, she thought she understood. "Really, Cole. I'll be fine. I'll have my rifle handy. I always do." She pointed to her reliable friend, propped up by the door.

He scratched his chin. "If you need anything, fire a couple shots."

"Will do." She rose and cleared dishes from the table.

In a short while, Cole and Toby had food, water and had saddled their horses. Blister barked in excitement when he realized he was going with them.

In truth, she looked forward to a change of pace. She so wanted to stitch a bandanna for Cole—and perhaps a scarf for herself?—but they'd been so busy with ranch needs that she'd not gotten to them. Maybe she could get some cleaning done while they weren't underfoot. Best of all, she wouldn't have to prepare a big noon meal. She would be content to eat leftovers and pan bread.

After they departed, she turned her attention to the stove and blackened it with wax until it gleamed. Next she cleaned the house. With those chores finished, she brought out her sewing and spread it across the table. The amount of fabric she'd purchased would be enough for two bandannas and a small scarf as she'd planned.

She ran her hand over the dark red cotton printed with small white dots. Would Cole think the design too feminine? He couldn't fault the fabric's softness. In no time, she'd cut the material and sewed the edges to keep them from fraying.

The sun had crested the halfway mark, signaling that noon had long passed, before she put her sewing basket away. She opened the door, allowing in fresh air as she waited for Toby and Cole. Their return had to be soon. She started a fresh pot of coffee, smiling as she antic-ipated his reaction to the bandannas. Would he be as pleased as she hoped?

After surveying the number of items she'd mended, she sighed in satisfaction.

A new pair of pants awaited Toby along with several pairs of darned socks, a repaired shirt and his nightshirt. She had created an apron from material scraps and her new scarf. And she'd repaired one of Cole's shirts.

Lenora lifted her scarf and draped it across her neck, enjoying the feel of the soft fabric. When she twirled in happiness, she caught sight of something by the door.

Shrieking in terror, she reeled back.

Standing on the threshold was Jeb Hackett. Watch-ing her.

While she clutched the scarf to her chest, he chuckled. "Don't stop. I enjoyed seeing you dance."

How had he come up to the house so silently? She'd not heard a horse or even his footsteps on the porch.

"I…" Anything she planned to say died in her throat.

"Didn't hear me coming, didja?" His grin spread.

Unable to find her voice, she shook her head.

"That's cuz I wanted to surprise ya." His gaze flickered over her form.

She glanced at her rifle, leaning next to Jeb.

"You wanting this?" He lifted the weapon and examined it. "Amos's favorite, if I recall. Not good for a lady like you, though." With deft fingers, he removed the shells and set the gun back where it was.

She finally found her tongue. "Did you—you come up the road?"

Maybe Cole had seen him. And perhaps he was now galloping her way?

God, please…

"Nope." Jeb grinned as he pocketed the bullets. "I came the back way so's I could visit my old friend, Amos." He pointed in the direction of her husband's tombstone.

Lenora's heart chugged to a stop. Had he found the money? Impossible. But did he suspect where it was? Again, impossible. She'd hidden it where no one would ever think to look.

"Where's your manners? Ain't ya going to ask me to sit?"

"Of course." Edging away, she indicated the seat nearest to him. Once he settled, she would escape.

As if anticipating her plan, Jeb pulled the chair away from the table and positioned it closer to the open door.

"Been a long time since we had a chat, you and I, all by ourselves." He rocked the chair back on two legs, pushing against the table with his foot.

She pulled the scarf off her neck and set it on the rest of her mending. "I suppose." With his dirty boot so close to the clothing, she gathered everything into the middle of the table.

"Don'tcha even want to know what I'm here to talk about?"

"I can't imagine." She sounded breathless, even to herself.

"I checked out that story you told me—of selling out."

She gulped, fingers tightening in the stack of mending.

"Frank Hopper and me had a nice talk. I told him he shouldn't even think of buying your ranch." Jeb smirked. "Besides, you weren't counting on that, were you? I knew you wouldn't be so foolish as to try to leave the area."

Again gulping, she slowly shook her head.

"Didn't think so." He ran his hands down his thighs. "But the real reason I came over is to talk about Amos."

Lenora grabbed her apron and tied it about her waist, like a protecting shield.

Where was her knife? Stupid to not have strapped it to her calf like usual. But somehow she knew a blade would be useless against Jeb. She shivered as she imagined him turning it on her. "Amos is dead. There's nothing to talk about."

"Something been bugging me for months now." As though pondering, Jeb rocked back and forth on the two chair legs. "He, the boys and me took a little trip into Cheyenne last November. If'n you didn't know. There we, uh, acquired some money. Gambling and such." He grinned, apparently amused by his own fabrication.

"I already guessed that's what Amos was going to do. Before he even left. He knew I couldn't abide his gambling."

Jeb's grin widened. Because he saw through her act?

"Well this particular day, our *winnings* were larger than usual. Amos was in charge of making sure the money got safely home. Funny thing though, the cash went missing."

She twisted her hands in her apron. "You know he didn't have time to spend it. He was found dead."

Nodding, Jeb studied her with narrowed eyes. "Bushwhacked. Or so the story goes."

"Then that's where you should look. For the man—or men—who held him up." She stuck to the story that Jeb and his henchmen had circulated. Somewhere to the northwest, they had said, Amos had been ambushed.

"Well, that's the odd part." Jeb ran his fingers and thumb down both sides of his mustache. "We didn't see no footprints or evidence of his being bushwhacked. And Amos, laying all peaceful next to his horse. But no money."

Lenora gripped the table's edge. No one had ever told her how they'd found her husband.

Jeb went on. "Someone knows something. And I've been asking around for months now. Even roughed up my own men too, to make sure they told the truth. But nobody's seen the satchel. And ya know, that used to be my ma's. Even had her initials engraved on the clasp." When he leaned forward, the chair thumped as it rested on all four legs. "Then I got to thinking. What if Amos stopped here? He worried about you not having anything to live on. So he came here and dropped off my money."

Her blood grew steadily colder. She clamped her teeth together to keep them from chattering. "*Your* money?" The words squeaked out.

"I meant our money." His lip curled.

What could she say? She drew herself up. Jeb had no proof, no way to confirm his suspicions. Even though he had guessed the truth, he would never find the satchel.

"Do I look like I'm living high off the hog?" She injected indignation into her tone. "I had barely enough money to pay for my supplies last week. Or didn't you hear?"

Of course he would have. Mr. Richards had all but proved he did what the Hacketts said.

Brow wrinkling, Jeb stared at her as though making up his mind about something. Slapping his hands on his knees, he rose. "Sorry to hear that." He turned and studied the row of tin cans lining one shelf. "Now where did Amos always hide his stash?" Without error, he grabbed the baking powder tin and shook it. The lone coin inside clattered.

He turned, eyebrows raised. "Sounds pretty empty." Jeb pried off the lid and peered inside. "Two bits and one dollar is all?" He dug into his pants pocket and pulled out a wad of bills. After peeling off a couple, he carelessly tossed them into the can and placed it back on the shelf. "There. Done my duty for my friend's widow."

She pressed her lips together, determined not to thank him.

His glance raked the room, then settled on the stove. "Coffee? Don't mind if I do." He grabbed a tin cup and poured the steaming, black brew.

Her hope that the interview had ended died as he settled back onto his chair.

"Have a seat, 'Nora."

Fists clenching, she controlled her temper with effort. "No, thanks." She took a shaky breath. "I thought we were done talking."

"Not by a long shot." He tasted his coffee, then jerked back as though he'd burned his lip. "I know you have that satchel. Don't know where you—or Amos—hid it, but I'm gonna find it."

What could she say? His speculations bordered on the truth.

"I can see your brain working, 'Nora, trying to create a lie. But it won't work on me."

She crossed her arms, determined not to answer.

"So here's my proposition. Either you give me my money, or I'll take you and your ranch in trade. Even though this place isn't worth that much." Sneering, he set his coffee on the edge of the table. "'Course, I'll have to shoot that mangy dog of yours first. And maybe your kid as well if he doesn't learn to shut his mouth."

Her heart hammered against her rib cage.

"But you…" His head tilted as he sized her up. "You're worth more'n any bankroll." Again, he tilted back on his chair, voice growing husky. "Poor Amos hadn't a clue. When he came back from Minneapolis, I was disappointed you two were already married."

She squeezed her crossed arms against her chest, trying to keep from hyperventilating.

"But now you're alone again, although not for long." He rocked back and forth on two legs once more. "You're gonna marry me, 'Nora. I decided. Not one of my boys, but me."

Without circumspection, she darted forward and slapped the cup off the table. Hot coffee splashed across Jeb's torso. With a yelp, he flew backward.

Lifting her skirts, she bolted past him and out the door.

A growl of rage followed the crashing chair. After nearly tumbling down the stairs, she regained her equilibrium and darted across the yard. Footsteps pounded behind her.

My shotgun. In the barn.

Thumping feet drew closer. Something swiped at her

arm, tearing her sleeve. She wrenched from his grasp. Off balance a moment, she righted herself.

Almost there.

Rasping breath drew closer. She'd taken a few more steps when Jeb latched on to her left wrist. Pain shot through her as he wrenched it. With brutal force, he twisted. She screamed as he forced her to her knees.

"Like I said," he panted above her, "I knew there was a spitfire underneath those petticoats of yours."

His grip tightened.

"Stop," she shrieked. "You're hurting me."

His face hovered over her, mouth thinning under the handlebar mustache. His teeth flashed with cruelty. "I want that satchel *now*. Either that or you. Your choice, 'Nora."

She clawed at the fingers that imprisoned her wrist. Gravel bit into her knees. Her whole existence focused on her agony. No words could form. A wail of pain rose to consume her.

"So be it." He jerked her to her feet, then swiveled. At the sound of gunfire, he crouched. As he grappled for his pistol, Jeb ducked behind her and let loose a stream of curses.

Wholly consumed with pain, Lenora tried to pry out of his relentless grip. When he shoved her, she crumpled to the ground. Face buried, she didn't lift her head at the sounds of creaking leather and Jeb's horse neighing in protest.

"I'm not done with you yet, 'Nora," he yelled.

Horse hooves galloped out of earshot as two other sets drew closer. Blister's frantic bark filled her ears.

"Ma!" Toby screamed the word. "Ma, are you okay?"

In moments, she felt him collapse next to her.

"Please say something." His young arms wrapped about her. "Please."

She raised her head, clutching her arm to her chest. "It's okay. I'm okay, Toby."

Looking around, she watched Cole disappear over the hill. Chasing Jeb? Cattle milled nearby. Had Cole and Toby driven them there?

She now recalled the shots—of warning? They must have seen her and Jeb in the yard.

Leaning her head back, she breathed a prayer of thanksgiving.

Tears streaked Toby's face. He wiped his nose on his sleeve. "Let me help you up, Ma."

Cradling her arm, Lenora awkwardly gained her feet. With her son's arm around her, they climbed the porch steps. When he tried to lead her into the house, she stiffened. "No. I'm not going back in there."

Brow wrinkled, Toby appeared as though unable to decide what to do.

"I'll sit here." She took the rocking chair instead.

Her son stood nearby, pulling at his hair as though in mounting helplessness. His lower lip trembled as he repeatedly sniffed.

Lenora took a deep breath. "I'm all right, son."

Again, he swiped his nose, chin quivering. Like all men, he needed a task to feel useful.

She closed her eyes for a moment. "Do you think you could get me a drink of water?"

His face lit up. "Sure." He disappeared into the house and was soon back. In his haste, he had spilled half of the water.

She finished it. "One more."

Again, he was soon back, this time with a full cup.

After Lenora drank that, she set the cup on the floorboards beside her. Still her son seemed barely able to contain his tears. So she did something she hadn't done in years. "Come here."

Taking care to protect her injured wrist, she pulled him onto her lap. He turned and buried his face against her neck and cried, huge sobs shuddering through his body. For a long time, she merely held him.

When he grew calmer, she said in a low voice, "It'll be okay, Toby. I promise you."

Gulping air, he kept his face hidden.

I will never let this happen again. Jeb Hackett would not threaten her like he had. No matter what, she had to protect herself. And her son.

As far as she was concerned, only one thing would stop Jeb. An idea seemed to come out of the blue. Because God gave it to her?

Jeb had spoken of marriage. Perhaps that was the one thing that would stop him. The moment she resolved what to do, peace washed over her.

Tonight. She wouldn't delay proposing to Cole for one more day.

Chapter Twelve

By the time Cole returned to the ranch, his anger had burned down into red-hot ashes. Jeb Hackett had escaped, the gap too wide to close. With night coming, Cole couldn't hope to find his way. But he determined to head over to Hackett's place at first light and call him out.

When Cole rode into the yard, he was surprised to see Lenora sitting on the porch. Not in the house? She cradled her left arm as she rocked, not even meeting his gaze when he mounted the steps.

A quick glance told him all he needed to know. Hackett had roughed her up a bit, but had not assaulted her in the way Cole first feared when he'd ridden over the hill. He would never forget the way her scream froze his blood.

Still, he had to ask. "You okay?"

She stopped rocking and met his gaze. In a frightening calm tone, she answered. "Yes."

He expected hysteria or at least tears. Again, she began rocking.

Toby was inside, doing something. Cleaning up a mess Hackett had made?

Cole glanced back at Lenora, then the animals that milled around the yard. It would be dark soon.

"I'm gonna pen the cattle while I can. Unless you need me here to…?"

Her deep brown eyes met his. "That's a fine idea. Toby and I'll be okay." She nodded toward her rifle, resting within easy reach. "He brought me that. Reloaded it too."

Reloaded? Cole gulped, resisting the urge to ask what happened.

Her serenity chilled him. Perhaps she was in shock? No doubt a storm of hot tears would come later. He wouldn't be so cruel as to force them now. But when the time came, he was prepared to hold her and let her crying wash away Hackett's brutal attack.

Cole paused to reassure her. "First thing tomorrow, I want you to give me directions to Hackett's place."

"Why?"

"I'm going to his ranch so that I can—"

"No." Wide-eyed, she gripped the rocker's armrest. "You'd never get to him. On his ranch or in town, he's always surrounded by a dozen of his cronies."

"I can't let this go, Lenora."

"You have to. There's no other choice. Jeb's men would beat you senseless if he ordered them to. I've seen it before."

He considered his options. "Then I'll go to the sheriff and—"

"And what? Say that you saw Jeb on my ranch?" Her voice rose. "Jeb could call twenty men to testify that he was at the saloon all day. And the results would be the same. He'd make you pay." She stood, chest rising and falling with anxiety. "Promise me you won't do anything foolish. I couldn't live with myself if Jeb…"

If Cole didn't agree, she might grow hysterical. "I'll think about it."

"No. Promise me." She gripped his arm. When he didn't answer quick enough, her fingers tightened. "I'd rather die than see you crippled for life because of me."

Cool reason swept over him. She was right, of course. Rumors abounded about how Hackett always managed to weasel out of a conviction. Cole needed hard evidence.

I will find it. That or...

Lenora's beautiful eyes pleaded. "Promise me."

"I promise I won't do anything stupid."

Foolish perhaps—like hang up his badge and step outside the law to take down Hackett. But not stupid.

"I'll see to the cattle." Cole stepped off the porch and climbed back into the saddle.

Dusk had fallen by the time he finished rounding up the herd and penning the cattle in the back pasture. Lenora hadn't moved from the porch, still rocking. Her mouth was set, but her forehead appeared calm. Though she no longer cradled her wrist, it rested on her lap. Even in the disappearing light, Cole could see her reddened skin.

He kicked himself for not taking care of her injury before the cattle. However, he doubted she would let him touch her. Perhaps now?

Without explaining first, he retrieved liniment from his saddlebags in the barn. He lit the lantern and carried it to the porch.

"Let me have a look at that." He nodded toward her wrist.

She hesitated before stretching it toward him.

Without touching her, Cole scrutinized her arm under the light. Didn't appear broken. After setting down the lantern and tin of liniment, he ran his fingers over her soft skin.

She hissed.

"I'm sorry." With care, he felt along the delicate bones. When he touched a couple spots, she jerked in reflex.

"Nothing's broken. But there's plenty of swelling." After scooping out some liniment, he carefully massaged it into her skin. Cole kept his voice low, like when he talked to an injured animal. "I usually use this on horses, but it should work on you too."

She wrinkled her nose, the first authentic reaction he'd seen besides her response to pain.

"It stinks." She pressed her other hand to her face and turned away.

"That it does." He watched her reaction as he attempted to joke. "I guarantee a direct link between how bad it smells and how good it works."

As he feared, she didn't smile. Pain—both physical and emotional—consumed her. In the countless times Cole had tended to injured animals, they had looked away, just like Lenora.

How he wished he could easily mend her hidden wounds.

He kept speaking even though she was likely aware of only a fraction of his words. "I know you'll be amazed at how good it feels by morning." Again he paused, assessing her as he continued to smooth the concoction over her delicate wrist. "The odor won't be as bad in a few minutes. Likely tomorrow or the next day, you'll think this liniment smells like some fancy, French perfume. You'll be begging me for the recipe."

A smile tugged at her lips. A good sign.

With care, he rested her hand against his palm as he stroked her skin. Not to apply more liniment, but to merely let her know he cared. Her arm was as delicate as a flower stalk.

Her dark brown eyes finally met his. Though her mouth spasmed, she didn't cry as he expected.

"It feels a lot better," she said in a low voice. "Thanks."

Why didn't she pull away? Again, Lenora didn't react as he expected, allowing her hand to remain on his.

Cole lurched to his feet. "Be right back." After he went inside, he blew out a breath. What was wrong with him? He seemed more affected by the contact than she. Wasn't *he* supposed to be comforting *her*?

The smell of overcooked beans made him take pause. Where was Toby?

A steaming pan sat on the stove. Before the food burned, he removed it from the heat and went back onto the porch with a towel.

Standing before Lenora, he clenched his jaw as he contemplated touching her again.

With parted lips, she looked up at him. "What is it?"

"I, uh…" He held out the towel. "Figured this would be better to use than my…well, since it's clean. For your…" He waved at her wrist, kicking himself for sounding so tongue-tied. After clearing his throat, he bundled her arm into a sling. "This should help. Try not to use your hand tonight, if possible."

Eyes huge, she nodded.

Toby bounded up the steps, hair wet and face scrubbed. "Supper's ready."

Scratching his chin, Cole nodded. "Sounds good." The gesture not only hid his consternation about Lenora, but covered his amusement about Toby's idea of making supper. Apparently the boy hadn't figured out he shouldn't leave food unattended on the stove. Washing up before a meal was so ingrained that he'd neglected the pan of beans.

After the youngster went inside, Cole paused to ask Lenora, "You coming?"

Mouth tight, she shook her head.

Couldn't blame her. Did she feel safer on the porch?

He stuck his head in the door. "We're eating outside tonight, Toby." While the youngster got dishes, he served up the beans. However, he left the blackened ones at the bottom of the pan. With bread slices and tin plates, they sat on the dusky porch to eat.

After one bite, Cole coughed, but he managed to hide his shudder at the burned taste that permeated the food.

Toby choked down some of his meal and ended up sliding his plate toward Blister who wolfed it down.

The only one who didn't appear to notice was Lenora. As Cole scooped the beans into his mouth, he watched her. She ate without really paying attention to her food.

Seemed like supper was finished in minutes.

"Toby, why don't you get ready for bed." Her eerily calm voice pierced the darkness.

Cole didn't miss the glance the boy shot his mother.

"Yes'm. Good night." Without a word, he went inside with his plate.

What? No prayers or Bible reading like usual?

"Let me clean up, and then I'll say good night." Cole grabbed the tins.

Lenora's voice rose. "I need to talk to you about something important first."

He couldn't help but hear the note of urgency—desperation?—that edged her voice.

"It can wait till morning. Sounds like you need rest."

"No. Now."

He'd heard that tone before—when she had pointed a

rifle at his chest. Her voice was cold, calm, daring him to argue with her.

Cole slowly set the tin plates on the porch, but he remained standing.

The light of the lone lantern shone on her face as she raised haunted eyes to his. "I've been thinking about this all afternoon. My mind's made up." She paused to lick dry lips. "I want to offer you half my ranch."

Were his ears playing tricks on him?

"Half your...?" He scratched his jaw. What was she talking about? For him to assume she wanted nothing in return bordered on ridiculous. He rallied. "In exchange for what? I have little money and just a few horses and guns. What could we possibly trade?"

Her mouth tightened. "Your name."

"Huh?"

"I said 'your name.' I'm willing to trade half my ranch for your name."

His jaw dropped as his brain scrambled for an explanation.

He must have looked as stupid as he felt because she added, "I'm asking you to marry me."

Hearing himself sputter, he stopped. A thousand protests rose at her foolish idea. He could never agree.

For starters, she was cheating herself by asking for so little.

Second, she didn't know him. Didn't know anything about him.

Third, he was a wanderer. Had she forgotten?

The list grew.

She ducked her head. "I know it's a bit unusual. But it's the only way...the only way to protect myself. If I was married, I would be off-limits to—to some men."

Jeb Hackett? Cole had no doubt she referred to him.

What had happened before he and Toby had arrived and interrupted Lenora and Hackett? What had the outlaw said and done that had driven her to such a drastic step?

"Naturally, the marriage would be in name only," she hurried to add in the same calm voice. "I'll draw up a contract, delineating all the details so there will be no misunderstanding between us. The day we marry, I will sign half the ranch over to you. In six months or so—after things calm down—you can go your way. Or stay and raise horses like you've said. No strings attached."

Six months? That was exactly how long he had been given to gather evidence of the Hackett gang. The eerie similarity caused a shudder to grip his body.

Was this God arranging the circumstances of his life yet again?

"Lenora. This is…" Cole paused to soften his words. "This is exceedingly generous of you. But you know nothing about me."

"Not true. You're a man of your word. You're kind. A hard worker. And Toby cares for you. Greatly. Why not you?"

"Because—you said it yourself—I'm restless. I can't settle in one place very long before I start looking at the horizon and wondering what's over there."

"I'm not asking for a lifetime commitment. Just six months. A year at the most." She rose, taking care to protect her injured wrist. "Just enough time to get the ranch back on its feet. If needed, I could always sell out. Give you half your share and…and we'd part ways. No hard feelings."

Tempted to say yes, he held his tongue. Reasons to decline deluged his mind.

He was in the area for one reason and one only—take Jeb Hackett down. Once that mission was accomplished,

Cole would move on to the next assignment. US marshals were needed all over the Wyoming and Oregon territories as well as California. He went where they told him to go. He couldn't if he was saddled with a wife and son.

As much as he cared for Lenora—and Toby—he wasn't ready to settle anywhere.

"I'd like your answer tonight, Mr. Cole." Lenora stepped closer. "If you don't agree, then I need to make other arrangements."

He straightened with a jerk.

Other arrangements? Did she mean she would find someone else to marry? A rush of fury rose at the thought of another man taking his place.

She moved closer yet. "Yes or no?"

Regardless of his personal feelings, he had to decline. No other option was available for a man in his position.

Prepared to refuse, he took a deep breath. "Yes." Astounded at his reply, he added, "I'll do it."

Her shoulders relaxed followed by a long exhale. "Fine. I'll draw up a contract right now."

Am I out of my mind?

What had he just agreed to? The ramifications of his *yes* crashed upon him. He shoved them aside. He already said yes. *What's done is done.*

In the moments after agreeing, he grew concerned about a ten-year-old who might not understand. Clearly Lenora had mentioned something to Toby before dinner. Cole felt obligated to speak to the youngster himself. Man to man.

She brushed by him, finally entering the house.

"Wait," he called. "Does Toby know?"

Lenora turned, her face once again in the light. "Not all the details."

"I'd like to talk to him before…" He stumbled over the words *we're married*. "Before we finalize our agreement."

"Very well. Oh, one more thing." She bit her lip, a deep blush spreading across her cheeks. "I would ask that you give me your word that you won't…" She gulped, her good hand pummeled the space between then. "You won't demand your husbandly rights once we're married."

He took care not to answer too quickly. Being intimate with her would only complicate his eventual departure. In a way, her request relieved him. His principles would demand he keep himself in check regardless of how tempting she might be. "I give you my word of honor."

Again, she sighed. "Thank you."

Before he knew it, Cole was congratulating himself on agreeing to her proposal. What if she'd chosen a less honorable man to marry? His *yes* had protected her from making a disastrous choice.

"Send Toby to the barn when you're ready."

She nodded. "He'll be down soon."

Less than fifteen minutes later, the boy showed up, dressed in nightshirt and boots.

"You wanted to see me, Cole?"

He hung the lantern on a nail. As he sat cross-legged on the straw, he waved for Toby to take a seat.

"Your ma and I've been talking." He studied the boy, trying to ascertain how much Toby knew.

"She told me."

"So you know we're gonna get married?"

The boy nodded. Raising his head, he peered at him. "Do you love my ma, Cole?"

For a moment, he opened his mouth, then shut it. "Can't say exactly I love her, but I do care for her. And you." When the boy didn't respond right away, he added,

"But I promise to treat you both right for as long as I'm here."

"Ma said you might someday move on."

Cole took a breath, debating how much to admit. "It's a possibility."

The youngster's mouth moved as he pondered the news.

"However, the reason I asked to speak with you is I wanted to ask your permission to marry your mother. If you say no, then I won't."

"Really?"

"Yep." Part of him hoped the boy would. That would solve a passel of problems since Cole hadn't the sense to decline.

Toby's jaw squared, mind apparently made up. "I'd like you to. Ma's happier than I seen in a long time."

His jaw tightened. "She is?"

The boy nodded.

"So, I have your permission?"

He took his time answering. "Yes."

"Something else you should know." Cole shifted on the straw. "I plan to keep sleeping here in the barn. So we can all get used to the new arrangement."

The boy's brow clouded. "I reckon that's a good idea."

Because he worried about what Hackett had done to his mother? It wasn't Cole's place to explain the way of a husband and wife. Or of a violent criminal like Hackett who had no concept of what was right or decent when it came to women.

Besides, Cole would only be guessing about what had happened on the ranch today.

He pushed the speculations away, knowing that if he thought about it too much, he'd be tempted to hunt down the outlaw and shoot him in cold blood.

Unclenching his fist, he blew out a breath. "Okay then. That's all I wanted to talk to you about."

Toby rose and brushed off the straw that stuck to his nightshirt. "Ma says you're getting married tomorrow. Do you think I can go?"

Cole masked his surprise by slapping the dirt off his britches. "Don't see why not." He straightened. "As a matter of fact, you need to be there."

A happy grin split Toby's face. Without warning, he threw his arms about Cole. "I'm glad you're gonna marry Ma."

Breath trapped in his chest, Cole fought to exhale normally. He patted Toby's shoulder, feeling out of his element. Why did the boy's reaction bother him so?

Because I'm a fraud.

He had no business agreeing to a marriage that he didn't intend to honor for a lifetime. Even if his motives were from a desire to protect Lenora.

But the truth was, the boy's hug of acceptance felt good. Cole battled the dual emotions of discomfort and joy.

"Good night, Toby."

Again, the youngster surprised him by holding out his hand.

With as much solemnity as he felt, Cole shook it.

Long after Toby went to bed, he stared up at the dark ceiling wrestling with his decision.

What if I'm wrong about Lenora? Again that worry rose to hound him. What if she knew more about Amos than she was sharing? What if she had the money? The thought crossed Cole's mind that he might be marrying an outlaw. How could he maintain his integrity if he grew attached to her? Impossible.

Rolling on his side, he clutched the blanket so hard his fist hurt.

If he grew attached? Cole's laugh of derision filled the dark barn. He was way beyond "attached" already.

Truth be told, no other man would marry Lenora Pritchard but him.

Chapter Thirteen

"Do you, Lenora Julia Pritchard, take this man…?" The preacher droned on.

Or was that the buzzing in her head that drowned out his voice, beginning the moment they had entered the church? She fought to concentrate.

"…for better for worse, for richer for poorer…" Lenora's tone sounded stilted, even to her own ears. In the quietness of the chapel, her words seemed to echo. She stumbled over the phrase, "To love and to cherish," worried about lying to the preacher. Lying to God.

But even if she didn't exactly love Cole, she could promise to look out for his best interests. That wasn't a lie, was it?

She cut her eyes toward his inflexible jaw and stern expression as he recited the vows. His red-rimmed eyes betrayed a fitful night. Was he also troubled?

Perspiration trickled between her shoulder blades. Another drop beaded at her temple.

A pesky fly circled the preacher as he talked, a nuisance the entire ceremony.

Everything about this wedding was different from her first. That morning, she had donned a clean dress, but no one would consider it "Sunday best." Long ago she had reconciled herself to work attire—the only clothing she owned. Lenora had woven a royal blue ribbon through her braid—her only adornment. Instead of flowers, she clutched a prayer book. No happy crowds crammed the pews. This event had been hurriedly arranged and carried out in secret.

Besides Toby, the only other person present was the preacher's wife. Several times, the woman licked dry lips. A frown marred her forehead.

"I now pronounce you man and wife." Preacher Jeremiah spoke with more speed than necessary. "Those whom God has joined together let no one put asunder."

"Amen," both Lenora and Cole answered at the same time.

Silence filled the church.

I'm married.

After shutting his book with a resounding *thwump*, the preacher wiped sweat from his brow. He swatted at the fly that zeroed in on his nose. "Let us pray."

Feeling faint, Lenora closed her eyes. *Dear Lord, what have I done?* How could she have thought marriage was a good idea? Where had her common sense fled to when she'd thought up this crazy scheme?

She jumped when the preacher's wife said in a loud voice, "Amen."

The officiant fixed his gaze on the groom. "You may kiss your bride."

Catching her breath, Lenora looked up into Cole's eyes. What would he do? Indecision flickered in the blue depths. It seemed like they stared at each other a full minute. The next, he inclined his head, but paused with his gaze fixed on her mouth.

Her heart pounded.

Before she could stop herself, she rose on tiptoes. His lips brushed hers with the lightest touch. In seconds, he stepped back, leaving Lenora feeling like she'd been cheated. Then she castigated herself. Hadn't she demanded Cole not touch her?

Swiveling away, he pulled a silver dollar from his pocket. He pressed it into the minister's hand. "Thank you, sir."

Without a word, Toby hugged her and Cole. After a few more requirements, the three of them were soon on the buckboard, heading out of town.

Body rigid, Lenora looked straight ahead, fingers clutched in her lap. A glance at Cole revealed him staring at the road, brow drawn, jaw set. Did he regret his decision? Neither of them spoke during the long ride back home. Even Toby remained sober.

When they reached the ranch, the day had nearly ended. Without a word, Cole helped her down from the buckboard, grabbing her about the waist and lifting her so that she wouldn't have to use her sore wrist.

"Thank you, Cole." She hoped he understood that she regretted unsettling him.

When he merely nodded, she grabbed his arm. "I mean it. Thank you."

His gaze shifted. "I'll see to the livestock." After climbing into the buckboard, he clicked to his horse.

Toby slipped one arm about her waist as they walked up the steps. "You did right, Ma."

She looked down at him, astounded at his comment. "You are getting much too tall, Tobias Joseph. And talking more and more like a grown-up."

He grinned when she mussed his hair. "Want me to set the table?"

"No. You go help Cole."

"'Kay." He bounded off the porch.

Smiling, she watched her son race across the yard. For some reason, seeing him act like a ten-year-old lightened her spirit.

As she scraped the ashes out of the stove and loaded it with wood and tinder, she considered the wedding ceremony. When Cole had given the preacher his full name, Jesse Phillips Cole, she had been surprised. Jesse? However, she suspected he still wanted to be called Cole.

It was late by the time supper was ready. All she had prepared was thin soup and hard bread. Cole and Toby came inside, the skin of their faces and hands scrubbed clean.

"Not much of a meal, I'm afraid," she murmured. "I'll bake tomorrow and cook up something special."

"This is a good enough wedding supper," Cole answered.

Lenora nearly choked on her soup. Not until she saw the dimple creasing one cheek did she realize he was teasing.

Toby grinned, his gaze darting between the two of them. What was he thinking? She didn't even want to imagine what ran through that young man's head.

For the remainder of the meal, Cole chatted about what he wanted to do around the ranch. They had cattle to brand and bull calves to castrate. He wanted to see about expanding the fenced-off pasture so that he could run the livestock in and assess their health. Most important, to get accurate numbers about how many head they owned so they could grow the numbers.

Hearing him make plans calmed her heart. When they were ready to part ways, the ranch might bring a better price. Or perhaps he would be more amenable to buying her out. For the first time that day, hope surged through her.

When he glanced her way, he stopped midsentence. "Am I talking too much?"

She shook her head. "I like it."

In truth, he sounded nervous. Like he didn't know what to do now that he was a married man.

Pulling on his earlobe, he made a face. "I didn't want you to think I'm showing off my greedy side."

"Not at all. I'm pleased you've taken an interest in your property."

"Sounds like a lotta hard work to me," Toby piped up.

They both chuckled, Cole's gaze again resting on her. When the telltale heat bloomed in her cheeks, Lenora pushed her bowl away. "Before I forget…" She went into her bedroom and returned, carrying the bandannas. "I made these yesterday. For you." She held them out to Cole.

He took them, fingers brushing hers. "They're right nice."

"I worried that they might be too fussy, but…" She bit her lip.

"I'm sorry I don't have a wedding present for you."

"Oh, they're not…" Mortification strangled her explanation.

"Appreciate it." Cole rolled one lengthwise and slipped it around his neck. "Perfect."

Lenora hastened to clear the table. "Well, it's about time for bed." She blew out an exasperated breath. Couldn't she say *anything* right? "Toby, change your clothes so we can do our prayers. First say good night to Cole."

"Can't he pray with us, Ma? He's family now."

She looked between the two of them. Surely Cole would decline, wouldn't he? "Of course. Mr. Cole is welcome to pray with us anytime he wants." Then she berated herself for calling him *mister*. Like she'd forgotten his preference.

Palms resting on the table, he met her gaze steadily. "I'd like that."

Hands shaking, she finished clearing the table, dishes clattering together in her haste. After retrieving her Bible, she set it at her place.

Cole surprised her by pulling the book closer. "Where're you reading from?"

Her mind went blank. "You pick."

While Toby climbed into the loft, she scraped leftovers into the pig slop bowl and stacked dishes. She pumped water into a pan and put it on the still-hot stove to heat. All the while, she was aware of Cole watching her.

By the time Toby clambered down the ladder, the dishes were soaking. She sat at her place while her son took his.

"I chose Psalm 4." Cole's finger marked the place on the page. He cleared his throat and began. "'Hear me when I call, O God of my righteousness…'" He continued reading, his voice rising and falling with expression.

Enthralled, Lenora leaned an elbow on the table. When he finished the last verse, he stopped and read it again. "'I will both lay me down in peace, and sleep: for thou, Lord, only makest me dwell in safety.'"

He fixed his gaze on her, eyes full of meaning. Was he assuring her he planned to keep his word? That she could rest tonight without fear?

Something fluttered in her chest. "Thank you, Cole." Folding her hands in her lap, she bowed her head.

As usual, Toby began the time of prayer. He thanked God for their day, the fact that Cole had married his ma and the welfare of the animals he cared about.

Lenora asked the Lord for His continued provision and

thanked Him for His grace. After pausing a moment, she prayed that Cole would find contentment on the ranch.

The room fell silent. Would he pray too?

He cleared his throat and said, "Amen." His chair scraped as he stood. "Thanks." He nodded to them both before turning on his heel and striding out the door.

Lenora didn't try to guess the reason for his abrupt departure. Holding out her arms, she waited for Toby's good-night hug.

"I love you, Ma," he whispered in her ear.

"Love you too." She caressed his cheek, tempted to snuggle with him like she used to when he was a little boy.

Silly thought. What was that saying about half-grown youngsters? Toby was between hay and grass. It would be inappropriate for him to crawl into her bed since he was no longer a child. Next week was his eleventh birthday. How the years had flown.

"Sleep well, my son."

For safety's sake, she closed the flues in the stove to suffocate any hot coals. The crossbar on the door was soon in place and the house secured. In her bedroom, she took her time unbraiding her hair and brushing out the long strands before shrugging into her nightgown. The thought struck her again, in a new way.

I'm no longer a widow.

So why did she still feel like one? Because her husband should be with her, not sleeping in the barn. Guilt pounded her. How could she have turned marriage into a mockery?

I had no choice.

She had to protect herself and Toby. The best way to let Jeb know she was off-limits was to remarry. Only a husband would stand in his way. Lenora turned down the lantern and climbed into bed.

Even as she excused her actions, she recognized the potential folly of her choice. Though Cole was a legal half owner, she couldn't stop him from selling the ranch and absconding with the proceeds. Where would that leave her? How would she and her son survive?

The bankroll. Buried with Amos.

"But it's not mine," she whispered into the darkness. For many minutes she rebuked herself for even thinking she could touch that money. Regardless, the idea worked on her. If the situation became desperate, would she be justified in spending even one dollar?

Cole paused to wipe away the sweat that stung his eyes. Who knew that branding cattle was such hard work? He straightened his aching back, tempted to call it a day. Seemed like calves lined up in a never-ending stream. However, if they didn't take care of this vital task, the cattle could be considered mavericks—and anyone could rightly claim ownership.

He wouldn't put it past Hackett to steal Lenora's cattle.

Correction—*their* cattle.

Funny how shared ownership kept barging to the forefront of his thinking.

"Okay, let 'er up." Cole backed away with the iron while Lenora and Toby loosened the ropes that constrained the calf.

Once freed, the bawling heifer staggered up and rushed to her mother.

He walked back to the fire pit to check if the branding irons were hot enough, giving his muscles a chance to unkink. A glance at his two partners proved they looked as tired as he felt. Since early that morning, they'd been working. Now the sun perched high in the sky, sending down waves of heat.

"One more calf, then I'm calling it." He spoke more for Lenora's sake than his own.

Despite the hat she wore, her cheeks appeared sunburned. What his mind kept having trouble with, though, was the way she dressed. Lenora wore a loose shirt and tightly cinched pants. Had they once belonged to Amos? Obviously, she had sized down the clothing, but they still appeared huge on her. Cole dragged his gaze away and searched for the next calf to lasso.

Pants on a woman were perfectly acceptable. No way could Lenora be such a help in long skirts. Besides, he'd concluded quick enough that he and Toby alone couldn't handle the job. Though willing, the boy didn't have the weight and strength to hold a wiggling calf so that Cole could seat a proper brand.

However, her pants-wearing was definitely a distraction. He found his mind wandering—a dangerous occupation considering his current task. More than one enraged mama had tried to gore him when he pushed his way through the herd to lasso another calf.

They finished the last one and released it. Castrating would have to wait another day. Besides, Cole figured that was something he would not let Lenora do.

"Appreciate the help." He spoke to them both.

"Glad to." With a delicate hand, she dabbed the perspiration on her forehead and cheeks.

"Toby and I'll finish up here. Why don't you go up to the house and rest up?"

"Rest?" She blew out a breath. "I need to make dinner. Or supper maybe?" She squinted at the sun.

"Biscuits and coffee would suit me just fine."

She licked parched lips. "I think I could manage that. Thanks."

"Thank *you*. For your help."

"How long before you come up to the house?"

Cole glanced at the cattle. Before he broke for the day, he wanted to separate the unbranded calves and mothers from the rest of the herd. And keep the bull calves to castrate another day. "Give us a half hour to an hour. You up for that, Toby?"

"Yessir."

"All right." Lenora let out a big breath. "I'll see you both after a bit."

He tried not to watch as she climbed between the fence rails and walked across the yard. Not for the first time he noticed what a comely woman she was. Even sunburned and covered in dust.

It took him and Toby over an hour to cut out the unbranded calves with their mamas. While Cole squeezed between the herds on his horse, Toby manned the gate and released the ones who were branded. A couple of times, a few cattle made a break for it and barged out with the others. Cole rounded them up again and returned them to the fenced areas.

Tired and starving, he finally called it a day.

"You worked hard today." He rubbed down his sorrel whose neck was crusty with dried lather. "Tomorrow you get a break, and Nips will get his turn. Maybe even Sheba."

His gelding snorted like he understood. Cole freed him into the pasture and grinned as his horse rolled in the dirt.

He was just heading up to the house when Toby appeared on the porch, a bar of soap and a towel in his hands.

"Where're you going?"

"Ma said I need a bath. I'm heading down to the stream."

"Huh." More than likely, Cole would end up there, as well. Otherwise, he might not get food.

He paused in the open doorway, waiting for his eyes to adjust to the gloom after the bright sunshine.

Lenora emerged from her bedroom, dressed once again in a white cotton blouse and navy skirt. Pressing a towel to her wet hair, she stopped when she saw him.

"Must be bath night." He waved in her general direction when he realized he'd been staring.

Her hair, usually pinned into place, hung in long, dark waves.

He clamped his mouth shut and forced himself to look away. "I don't suppose you have more soap? In case Toby loses his bar in the creek."

"And a towel?" She moved nearer. "I'm sure a feed sack wouldn't feel good."

"No, ma'am."

She went back into her room and returned with two thin towels. "This is the best I can do." After setting them on the table, she searched the shelf in the kitchen for soap. "I thought I had another bar around here someplace." She stood on tiptoes.

"I see it." He stepped beside her and easily reached the soap that was out of her sight.

They were standing so close, he could count the number of freckles sprinkled across the bridge of her nose. Her brown eyes were lighter than he'd originally thought, with a dark ring encircling the iris. But her lips were the most tempting—soft, moist, parted. That brief and oh-so-tantalizing kiss they'd shared on their wedding day had merely fired his yearning for another. And the next one, he promised himself, wouldn't be a namby-pamby peck on the lips.

She's my wife.

The idea startled him anew. And in that moment, he was tempted to take her into his arms and kiss her so roundly that she would swoon.

He straightened his shoulders.

In name only, he reminded himself. He had given his word that he wouldn't touch her.

Cole was halfway to the stream before he realized that though he clutched the bar of soap, he'd forgotten the towels. However, he wouldn't risk returning to the house. Not until he lectured himself good and long.

No matter how alluring Lenora Julia Cole was, he would keep his promise. Even if it killed him.

Chapter Fourteen

"'A good man out of the good treasure of the heart bringeth forth good things,'" Lenora read. "'And an evil man out of the evil treasure bringeth forth evil things.'"

Cole rested an elbow on the table, growing sleepier by the moment. Not that he wasn't interested in the topic, but the day had been long. At least they were done branding. He and Toby also had castrated the bull calves while Lenora had worked in the garden.

No doubt there were more chores that needed to be taken care of, but in light of Hackett's visit almost a week ago, Cole wouldn't chance leaving her alone again.

When he yawned, she paused and looked up.

"Sorry," he mumbled.

"I think we're done for the night." She pointed to Toby, whose head rested on the table. His sudden twitch proved that he indeed slumbered. Lenora smiled softly at her son.

Nodding in his direction, Cole held up his hand. "Let me." He rose and lifted the youngster, who seemed barely aware of what was going on.

"Is it time to get up?" Toby mumbled in a groggy voice. Without waiting for an answer, he leaned his head on Cole's shoulder and appeared to fall back to sleep.

He carried the boy to the ladder. "Hang on."

Rousing just enough, Toby put his arms around Cole's neck while he climbed up to the loft. He stayed long enough only to remove the boy's boots and tuck him under the blankets.

"Did he go back to sleep?" Lenora asked when he returned to the room below.

"I don't think he even woke up." Cole stretched, removing a knot from his back. "Tomorrow we'll take it easier."

"I'm sure we could all use the rest." She flexed her wrist as though it bothered her.

Cole pointed. "That still giving you trouble?"

She shrugged and pushed back her sleeve. "I might've strained it when I lifted a full bucket of water. But the bruising is nearly gone."

"Let me look." He took her wrist in his hands before considering the foolishness. For four days, he'd been careful to guard his thoughts and actions. How quickly he could forget his resolve.

With care, he felt along the bones. Like she said, the swelling had gone down quite a bit, and the bruising was all but faded.

"Does it hurt here?" He pressed gently.

She hissed. "Yes."

"You might've reinjured it a little." He stepped back. "Want me to get that liniment?"

She appeared as though she would agree, then shook her head. "I'll just wrap a cool cloth around it." Before he could excuse himself for the night, she asked, "Would you like a cup of coffee? We could set a while on the porch."

"Sure." As soon as the word left his mouth, he chastised himself for agreeing so quickly.

Since the wedding day, he had not stopped beating

himself up for making such a hasty decision. It would do no good at this point.

What's done is done. Still.

While he stood on the porch and waited for her to join him, he looked out across the landscape. With the moon hiding behind the clouds, darkness shrouded everything.

Were Jeb Hackett and his men out there? Watching? No doubt the outlaw knew about their marriage by now. How would he retaliate? Or perhaps he would leave Lenora alone as she hoped.

Regardless, Cole still had a job to do. His marriage had not changed his plans to solve the mystery and find the money if possible—only rerouted them for a bit. Now that he had finished the branding and castrating, he was ready to turn his energies back to the investigation.

Lenora had once said that her husband's body was found northwest of the ranch. Hackett's place was northeast. So where had Amos been heading? Cole would stake his reputation on the gang having some rendezvous point. Or a hiding place. Coupled with the campfire evidence, it was likely the men holed up somewhere not far from this ranch.

"Here you are." Lenora held a cup toward him while she gripped one of her own.

"Much obliged." The strong coffee seemed the perfect temperature.

Instead of sitting on her rocking chair, she remained standing beside him, looking out into the night. The gentle glow of the lanterns from inside the house spilled onto the porch, creating a haven of soft light.

He threw her a sidelong glance. "How're you holding up?"

She smiled. "Good." After a tentative sip, she cradled the cup. "Actually, very good. You?"

"Haven't worked this hard since…" Pausing, he sought to recall. He thought about a posse chase he had once led through Missouri. Ten days of pushing hard with little rest. Though mind-numbing and rump-bruising, it had not been as physically demanding as what he had done the last four days.

"Since…?" she prodded.

"Actually, I might've imagined laboring this hard as a kid, but I can't recall any particular event. For a couple years, my pa hired on as a ranch hand. I helped."

She turned, leaning against the porch rail. "There's something different about working for yourself though, isn't there?"

"Hadn't thought about it before, but you're right." He faced her.

In the darkness, tiny stars danced in her eyes. The peace of the night wrapped around him. But instead of getting sleepier, he felt like his senses heightened.

She took a sip of her drink. "I wanted to thank you—again—for agreeing to my outrageous proposal. And tell you that I'd do it all over again if I had to."

"We haven't been married a week. You don't know what I'll be like in a month or two."

"Yes, I do." She took a deep breath and hurried on. "You'd still be a man of your word. A gentleman. A good role model for Toby. A man that I…" She sucked on her lower lip.

Admired?

He shifted in discomfort as he imagined what she almost said. Truth was, Lenora deserved a man who would love and cherish her. Not someone like him who had too much of his father's blood running through his veins. He wasn't good enough for her. Certainly he didn't merit her admiration.

In the darkness, he could barely make out her more subtle expressions. He spoke softly. "I hope I don't disappoint you in the future."

She ducked her head as though studying her coffee. "I doubt you will."

Not true. The day he completed his mission—taking down the Hackett gang—was the day he would ride out of her life. To keep his oath to the US Marshals Service would require him breaking his bargain with her.

She sighed, ever so quietly, as though working up the courage to ask him something. "Tell me about Andrew."

Cole straightened. That was not what he was expecting. He struggled to answer. "Not much to tell. I was pretty young when…" He took a hurried drink of his coffee as he contemplated how to continue. "Guess he was much like Toby. Bright. Inquisitive. Loved to follow me around."

And that's how they'd ended up behind the mercantile. Cole had told his kid brother to go home, but he wouldn't listen. Finally, he had given up.

"I don't want to hear of you taking that shortcut again." His mother's voice rang in his memory. Why hadn't Cole listened?

As he looked back, he realized the mercantile had acquired a bad reputation. Ma didn't want them anywhere near that place. Hence the warning to avoid taking a shortcut behind it.

The silence wore on, but Cole didn't know what else to say.

"You blame yourself for his death, don't you?" Lenora's soft voice came out of the darkness.

His jaw tightened.

She turned toward him, her gaze searching his face. "My husband…" She shook her head as she clutched her cup with both hands. "I mean my *first* husband did things I felt responsible for."

Was she talking about Amos's thieving? Cole couldn't say anything about it, knowing that to ask would reveal he knew a lot more than he should.

She chewed her lip as she gazed into the dark night. "I nagged. Trying to change him, I suppose. And I prayed. Oh, how I prayed. But Amos kept right on…" Her lips pursed.

"What are you saying?"

She blew out a breath. "I finally reached the point where the guilt got to be too much. And one day…" She opened her mouth but didn't continue right away. "One day, it was like God knocked me off my high horse. I saw so clearly that Amos's behavior wasn't my responsibility." Her gaze met his. "I guess I'm trying to tell you not to blame yourself for Andrew's actions."

"Now hold on." Cole held up one hand. "It was my duty to watch him that day. I shouldn't have—"

"If he was about Toby's age, then he had a mind of his own. Lately I've been learning that about my son. I can't control him any more than you could've controlled your brother." She set her cup down before drawing closer. Her wistful expression silenced Cole's next protest. "I'm trying to help you not be so hard on yourself."

Still not convinced, he clamped his jaw.

Her gentle hand on his arm distracted him from his black thoughts. "I didn't mean to pry. I just…" She pressed her lips together. "I recognize some of the burden you've been carrying around for years. The Lord knows how long I did."

She blew out another breath, as though finished with that topic, and turned again to the darkened landscape.

Slowly Cole unclenched his fingers from around the

coffee cup. He might have dented it, he'd been gripping it so hard.

"I should probably get to bed," she announced in a bright tone as she set down her cup. "Lots to do tomorrow. Now that Porky's producing so much milk, I have to churn butter almost every day."

"About tomorrow," he began, trying to figure out how to word his plans without alerting her of the secondary reason. "I want to take off early to do some scouting around the ranch."

She twitched. "Why?"

"Because...well, Toby and I ran across evidence of poaching. I'd like to investigate that more."

Her widening eyes glittered. "You will be careful, won't you?"

"Always. But I'm more concerned about leaving you alone." He half sat on the rail. "Please keep Toby close. And Blister. Until I come back. I should only be gone three, maybe four hours at the most."

She spoke slowly. "And if you're gone longer?"

"Then I'll likely be hauling a body to town to show the sheriff." He'd meant it as a joke, but Lenora sucked in a quick breath.

She wrapped one arm about the porch column, her body tight with stress. "Don't expect help from the sheriff. He's..." She paused to gulp. "He's friends with Eli. Close friends."

He pretended ignorance. "And Eli is...?"

"Jeb's father." Her tone grew bitter as she clutched the column with both hands. "The man who owns ten thousand cattle and countless souls."

He covered her fingers with his. "At least he'll never own yours."

For endless moments, she studied him.

How easy it would be to slide his arms about her—to comfort her. Or to comfort himself? For once in his adult life, he saw so clearly the life he was missing because of his choices. But couldn't he change the course of his future? Right now?

Before he did something regrettable, Cole brushed by her. "Thanks for the coffee." He set the empty cup inside and with a quickening step strode toward the barn.

Lenora, no doubt, stared after him. Straightening his shoulders, he made certain not to look back. The sooner he solved the bank robbery and arrested Jeb Hackett, the better.

Cole clenched his jaw, forcing himself to continue to walk away as one question hammered his mind—how could he hope to keep his promise to stay for six months if he couldn't keep his promise to want a real marriage from her?

He had to get away from Lenora Cole. Away from the burgeoning feelings that entangled his mind. And heart.

A dozen times, Lenora peeked out the door to see if Cole's outline crested the horizon. Her heart pounded when she thought she spotted him. But no. It was only a cattle's form, bobbing in the distance. Or a deer. Or the teasing wisp of a cloud.

What time had he left that morning? She kept guessing, trying to determine when he would return.

By late morning, she stood in the center of the room, twisting her hands in her apron. What if he didn't come back? She'd never thought to check if his horses were still in the back pasture. But would it matter? Perhaps he'd left them in her care and would someday return to claim them.

"It's my fault he's gone."

Last night, she had thought they were growing closer. Yet she had pushed him into confessing his guilt about Andrew's death. He had seemed to accept her words, evidenced by the fact that he had lingered on the porch afterward.

And when he had touched her hand...

Closing her eyes, Lenora relived the tenderness of that moment. She had so wanted him to take her in his arms. The way his breathing had slowed and his eyes hooded told her he was tempted.

And I wanted him to.

A foolish desire. Hadn't he given his word that he wouldn't kiss her? Yet she enticed him to break his oath.

She needed to pull back. Give him space.

How many times had she caught a faraway look in his eyes—because he longed to move on? Because he regretted his rash decision?

She stared out the window. "How could I have been so selfish to trap him into a marriage he didn't want?"

Yet now that they were married, she couldn't imagine going back to her lonely life.

Then guilt washed over her about the secrets she kept. Last night, she had wanted to tell him about Amos. About his thieving ways, but somehow they'd gotten sidetracked.

What about the hidden satchel?

"No," she whispered as she leaned her hand on the windowsill and wrestled with herself. What if knowing about that money proved to be too great a temptation? Even to a man of integrity like Cole? That secret needed to remain buried.

But all the rest...

She needed to tell him. Soon. She owed Cole that much.

"Hey, Ma." Her son's footsteps tromped across the porch. "Look what I found."

In his dirty hands, he held an enormous toad. Clearly happy to have a break from ranch chores, Toby grinned.

"He's…quite a specimen." Lenora fought to insert interest into her tone.

"Found him by the side of the house. Probably looking for bugs."

"Probably." It was likely the one that had frightened her that one day when she was collecting eggs.

Toby peered up at her. "Can I go fishing yet? You said I could."

"Maybe later." She cleared her throat. "Let's wait till Cole gets back. He said…" She paused when her ears picked up a sound in the distance. "Stay here."

Lenora grabbed her rifle and peered out the door. Up the road rattled a buggy. One of her neighbors was coming to call. From the looks, it was Frank Hopper.

To explain his and Jeb's "chat" about her ranch? Perhaps apologize that he could no longer consider buying it because of threats?

After setting aside her gun, she stepped onto the porch.

Frank pulled up beside the hitching post. "G'morning, Lenora."

"Good morning. Care to set for a spell? Coffee's fresh." She nodded to Toby to get him a cup as she stopped on the top step of her porch.

"I can't stay long. I'm on my way to town."

She chewed her lip, taking care to form her next words. "My ranch is kind of out of the way. Everything all right with your wife? Children?"

"Yes. Thanks." He nodded in thanks as Toby handed him a cup of coffee. His gray eyes pierced her. "Heard congratulations are in order. You remarried?"

Her cheeks grew warm at the way his eyebrows rose. "Yes."

"The missus never heard about the wedding till it was a done deal."

She clenched her hands. "We were behind on so much work, we couldn't take time to throw a party."

"Huh." Frank glanced around. "And where is Mr. Cole? I was hoping to meet him."

"He's checking the herd." Why did she feel embarrassed that he wasn't there? An odd tingle at the base of her skull forced her to add, "He should be back soon. Anytime now, as a matter of fact."

Nodding, Frank leaned forward to rest an elbow on his knee. "You know, folks in town are talking about him. Everyone's saying he's a drifter. Took advantage of you."

Everyone? The heat from her cheeks spread.

"Cole's no drifter," Toby piped up. "He's a horse trainer. You should see his horses. They're the best mannered in the country."

"No doubt." Frank's smirk disappeared behind the cup as he sipped his coffee.

"I'm telling the truth. I can show you if you'd—"

"Toby, Mr. Hopper said he was in a hurry. Likely he doesn't have time." Lenora hoped her neighbor would get the hint and tell the real reason why he was there. Surely it wasn't to castigate her for not throwing a party or to question her husband's character.

"You're right." He straightened. "So I'll get to the point. Heard tell that Jeb Hackett's after your ranch."

Even though she knew that, a chill still slid down her spine. How had he heard? And from whom? She spoke slowly. "Jeb's made that clear a time or two."

"Folks are saying he's gotten his father involved. Apparently there's some irregularity with your paperwork. And they're going to challenge your claim."

"That's preposterous." Lenora jammed her hand into her apron pocket. "Amos got this land more'n twelve years ago. The *Homestead Act*, like most folks around here. They can't—"

"They can and they will." Frank's mouth tightened. "You know that."

Though the hot sun climbed high in the sky, Lenora felt like a winter storm passed through her heart. She recalled stories she'd heard over the years—one in particular. A family, sitting on a nice piece of land near the river, mysteriously disappeared. No word for when or why they moved. Whispers abounded that Eli Hackett had wanted the property and naturally, when the family left, he suddenly possessed that stretch.

Of course, he claimed he'd bought it from the previous owner.

If Jeb recruited his daddy, she wouldn't be able to stop them.

She glanced at Toby, then at her neighbor. "What'm I going to do? I—I can't let them take our land."

The admission surprised her. Since when did she claim this property as her own?

"If I were you, Lenora, I'd head down to Cheyenne as soon as possible. Before one of Eli's highfalutin lawyers gets there first. Make sure your claim is rock solid."

"All right. Thank you."

"Don't wait." He shook his head for emphasis. After taking a couple gulps of his drink, he poured the remainder on the ground. "Thanks for the coffee. I'd best be going." He tossed the cup to Toby.

Frank undid the brake, then clicked to his horse.

"Thanks again," Lenora called.

With a wave, he and his buggy disappeared down the road.

For a long time, she looked after the small cloud of dust. Should she grab the buckboard and go? A glance at the sky showed it was almost noon and still Cole hadn't returned. A nagging fear came back—what if he didn't?

Ironic that she had been so anxious to get rid of her ranch a month ago. Jeb's threats about taking the ranch did not stir the same kind of worry she now felt. Because of Cole's involvement? She had to protect his interests as well as her own.

If she and Toby left within the hour, they could make the eight-hour trip to Cheyenne before nightfall. Maybe. Assuming they had no mishaps or delays on the road.

Her son watched her with wide eyes.

She made up her mind in an instant. "Toby, untie Porky. Lead her and her calf out into the back pasture. Make sure the pig has food. I'll take care of the chickens."

"Why, Ma?"

"We need to head to Cheyenne as soon as we can."

"But shouldn't we wait for Cole? Didn't he say to stay close to the house?"

"We can't, Toby. I won't take a chance that…" She bit her lip, not wanting to frighten her son. "Go take care of the animals. Hurry. I need to pack us some food. It's a long trip." When her son still hesitated, she spoke sternly. "We don't have time to waste."

His young face screwed up. "Yes'm." He ran toward the barn.

Lenora blew out a breath as she ran her hand across the back of her neck.

Money. We'll need money.

As she contemplated where to find some, she grew calm. All she had to do was dig up that brown leather satchel to find plenty of money. Enough to hire a lawyer, if needed. Enough to live high off the hog for the remainder of her life.

She pressed her forehead to the porch column. The forbidden memory barged into her mind.

"Take it," Amos rasped. He loosed the leather strap that bound the satchel to his saddle. It fell heavily to the ground...

At the time, Lenora hadn't opened the bag. But could this be the right time? While Jeb busied himself trying to steal her ranch, she would use some of the money and make certain he didn't.

"No." She spoke aloud. With determination. "No. We don't need it."

A thought struck her—Jeb had put money inside her baking soda tin. With shaking fingers, Lenora pried open the lid. Two crisp five-dollar bills lay inside. Though loathe to use the money, she shoved it into her apron pocket.

Ten dollars would be more than enough to put them up in a Cheyenne hotel and stable the horse for a couple of nights.

Chapter Fifteen

All morning, Cole traveled in a northwesterly direction, cutting back and forth across the terrain. Several times, he stopped and studied tracks, unable to identify what bothered him about them. Finally, when he came to what those down south called an arroyo, he took his time examining the signs.

From all appearances, cattle wandered through the region. Problem was, this particular area had little good grazing. So why were they there?

"Because someone's rustling cattle." Speaking aloud made it clear what was going on. The intermittent horse tracks—ones with shoes—confirmed that roaming cattle passed this way. Did some of them belong to Lenora?

He followed the trail for a little while, careful to keep his ears and eyes open. When the tracks disappeared, he stopped. Likely the cattle had been forced up the side of one hill to be rounded up. But someone had been very careful to cover the evidence.

A premonition slithered down his spine as he pushed Nips into the brush, out of sight from anyone above. Cole dismounted and put fingers in the horse's nose to keep him from whinnying.

As he listened, he watched Nips's ears flick and eyes widen. Though his pinto didn't neigh a greeting to the horses he clearly heard, he blew a little.

"Easy, boy," Cole murmured. He ran his hand along his horse's neck, calming him. Nips had been a better choice than Rowdy, who would have stamped his feet in protest at having to be quiet. "That's it."

Hearing the *clop-clop* of a horse—or two—Cole concentrated. Men's voices wafted toward his position, but he couldn't understand what they were saying. If they were on the ledge above him, it was only a matter of time before they spotted him. A few tense minutes later, he confirmed they weren't in the arroyo with him. The sounds definitely came from above. And they were drawing closer.

Greet them or run for it?

Instinct told Cole to flee. If they were indeed cattle rustlers, they would have no qualms about shooting him. If they weren't, they might assume he was a thief and the results would be the same. He yanked his bandanna over his face to hide his identity and pulled his hat low and tight.

Ignoring the branches that clawed him, he climbed into the saddle. With a jerk on the reins, he turned Nips toward a direction that would mislead possible followers. However, one stirrup caught in the scrub brush. Startled, his horse squealed and shied as he tried to escape the invisible hold. Sand churned and branches snapped. Finally, his pinto bolted, nearly unseating him.

"Hey, you!"

Cole heard the yell but didn't pause. Hunkering down in the saddle, he kicked Nips hard. "Go, boy," he growled. "Go."

In moments, his gelding moved into a flat-out gallop,

giving all he had. When Cole heard shots, he instinctively ducked. Over a rise and down a steep hill he rode, trusting that Nips wouldn't hesitate to obey his commands no matter where he guided him.

After nearly two miles, he finally slowed to look behind. Had he lost them? Only a fool would have followed down the dangerous inclines they'd traveled. And he'd ridden far enough away from the direction of Lenora's ranch to throw anyone off his trail.

White lather covered his mount. Cole took a moment to grab his binoculars and pan the area. No one was in sight.

He swallowed the parched feeling in his throat, tempted to walk Nips back to the ranch so the horse could have a breather. But something told him to hurry.

"Come on, boy." Cole kicked him into a stiff trot, then a canter.

"Lenora," he called when he reached the ranch. The place appeared deserted. The barn door swung lazily on its hinges, batted by the ever-present breeze. Porky and her calf were in the back pasture. Why? Usually they kept her on a long rope, tied by the house. During the day the cow fed on the lush grasses while her baby napped nearby.

A quick glance told him Sheba and Rowdy were in back, as well. What about Lenora's horse? Cole couldn't see him. Blister was nowhere to be found.

A chill gripped him when he saw the door to the house open. Cole rode his horse up to the porch and leaped off. A look inside proved the place was empty.

"Oh, God, please…" Closing his eyes, he stood inside the large room, not knowing what to ask for. Not daring to imagine what had happened. Again, he stepped into the bright sunshine.

Swiveling on his heel, he looked for some clue for where Lenora and Toby had gone. Cole pushed his hat off and nearly yanked out a handful of hair as he castigated himself. How could he have been so stupid to think Lenora would be safe for even a few hours? No doubt Hackett had been watching the place and had swooped down the minute Cole was out of sight.

With an effort, he calmed himself. He had only one choice. Pin on his badge, ride to Silver Peaks and speak to the sheriff. Identify himself as a US.marshal and deputize men to rescue Lenora from Jeb Hackett.

That decided, he blew out a breath.

After he cooled Nips, he would saddle up Rowdy and be on his way.

The distant muffled bark of a dog caught his ear. Blister? It took Cole a few minutes to figure out the sound came from the root cellar. So Hackett hadn't shot the dog? Perhaps in a strange, twisted act of mercy he'd allowed Toby to lock him up.

When Cole yanked open the door, he yelped and jumped back. Two gun barrels pointed straight at him, from a rifle and shotgun. The next moment, a wiry form flew at him.

"Cole!" Toby threw his arms around him.

A pale-faced Lenora emerged from a dark corner a second later.

Cole gripped her hand, tempted to yank her into his arms. "Thank…thank God." He shot the prayer upward.

They were all right. He could breathe again.

Brown smudges dusted her, but she looked okay as she squinted up into his face. Relief soon gave way to horror as she stared at him, mouth agape. "Cole! What happened?"

"I came back as soon as I could. I'm sorry, I—"

"No, no. You've got blood all over you." Her face had gone white.

"I do?" He looked down, now noticing his torn shirt and the multiple scratches on one arm.

Pressing her lips together, she gingerly touched his face. "You've a nasty gash here."

As soon as she mentioned it, the wound began to sting. In his concern for her, he'd not even noticed.

He flexed his cheek. Yep, it definitely burned. And now in earnest. "So why were you and Toby hiding in the root cellar?"

"That can wait." She spoke with a firmness he wouldn't dare oppose. "Your wounds need tending first."

"I don't s'pose you know of anyone around here who has some good salve, do you?"

A tense smile broke on her face. "Maybe. Let's go up to the house." Then she sobered as she gripped his un-injured arm. "I—I'm really glad you're all right." She seemed to have difficulty saying the words.

"I'm glad you are too."

She smoothed down her hair. "Toby, take care of Nips for Cole, would you?"

"Yes'm." He had not made a sound the whole time they'd been talking.

"Wait a sec." Cole grabbed his binoculars and panned the area. Before he took the time to tend to his wounds, he wanted to make certain that Hackett wasn't barreling down on the ranch.

No one was in sight in the nearby hills. The road remained empty. Good. Cole hadn't been followed. Only then would he allow himself to relax.

In the house, he took the chair Lenora indicated. With his head tilted back, he let her clean the gash on his face with water and a soft cloth.

Biting her lip, she studied him. "This needs to be stitched. It won't stop bleeding."

"Who knew a tree branch could do such damage."

She grimaced as she took care to dab his cheek.

"Lenora." He grabbed her hand. "If you want, I can do it myself. Got a mirror?"

"No. Yes, but…" She passed her other hand over her forehead. With a visible effort, she squared her shoulders. "I'll do it."

"I've got some astringent powders. That'll deaden the wound some. Why don't you get a needle and thread."

Looking braver than she apparently felt, she nodded.

He was soon back and seated, cheek dusted with powder. The sting had abated somewhat.

"I think… I think one stitch should be enough." If possible, she looked whiter than ever. Her lips appeared bloodless.

He met her gaze. "Skin is pretty tough, so do it quick. Don't think. Pretend you're sewing up my leather gloves."

Nodding, she gulped as she again peered at the gash.

He put one hand on her waist to steady her as she leaned toward him. Balling his other fist, he clenched his teeth, determined not to flinch at the needle's first bite.

The powder had done its job, dulling most of the pain. She did as he bade, working quickly. After several tugs, she was tying off the thread and knotting the ends.

"Hold still." She took care to cut the excess. When she straightened, she wore the look of someone who couldn't believe she'd just done something extraordinary.

She automatically wove the needle through the collar

of her blouse, like he'd seen her do a dozen times after she was done mending.

"Congratulations." Cole tried not to grin too broadly because of the odd pull on his cheek. "You survived."

"Thank..." Swaying on her feet, she suddenly dropped the scissors and bolted out the front door.

He leaned forward to see her retching over the railing of the porch.

Still queasy, Lenora tried to stifle her groan as Cole and Toby ate. Food appealed to her not one bit.

"So you gonna tell me why you were hiding in the root cellar?" With apparent relish, Cole stuffed a bite of pie into his mouth. He smacked his lips and made a face. Because the berries were tart?

Sipping her weak tea, she averted her gaze from the gash on his cheek. The black thread, holding skin together, stuck up like a flag. And reminding her again that she'd sewn Cole's face like fabric.

"On account of Mr. Hopper coming to visit," Toby answered for her. He also seemed to have no lack of appetite.

Of course, her son probably loved the fact that they were having pie and bread for dinner. That was all Lenora could scrounge up without feeling sick. The tea, steeped from dried mint, settled her stomach so she could at least look at Cole without vomiting.

I'm such a weak-kneed baby.

"What did Hopper have to say?" Cole looked between them.

Lenora quickly filled him in, as well as her decision to go to Cheyenne. "I was all set to leave, but I got to thinking. What if Jeb was on the road somewhere?"

Cole's jaw tightened. "Hopper is one of his men?"

"No." She shook her head. Had Jeb gone over to Frank's house and had another little "talk" with him? "I just wondered if maybe Frank overheard a rumor that made him think that the Hacketts were about to take my ranch. Something Jeb *wanted* him to hear."

His eyebrows rose. "Good thinking."

"Then I got scared." She traced her finger along the china cup's delicate handle. "Since you weren't back, I worried that maybe I wasn't safe on the road *or* at the ranch. So that's when we hid."

"You did well." He took another bite of pie and seemed deep in thought as he chewed it. "Likely Hackett used your neighbor, just as you suspected. I wouldn't put it past him."

"So I did right staying here?"

He nodded. "But I'd suggest the next time you get scared, lock yourself in the house."

"But it's the first place he'd look."

"True. But you'd have a much more defensible position in here. The door to the root cellar is pretty rickety."

"But I'd shoot a few of them before they got to me."

His expression grew grim. "Their first couple shots into the cellar would kill you *and* Toby."

She closed her eyes, terrified of that possibility.

When his hand briefly touched hers, she met his gaze. "All right. If danger comes a'knocking, I'll barricade myself with Toby in here."

"Good."

She glanced at her son, who stared at them with round eyes. "I guess Amos always expected trouble."

"What do you mean?" Cole scooped the rest of the pie into his mouth.

Lenora pointed. "He built shutters for the windows—

but they go on the inside. I never understood why he'd made them that way."

"You have some in the bedroom for your window?"

"Yes."

"And ones for in here?"

She stepped toward the wood bin and rested her hand on the four single panels that stood against the wall. "These go in here."

"Then I rest my case."

"Is Hackett going to come here and start a gunfight?" Toby's mouth quivered.

"Unlikely." Lenora hastened to his side and placed a hand on his shoulder. "Cole and I were talking 'what if.' I learned my lesson about the root cellar."

Her son didn't seem convinced, a worried pinch forming between his brows. Staring at Cole, she pleaded in silence for him to say something.

He cleared his throat. "I think your pa was pretty smart when he made this house. You know, I always wondered about it and finally decided that it's just like Noah's ark."

"What?" Toby swiveled in his chair.

"It's obvious, isn't it?" Cole flashed a grin. "Shutters for the windows? And the house built so high off the ground? Your pa was expecting floodwater."

Her son made a face, but was clearly distracted from the discussion about Hackett. "The stream sometimes gets high in the spring, but it never comes near the house."

"Doesn't matter." Cole held up a finger. "Don't forget that trapdoor on the roof. You thought it was for fires. But I get the feeling your pa told you that so you wouldn't worry."

When Toby scratched the top of his head with a closed fist, Lenora pressed her lips together to keep from smiling.

"Think about it." Cole leaned forward in his chair and lowered his voice like he was sharing a secret. "He didn't tell anybody else about it, right? Because he knew that at the first sign of rising water, everyone would stampede over here. After this whole area got flooded, your house would float just fine. And that trapdoor? Obviously that's what you'd use to spot dry land." Nodding to affirm his explanation, he sat back with a serious expression.

Pressing her fingers over her lips, Lenora waited for her son's response.

Toby suddenly made a sound of derision as he sat back on his chair. "That's the dumbest thing I ever heard. I mean, we don't even have a dove like Noah."

Lenora couldn't help but giggle.

Glaring at them both, her son reiterated. "Well, we don't."

She chuckled until her sides ached. Cole, too, laughed, wiping his eyes after several minutes—taking care around his sore cheek. Only her son seemed to have no idea what was so funny. Crossing his arms, he glowered at them both.

When she finally quieted, Toby said with no small indignation, "The house wouldn't float because the floor would leak."

She and Cole lost themselves in laughter all over again.

Chapter Sixteen

Cole stretched his chin upward as he watched himself in the small mirror. With care, he shaved around the gash on his cheek. Though Lenora's salve had worked wonders—along with the one stitch—the area felt extra tender. And he didn't want to accidently reopen the wound.

With the early-morning light, he stood at the side of the house while he took care of his morning ablutions, stripped down to pants, boots and his undershirt. A basin of water on the stand sufficed to rinse his razor. Inside, he heard Lenora move around, stoking the fire in the stove and preparing to do her cooking. Two days had passed since his little scouting expedition, and they'd heard and seen no one.

No doubt Jeb Hackett was out there, plotting his next move.

He wanted Lenora off the ranch—so he could waylay her on the open road? Possibly. Cole doubted he would ransack the house again. Whatever he was looking for wasn't there. That was proved when Cole himself had found nothing.

That left only one possibility—Hackett was trying to

get his hands on her. And her marriage to Cole apparently hadn't deterred the outlaw in the least.

Did she know where the bank robbery money was? Cole cleaned his razor, debating about asking her. But would she tell him the truth?

She would want to know why—and he'd end up telling her who he was and why he was there.

Her likely reaction had kept his mouth shut.

She would accuse him of marrying her just so he could solve the bank robbery mystery. Not because he was interested in the ranch or horses or even building a life for himself.

He dabbed his face with the towel, then clenched it between his hands. In truth, why *had* he married her? And now that she was his wife, was he ready to do anything to keep her?

No matter what, he needed to tell her the truth—the real reason he'd come to Wyoming Territory. And how over time, things had changed, specifically because of her. If she was willing to accept him as a US marshal, then perhaps they had a future together.

Once planted, the idea began to grow on him.

"Oh, I'm sorry." Lenora's voice startled him from his musing.

She stood at the corner of the house, face turned away. Because he was in his undershirt? Her cheeks were suspiciously rosy in the morning light.

"Good morning."

"I, uh…" She cleared her throat and threw a quick glance at him. "I mended your shirt. And washed it. But I'm afraid it's in pretty bad shape." With the clothing in her hand, she stuck out an arm in his direction without looking at him.

Finding her modesty charming, he grinned. "Appreciate it." After hanging the towel on a nail, he slipped on his newly mended shirt and buttoned it.

She was right. The bloodstains likely would never come out though she'd done a fine job sewing the tears.

After she glanced his way again, she moved closer.

Cole made a show of examining the stitches on his sleeve. "Huh. You do fine work."

"Thank you." Clearly pleased, she smiled.

"I should've insisted on three stitches instead of one." He touched his cheek. "Less scarring."

She blanched. It took her but a moment to recover. Grabbing the nearest thing, which happened to be the towel, she flung it at Cole.

The material hit him square in the chest before fluttering to the ground.

He let out a bark of surprise. "Good thing you didn't have a shovel or rake handy."

They both bent for the towel, but he beat her to it and snatched it off the grass. Holding up his hands, he backed away. "Whoa, now. I was only kidding."

Cheeks flushed and hair a little askew, she fought to catch her breath. "How terrible to tease me about that."

"Couldn't help it. You're irresistible." He stepped closer to rehang the towel on the nail.

Instead of moving aside like he expected, she stood her ground. Cole pulled up short, a mere foot from her. Suddenly realizing what he said, he amended, "I meant that the situation was..."

Words dying in his throat, he looked down at her.

She is so lovely.

Not just externally. He'd never forget the fierce look on her face when he'd opened the root cellar door—protecting her son. Or the way her chin had trembled as she'd fought to be brave while stitching him up.

Or the way she read the Bible to Toby every night. They weren't just words to her. She believed. And when she prayed, something always seemed to squeeze in his chest at her simple but trusting requests.

For the first time in Cole's life, he longed to share in the faith she so effortlessly exhibited. Again, he was struck by the circumstances that had brought him to the ranch. What if God had directed Cole there? The truth humbled him.

The sun burst around the corner of the house. In the golden light, she glowed while her soft smile captivated him anew.

Lovely.

"Lenora…" He breathed her name like a prayer as he moved closer to her still. Would she pull away?

Eyes widening, her mouth parted as she raised her chin. Inviting.

Anticipating her sweet lips, he bent his head. Just another couple inches and…

"Ma? Cole?" Toby's shout shattered the moment.

Lenora jerked away, palms pressing her face as she turned aside. Because she was shocked she'd forgotten herself? And they'd almost kissed?

"Back here." Cole grabbed the basin and dumped the water as Toby careened around the corner.

"Can I go fishing?" He glanced between them. "I never got to the other day."

Head ducked and shoulders hunched, Lenora didn't answer.

"'S'okay with me," Cole volunteered. "But better check with your mother."

"Ma?"

"Maybe after breakfast." She slowly turned, smoothing her hair into place.

"Aww." Toby kicked at a clod of grass.

Cole measured the distance between himself and the woman he'd nearly kissed. Too far. It seemed obvious their tender moment had passed. He sighed, more disappointed than he expected.

"Didja ask him yet?" Toby's question aimed at his mother.

Lenora blushed, her gaze cutting toward Cole then back at her son. "No."

"Ask me what?" He strapped his gun belt around his waist and adjusted it.

Apparently distracted by his actions, she didn't speak.

Toby answered for her. "If you'd teach my ma how to ride good like me."

Cole straightened. "Horse riding lessons?"

"Why not?" She lifted her chin.

He pulled on his ear. "But you already know how to ride, right?"

"Of course." She caught her upper lip in her teeth as she glanced away. "Just not very well."

Toby's eyes glittered with excitement. "You gonna teach her to ride bareback like me?"

"Well, I…" He squinted Lenora's direction.

Her shoulders squared as she apparently anticipated his objection. "I plan to wear pants."

"G-good." Cole passed a hand over his clean-shaven face to keep from saying more.

"Is that a problem?" Folding her arms, she stepped closer.

"No, no." He shook his head and added another for good measure. "No."

"All right then." She stuck out her chin as though the matter was settled. "We'll begin after breakfast."

She marched away.

"Fearsome." Toby's fist shot into the air. "I can't wait to watch."

He hurried after his mother, yelling, "Cole's a great teacher, Ma. You'll see."

He laced his fingers on top of his head and rubbed his hair with vigor. Teaching Toby to ride was one thing, but Lenora? Cole gulped at the thought of being so close to her.

During breakfast he would have to figure out a way to gracefully bow out of riding lessons.

As Lenora poured more coffee into Cole's cup, she studied his pensive expression. All during breakfast, he'd barely spoken. Of course, she had little to say as well. Especially as her thoughts kept returning to what had happened earlier.

Had he really been about to kiss her? They'd been talking and the next thing, the sun peeped around the house and blinded her. Then he was standing so close that she couldn't get by him and…

That wasn't exactly true. When he'd teased her and spoken to her with a strange, soft smile on his lips, her heart had nearly stopped beating. Then he had drawn closer and…

Lenora gulped. Now was not the time to dwell on that. She had more important things to think about—like bowing gracefully out of riding lessons. But nothing came to mind. How had she been snared into agreeing to this? After noticing how much Toby's riding had improved, Lenora had dropped a casual comment, which he took to mean she wanted to learn.

What a time for him to bring that up again.

All too soon breakfast ended, and the three of them

headed to the corral. Still she hadn't come up with a good reason to delay lessons. Indefinitely, if possible.

Toby perched on the fence while she stood by the gate, hands clenching and unclenching.

When Cole led his pinto from the back pasture, she frowned. "Not Sheba?"

"I trust Nips a little more. And he'll watch me instead of trying to show off." Again he surprised her by bridling the gelding.

"I thought…" Biting her lip, she told herself to be patient. He was the teacher, and she was the student.

Cole apparently didn't hear, brow drawn as he adjusted the cheek straps. After he draped the reins over the horse's neck, he threw a glance over his shoulder. "You riding or not?"

Hurrying to his side, she stared at his laced fingers as he waited to boost her to the pinto's back.

"Oh, I…" She had assumed she would use the fence to mount the horse. Nothing was going as she expected.

With difficulty, she placed her foot in his hands because he hadn't bent over far enough. She ended up losing her balance and grabbing his neck. Together, they nearly toppled to the ground. After a couple tries, she finally got on Nips. She fanned herself with one hand and glanced at the sun. The day seemed overly warm already.

"You're too far back." Cole swatted the air as he grabbed the bridle. "Scoot up. Forward some."

She did so, but ended up kicking Nips in the sides. The gelding jumped, nearly ramming Cole while Lenora grabbed for a handhold.

"Whoa." He tightened his grip and placed a palm on the horse's flank to calm him.

"Sorry." When he didn't look at her, she repeated, "Sorry, Cole."

He pushed back his hat and peered up at her. "I'm gonna hang the reins over his withers, but don't hold them. Use your—" he paused a second "—legs to guide him."

After that, he stepped back.

How to do that? She'd received only the most rudimentary instructions about riding when she was a child. Most of the time, she drove a buggy or buckboard. Her father had taught her that much at least.

Lenora gave a tentative kick. Again, the pinto seemed to overreact, causing her to grab wildly for whatever was within reach—his mane and the reins. After a moment, he slowed to a walk.

As far as guiding him…

Hanging on for dear life, she let him go where he wanted.

She was aware of Toby yelling encouragement and of Cole's near-scowl, but she concentrated so hard on staying atop the horse that she thought of little else. The other thing she grew aware of was how high up she was. Nips was big, to be sure, but she hadn't realized how tall.

Eventually, he settled into a sleepy walk around the perimeter of the corral. Lenora suspected it had something to do with the hand signals Cole gave him. His ears pricked forward, but he always seemed to be watching his master. And ignoring her when possible.

After a few minutes, she began to relax, enjoying the movement—almost a rocking motion.

This wasn't so bad.

"All right," Cole piped up. "See if you can guide him into making an eight without using the reins." He drew the number in the air.

Her expression must have betrayed her ignorance because he added, "Use your knees to signal him." When

Nips tossed his head and snorted, Cole raised his voice. "Just one, not both."

Lenora pressed her left leg against his side. The horse seemed to understand what she wanted him to do. Somewhat. After several frustrating moments, he ended up crossing the middle of the corral, but resumed circling the perimeter.

"Whoa." Cole stepped in front to stop the gelding. Though he frowned, he seemed to have trouble controlling the movement of his jaw. Like he had a huge mouthful of food that he couldn't swallow. Finally, he peered at her. "How much riding—exactly—have you done?"

She pushed back the hair that blew into her eyes. "Enough."

"Which means what?"

"S-some."

He looked away, face hidden by his hat before squinting back up at her. "My guess would be twice. If that."

The truth made her squirm. "Actually, three times."

He didn't bother to hide his grin. "How come you didn't tell me?"

"You didn't ask *that*. You asked if I could ride."

"I might argue that point." He scratched his forehead with one thumb, like it kept him from laughing. Apparently making up his mind, he pulled the brim of his hat down with a jerk. "All right, let's start again. This time, use the reins."

Lenora wouldn't deny the concession boosted her confidence. Toby, she noticed, had disappeared. Apparently, this was a lot more boring than his riding lessons.

Again, Cole had them circle the corral. "That's it. Feel the horse underneath you. Move with him. Don't treat him like he's hitched to a plow."

In no time, Lenora's self-assurance grew.

"We'll try eights again. Gently ask him. Don't yank the reins." He continued to give directions as Nips obeyed.

She couldn't help but think her son was right—Cole was a great teacher.

As the pinto moved into a trot, she bounced on his back. Every time she tried to get a breath, the movement pounded the air out of her.

"Push him into a canter, Lenora. It'll be less jolting."

She did as he bade, wrapping the reins around one wrist for security.

"That's it."

She caught sight of Cole's grin as Nips cantered around the perimeter. A sense of exhilaration swept over her. Is this what Toby felt?

One-two-three, one-two-three—the rocking-horse gait mesmerized her.

She heard Cole say something, but she didn't quite catch the words. Somehow she felt like she was off balance one moment, and the next slipping from the gelding's back. She grappled for a better hold of the mane.

"Lenora!" He ran toward her. "Whoa. Whoa!"

As she slid sideways, the reins tightened around her left wrist until she dangled. Lenora cried out. Massive hooves churned as Nips gradually slowed.

Cole grabbed the bridle and stopped him. In a second, he was beside her, lifting her around the waist.

"My wrist," Lenora whimpered.

It took several moments until he untangled her arm from the reins.

"Are you all right?" Anxiety etched his face.

"Yes, ouch!"

As he lowered her to the ground, she rubbed her wrist.

"I should never have..." He spoke through clenched teeth.

"It's fine. Just a little sore from…from the other day."

His jaw set. "You could've been seriously injured. If you'd fallen the wrong way—"

"But I didn't." She realized that he still held her.

Ever so slightly, his hands moved, almost in a caress. Had he truly been that worried?

"Cole…" She laid her palm against his shirt, to reassure him. His heart pounded against his rib cage. She dragged her attention back to his face. "I'm okay. I have only myself to blame. I let my mind wander."

Still he didn't seem convinced. His eyes were screwed to slits, face tight.

"Next time, I'll use a saddle."

His hold loosened while his shoulders relaxed a tiny bit.

"Hey, Ma. You okay?" Toby climbed the fence, face worried. "I thought I heard you yell."

"I'm fine."

After glancing over his shoulder, Cole stepped back.

Lenora spoke to her son. "But I think riding lessons are over for the day."

Never had Cole looked so relieved.

When she reached for the reins, he spoke. "What'd ya think you're doing?"

"Going to brush Nips."

He held up a hand. "Please allow me."

For a moment, she thought of refusing. Instead, she nodded. "Very well. I'll go start dinner."

"I'd feel much better about that."

Feel?

Before he had a chance to see her confusion, she hurried to the house.

Chapter Seventeen

After the meal, Toby headed back to the stream to try to catch the "big one" that had escaped earlier.

Cole seemed in no hurry to rush out. Sipping his coffee, he leaned back in his chair while Lenora cleared plates. What was he waiting for?

The need to apologize pressed upon her. "I'm sorry the riding lesson didn't go quite as planned."

He grinned, that prominent dimple in one cheek deepening. "Don't know as I'd call it that."

"I definitely learned *my* lesson."

He squinted at her. "Which is what exactly?"

"Well, for starters, listen to my teacher. Pay attention." She gulped. "Be truthful."

Nodding, a frown settled on his forehead. "Truth is always good." His jaw flexed. Because he knew she kept secrets? Cole might be a man of few words, but she would never accuse him of being simpleminded.

As Lenora cleared the dishes, guilt pressed upon her. She needed to tell him the truth about so many things—about the reason Jeb harassed her, about Amos's criminal activities, about the hidden money. It was time.

She wanted Cole in her future. Now that she knew he

cared for her—and hadn't he proved it over and over?—she needed to be honest.

"Cole, I—"

"I have to—"

They began speaking at once. And both stopped.

As before, he nodded to her. "Ladies first."

She took the seat across from him. "I need to tell you something." She ducked her head. "Something important."

Where to start?

"My husband—first husband—was an outlaw." She glanced at the door to make certain Toby wasn't in sight. "Though I don't know the extent of his activities, I do know he was a thief."

Cole's face grew rigid. "Go on."

"I should have told you this before we married." She stared at her white knuckles. "But I was so ashamed."

It seemed forever before he spoke. "What did Amos steal?"

"Cattle. Horses." She stumbled over the words. "I don't know for certain if he stole money before...before last November."

The chair creaked as Cole leaned forward. "What can you tell me about that?"

She met his gaze. Why did he want to know? Since she'd already spoken, she needed to be as truthful as possible. "I don't know where they went."

"They?"

"Yes. Jeb Hackett is the gang's leader. Amos was his right-hand man. They'd been friends a long time. There are others, but I don't know for certain who went, although I have a good idea."

"Go on."

"The day Amos died..." She gulped and chickened

out. If she told Cole too many details, he might insist they go to the sheriff—a man she didn't trust. Though she didn't know for certain, she suspected he retained his office because of Eli Hackett.

She took a deep breath. "I believe Amos was shot during a robbery."

"What did they rob?"

"I think they held up a bank. Amos never told me…" She refused to know details.

Cole sat back, a speculative look crossing his face.

Again, she ducked her head. "Jeb came over late one night beforehand. He and Amos talked. I guess they thought I was asleep. I heard them plan. They spoke of a place off Main Street that wasn't 'too heavily guarded.' And that this payoff would be the best ever. I know they weren't talking about Silver Peaks—someone would've recognized them or their horses. So I'm guessing somewhere farther away. Perhaps Cheyenne."

"Have you told this to anyone?"

"No." She clenched her fist. "Who would believe me? Besides, I couldn't ride five miles before Jeb or his cronies intercepted me and demanded to know where I was going and why." She bolted up to carry dishes to the washbasin.

Cole's chair squeaked as he shifted his weight.

With her back still to him, Lenora held a tin plate in her tightening grip. "I'm sorry I didn't tell you before we married. It was wrong of me."

When the silence wore on her, she turned. What was he thinking? Would he tell her he was going to leave?

Brow lowered, he stared at her. As though making up his mind about something. When he abruptly rose from his chair, she jumped at the loud scraping sound.

"Since we're confessing…"

As he drew closer, she gulped. What was he trying to say? Cole had already shared painful secrets, ones that he perhaps had never spoken about before. Did he, too, feel the need to be completely open because he looked forward to a future of them together? Did he—like her—long for something more than an *almost* kiss?

The impending confession both excited and scared her.

He pursed his lips. "I'm not just a drifter with a couple nice horses." Resting a fist above his gun, he met her gaze. "I'm an undercover US marshal. I was sent to investigate Jeb Hackett's possible involvement in a Cheyenne bank. One that was robbed six months ago."

When her lips went white, Cole thought she was going to faint. The tin plate in Lenora's hand clattered to the floor.

"You're a…?" She seemed to have trouble getting the words out. "A…marshal?"

"Yes, ma'am." He clamped his lips together, reprimanding himself for giving her the rote response.

Openmouthed, she stared at him. He read shock, fear and even revulsion on her features.

Not what he was expecting. Disappointment hammered him as he picked up the dish and set it in the washbasin.

Her hands twisted in her apron. "And you came to find out about Jeb?"

He nodded.

"Tell me the truth, Cole. Did you come here to investigate Amos, as well?"

Ire, like a storm, rose inside him. Did she expect him to lie? Nevertheless, he looked for some way to soften the truth. Nothing came to mind. In a low voice, he answered, "I came to learn about Amos too."

She appeared to totter. When he reached to steady her, she threw up her hands and avoided his help. "No. No, don't…"

Touch her? Like he was diseased?

Something inside him withered.

She slumped into a chair, head bowed.

For what felt like minutes, he stared down at her. Pride demanded he respond to her silent accusations. Or was it because he felt desperate enough to try to win her back?

Cole crouched beside her. "Lenora, I had no idea this was Amos's place. I didn't even know your name until you introduced yourself the next morning. By then…" He shook his head, still confounded by the events that had stampeded out of his control. From the moment he had cut Blister loose to this very day, nothing had gone as planned. Because God directed him?

With her head so low he couldn't see her face, she remained silent.

He continued, helpless as his future—one that he had begun to hope for with Lenora—seemed to evaporate. "Sheba had gone lame and things…well, things just went from there."

The gaze she raised to him was full of hurt. And anger? Or was that fear?

He reached for her hand but pulled back at the last second. "Please believe me, Lenora."

For many moments, she didn't speak. However, he detected a softening of her expression.

He spoke slowly, praying she would accept his explanation. "I don't have proof about Jeb being part of the bank robbery, but the details you gave may help prove he was one of the men involved."

"I know Amos was." Her voice was sad, expression faraway.

"You know?"

"Yes." Her voice came out barely above a whisper. Did she feel guilty by association?

"Amos was the outlaw, Lenora. Not you. You were only married to him." When she shook her head, he went on. "Didn't you tell me that the other night? The shame rests on him, not you. And you don't carry that guilt any longer. Remember?"

Chin puckered in sorrow, she nodded.

"And if I can find some way to prove that Jeb was involved in the robbery, you will be rid of him forever. You can live without fear."

Head lowered, she bit her lip. The muscles in her throat spasmed.

What else could he say? Nothing.

He rose. She surprised him by grabbing his wrist. "But once you arrest Jeb, you'll be finished here. You'll leave."

"But our bargain…"

She shook her head. "That no longer matters. You have more important things to do than hang around my ranch for six months."

The reality of her statement slammed into his mind.

He had no answer. That was the way it had always been. Accept the job. Deal with the criminals. Move on.

That had been his life for nine years. He had no time to settle down. Not while outlaws roamed the land. He had a duty to himself—and to his brother—to remove any and all who threatened the health and wellbeing of those in this great country.

Didn't he?

Releasing her hold, Lenora rose and brushed by him. She slowly began to wash the dishes.

Since his arrival at her ranch, he had been constantly distracted from his goal. He'd made little progress on the case. Lenora's testimony was the first real evidence he'd gotten that Jeb Hackett had been involved in the Cheyenne robbery.

But was it enough to arrest and convict the man?

Already Cole knew the answer—*no.* He needed hard evidence so that Hackett would not be able to weasel out of a conviction.

That meant going back to where Cole suspected their hideout was. Find it and perhaps discover something that would incriminate Jeb and the others.

"What are you going to do?" Lenora's question jarred him from his reverie. Strange how she always seemed to know.

"For starters, try not to get killed."

He meant it half seriously, but she whirled and clenched her hands together as though in prayer. Water trickled down her arm and dripped to the floor.

"I need to see if I can find the gang's hideout. I think I got close the other day. When I got this." He pointed to his stitched cheek.

"I don't know if they have a hiding place." Her voice hardened. "Amos never told me much. And I didn't want to know."

Her expression revealed she spoke the truth.

"I should go soon," he said in a soft voice. "See if I can find it."

"The sooner you stop Jeb, the better." Her mouth tightened. "Are you planning to go tonight?"

Cole considered. "No. I don't know the terrain that well." Besides, how could he find a place in the dark that he only suspected existed?

"Toby's birthday is tomorrow. Would you consider staying at least through then?" Her beautiful eyes added a weight to her plea that he dared not disappoint.

His impending departure hung in the air like smoke from the stove. He had to leave. They both knew it. Humor seemed the best way to ease the pain in both their hearts.

Cole managed a small grin. "Are you baking a cake?"

A smidgen of worry melted from her face. "Yes."

"Then wild horses couldn't drag me away."

Though she smiled, her mouth trembled. When the time came, would she really be sorry to see him go?

The bigger, more daunting question was—would he have the strength to leave her?

At supper that night, Lenora tried to be cheerful, but she found it hard to smile at Toby's antics and Cole's banter. Not when his departure loomed ever before her.

How had she not seen the obvious? The way Cole walked with authority? The way he wore his gun on his hip? The way he had stared down Mr. Richards?

Outside, the rooster's repeated crow signaled the ending of the day. Dusk crept into the house. Despite the lit lanterns, darkness enveloped her heart.

Cole would soon leave. The ominous portent clanged in her mind.

Would he return from his task, victorious? Or would he merely melt away—killed by Jeb or his men? She would know soon enough. The outlaw wouldn't waste a day before he came to the ranch, gloating over his victory.

And forcing her to make a horrendous choice.

I can't let that happen.

She would have to run. Go anywhere to escape the long reach of the Hacketts. Perhaps Minneapolis where she knew the lay of the land? Or somewhere new like San Francisco? She could work in a small restaurant, where she and Toby could live in peace.

As she pondered leaving the graves behind the house, a poignant ache welled inside her. Could she leave her two babies? Her home?

She would have to.

Her eyes rested on the things that she'd have to abandon. Her mother's remaining dishes. The tambour mantel clock. Best to go on horseback with as little as possible. She couldn't chance taking the buckboard. They would have to travel with all secrecy and speed.

Could they reach Cheyenne without being intercepted by Jeb or his men?

"Ma." Toby made a face, voice betraying puzzlement.

"I'm sorry?"

"I asked what kind of cake you're gonna make."

Lenora glanced between him and Cole. "Well, I think that is something for you to decide."

"Spice cake." Her son didn't hesitate. "With lots of frosting."

"Hmm." She pretended to think. "You mean, the kind with cinnamon and nutmeg?"

He shrugged. "I don't know. I just like spice cake."

Though Cole chuckled, it sounded forced. His deep blue eyes met hers.

"Do you like spice cake, too, Cole?" She caught her breath, dying to know. After all, this might be the last thing she baked for him.

"Anything you make, I like."

"But is there a type of cake you prefer above all else?" For some reason, she desperately needed to discover his favorite. If necessary, she would bake two cakes. Who cared about the extravagance?

"Chocolate is too rich. Some sponge cake is too boring. Spice sounds perfect."

"Ma makes the *best* spice cake." Toby clutched his stomach and groaned in exaggerated ecstasy.

"I know." Cole nodded. "The best in Laramie County, I'm sure."

Her son giggled.

Again, Cole's gaze met hers. Wouldn't he miss this? The times he had with her and Toby?

A moot point. He had a job to do. Obviously that took precedence over everything else. Including his personal life.

Then one unanswered question pierced her soul.

What would he do when he found out she'd hidden the bank money? She wouldn't be able to bear the disgust on his face. Her heart would split clean in two because…

Because I love you, Cole. She swallowed the words even as she admitted them to herself. *So very much.*

Lenora rose, the dishes clattering as she bumped the table. If she didn't get away from him, she would begin to bawl. "I'm tired. Please just…just leave the mess. I'll take care of it in the morning."

"But what about our reading?" Toby's young face wrinkled. "And prayers?"

"I'm sorry." She waved in Cole's direction unable to risk pleading for help. "Good night."

She hurried into her bedroom and shut the door. To her credit, she managed to stave off tears. As dishes clattered and chairs scraped, she pressed the blanket to her mouth.

Dear Lord, how she loved him. For the thousandth time she wished Amos had never dropped off that satchel of money. Because now she knew if she admitted to having the money, she would lose Jesse Phillips Cole forever.

Chapter Eighteen

"That's it. Keep a good, steady rhythm." Cole demonstrated how to swing a lasso. Though he wasn't very good at it, Toby excelled after his brief instruction. "Hey, I think you've been practicing behind my back."

The youngster laughed.

The morning sun momentarily blinded Cole as they stood beside the corral, lassoing a fence post.

"It'll be a whole different matter with a moving target." He coiled the rope and merely watched the brand-new eleven-year-old.

All the while they practiced, Cole kept attuned to the house. Though Lenora had not yet called them for breakfast, they were passing the time as they waited. All the pressing, early-morning chores were done. Cole had even removed the one stitch on his cheek since the gash had healed enough.

Even though he was prepared, he still jumped when Lenora yanked open the door and called her son.

"Yes, Ma?"

Cole followed him to the porch. It took no great powers of discernment to see she'd had a bad night. Pink blotches marred her pale cheeks. If he'd had any doubts about her crying, a chafed nose attested to the handkerchief that had scrubbed her skin raw.

"Could you collect the eggs for me?" She avoided looking at Cole. "And I need my apron. I think I left it hanging in the root cellar."

"I'll get that," Cole volunteered.

She barely met his gaze. "Thanks." Without another word, she went back inside.

When Toby stood staring after her, a worried frown on his face, Cole put his hand on the youngster's shoulders. "Let's do as she says."

Together they walked down the porch steps.

"Has Ma been crying?" He screwed up his face as he looked at Cole.

"I reckon." He clenched his teeth to keep from saying more.

"Why do you suppose?"

Cole took care to form a reasonable explanation. "Maybe she's worried about your growing up."

"What?" He scratched his head.

"You know that talk we had about women's feelings? Well, mothers are even more sensitive. If your ma imagines you growing up and moving away, she's bound to be sad."

Toby's mind worked on that a bit. He clenched his fists. "I'm never leaving."

Cole smiled. Hadn't he himself once said that to his mother? As a twelve-year-old, he had declared with youthful assurance that he would always stay by her side. He never understood her chuckle at the time. Because it hid tears?

In the years since Andrew's death, he had said goodbye to her over and over. Now he understood her stoic

face and red-rimmed eyes. Did she worry if that would
be the last time she saw him?

"Make sure to say that to your ma, Toby. Tell her you'll
never move away. And give her a big hug when you do,
okay? Right after you collect the eggs."

The youngster looked taken aback by his fierce tone.
"If you want."

"I mean it. I want you to vow to me you'll do that."

Toby's eyes widened. "I'm not supposed to swear."

"A vow isn't swearing. It's a real serious promise.
Okay?"

"Sure. I promise."

"Okay then." Cole strode to the root cellar.

He stood just inside the door, waiting for his eyes to
adjust to the gloom. Why had he said such a fool thing?
Because he felt guilty about leaving Lenora. Like he
could assuage that by having her son declare the very
thing Cole himself should say to her.

He leaned his hand on a rough, wooden column.
"God," he prayed aloud, "how can I leave her?"

If the Lord had indeed led Cole there, wouldn't it be
foolish to go?

In moments, a plan formed. The next time they went
into Silver Peaks for supplies, he would send a telegram
and resign as a US marshal. He would drop the Hackett gang investigation. Since Cole had no evidence, he
couldn't pin the robbery on him. No doubt the man would
slip up in the future, but Cole didn't need to be the one
to bring him to justice. If Hackett showed up again on
the ranch, he would deal with the outlaw as befitting the
situation.

At peace with his plans, Cole sighed.

Lenora needed him. And Toby.

He bowed his head. "And Lord, You know *I* need them."

It was time to hang up his star and settle down. Right here. Starting today.

The moment he made the decision, a huge weight lifted from his soul. He smiled as he anticipated the look on Lenora's face when he shared the news. The next tears she shed would be ones of joy.

He edged into the narrow root cellar, looking for her apron. The dark blue item hung from a nail toward the back. As Cole grabbed it, a piece of paper fluttered to the ground.

What was that? When he picked it up, his fingers ascertained it was money. He carried the paper outside and squinted at the bank note. Breath caught in his throat.

The five-dollar bill was from the Cheyenne bank robbery—the series date and charter confirmed it. The red seal and serial numbers seemed to blaze in the sunlight.

Realization slammed into his mind. Then the next thought, even more piercing, followed quickly.

Lenora lied to me.

Crushing the note in his fist, Cole looked toward the house. His heart—so tender and open moments before—hardened into a block of stone.

Lenora jumped when the door slammed open so hard it banged against the wall. Even Toby stopped talking midsentence as they both turned to see Cole standing in the doorway. A chill ran through her. She had never before seen such cold fury. The still-healing cut on his cheek throbbed red.

She brushed off her hands. "What is it?"

"Here's your apron." He thrust it at her.

Without a word, she took it and put it on. What was wrong with him?

Expression tight, he avoided her gaze as he yanked a chair out and sat down.

The eggs, popping in the frying pan, drew her attention. Lenora returned to the stove and dished them onto three plates. A quick check of her biscuits showed them nearly done. As she hastened to finish preparing the meal, she half listened to Toby and Cole chat. Her son bubbled with excitement while Cole answered in monosyllables.

Finally she had assembled everything on the table.

A little out of breath, she sat. "Toby, would you please say the blessing?"

Lenora held out her hands for prayer. When Cole didn't reach across the table as usual, she glanced at him. His eyes were hard, jaw set. Not only that, but his fist remained balled on the table's surface. She gulped. The message blared loud and clear. He would not hold her hand during prayer. Her fingers shriveled back into her lap.

As she clasped her son's palm, she ducked her head. Was Cole angry at her? Why?

She squeezed her eyes shut, imagining she understood. Last night, he must have heard her crying. Perhaps he was irritated that she didn't control her emotions.

Amos had often said she wore her feelings on her sleeve. More than once, he had chastised her about it being bad for Toby. A blatant display of womanly emotions would only stunt his growth as a man.

As her son prayed, she vowed to hide what Cole's imminent departure did to her heart.

I shouldn't be so selfish. I need to be braver.

His task was noble. She shouldn't allow her personal feelings to get in the way of his very important job.

But after he left on the morrow, she would immediately begin preparations to travel to Cheyenne—and pray Jeb wouldn't show up at the ranch first. She and Toby would have to wait until dusk before departing. It would be safer.

Before he finished his prayer, she dared to interrupt. "And Lord, thank You for my son, Tobias Joseph. Thank You that he's turning out to be such a fine young man. I pray..." She paused as her voice cracked. "I pray that he would grow up to be like Cole. A man of integrity and high ideals. One who pursues what is right no matter the cost." Again, she stopped, afraid she would burst into tears. "Amen." The word squeaked out.

She kept her head lowered to hide her stinging eyes. When she glanced at Cole, she expected to see a softened expression. At least one of understanding. But no. If nothing else, his face seemed even more chiseled in stone.

Did he think she was trying to manipulate him by her prayers?

She tried to swallow the huge lump in her throat. If only she could explain. Tell him that no matter what, she supported his mission to hunt down Jeb Hackett and others like him.

But not now. She wouldn't spoil Toby's special day. As far as her son knew, Cole was there to stay.

After picking at her fried egg and biscuit for several minutes, she pushed her plate away. Toby and Cole seemed to eat with relish. Good. That was the way it should be.

"Before I forget..." Lenora went into the bedroom and soon returned with her son's gift tied in a kerchief.

Toby's eyes widened. "A present? Now?"

"Why not? I figured you'd want it sooner than later." He unwrapped the gift. "Wow. This was Pa's." He held up the bowie knife sheathed in leather. With care, he slid out the long blade.

"I hope I don't need to remind you to take care handling that."

"No, ma'am." Toby's voice betrayed his awe as his gaze fixed on the shiny metal.

Lenora grinned at his phrase, one he likely picked up from Cole. For his sake, she explained to Toby, "Your pa had that before he and I married. It may have once belonged to his father."

"My grandpa who died on the Oregon Trail?"

"Yes. Grandpa Joseph." From what she knew of the bits and pieces of history, Amos's mother had made it to North Platte where she settled before her death. He was only fifteen when he became an orphan.

Not much older than Toby.

Struggling with the similarities, she cleared her throat to circumvent tears.

"I have to finish your present." Cole spoke quietly as he looked at her son. "That snakeskin hatband. Sorry it's not quite ready."

"That's all right." Toby grinned. "Hey, Ma, can I go out and try my new knife?"

Since he was already halfway to the door, she couldn't find it in herself to tell him no. In a way, she hoped Cole would accompany him, but he seemed content to remain. He even slouched in his chair as he stretched out one leg to the side of the table.

"Go ahead," she finally answered. "But be careful. I don't want to have to stitch you up."

Toby's footsteps clomped out of earshot, followed by Blister's excited bark. That too faded. Except for the persistent chirp of a bird outside, nothing sounded.

Lenora slowly began to clear the dishes. The tin plates

rattled dully while the pottery clattered. A glance proved Cole watched her, eyes narrowed, mouth pursed. The absence of talking wore on her until she thought she would scream.

She was nearly finished cleaning up when he coughed. "Found something of yours."

Lenora swiveled and gasped at the two crumpled bills that lay on the table. Immediately she recognized them. The ones Jeb had left.

She raised her eyes to Cole. "Where did you get them?"

"Root cellar. One fell out of your apron pocket when I picked it up." His eyes narrowed as he studied her.

She shuddered as though the bills were two rattlers preparing to strike.

"Take them away. Do whatever you want with them." Pushing out her hand, she backed away. Now she recalled shoving them into her apron after she'd retrieved them from the tin can.

"Don't you need them? I seem to recall you lacking funds."

"I don't care. I don't want that money." She stared at the bills, disgusted that she even considered using them.

"Why?" Cole rose from the chair, his voice like flint steel.

"I…" Intent on the paper, she barely glanced at him. "I want nothing to do with Jeb or his so-called generosity. Get them out of my house."

"Hackett? What does he have to do with this?"

She backed away even more, as though to distance herself from the memory of Jeb's visit. "Last time he was here, he pretended concern for my welfare. He left that money. Like he was trying to buy me or…" Revulsion rippled through her. "That was before he decided to just take what he thought was his." Her voice rose. "If you don't want them…"

She brushed by Cole and grabbed the bills. In three steps, she twisted open the stove's door handle with her apron.

"Lenora, stop." Cole grabbed her arm before she could throw the bills into the flames.

"Let me go!"

One moment his grip tightened and the next he yanked her into his arms. He held her so tightly she could hardly breathe.

For mere seconds, she allowed his embrace. The next, she shoved against his chest. "Don't do this to me, Cole. I can't… I can't…" A sob choked her words.

He didn't heed her cry, but merely tightened his arms about her. "I'm sorry. I'm sorry," he whispered over and over.

Because he regretted what Jeb had done to her? She had no idea what else he could mean.

With all her strength, she shoved herself from his embrace. "Please, *please*, burn that money."

"I can't do that."

"Why not?" Why would he want to keep it, especially now that he knew where it had come from? Those bills represented only pain to her.

Cole uncrumpled one banknote and held it between fingers and thumbs. "Because this money—that you got from Jeb Hackett—*proves* he was one of the Cheyenne bank robbers."

Chapter Nineteen

"Do you have everything you need?" Lenora's eyes appeared coffee-colored in the noonday sun.

She is so beautiful. Cole's heart tightened in longing. "I believe so."

"And you remember the names of the other gang members?"

He nodded as they lingered beside the corral. Rowdy blew air through his nostrils, tossing his head and letting Cole know he was raring to go.

His saddlebags were packed with extra ammunition for his pistol and rifle. One incriminating bill remained with Lenora while he carried the other—a precaution in case things went wrong. He had water and food. Nothing else remained.

Except his goodbye.

Cole devoured her with his gaze, memorizing every beloved feature. Her honey brown hair, curls woven with gold. The trembling of her lips as she tried in vain to appear brave. The soft curve of her cheek.

He swallowed, trying to dislodge what his departure did to his heart. "And you'll explain to Toby why I had to go?"

"Yes." Her word barely came out above a whisper as her hands twisted in her apron.

"Tell him I'm sorry I couldn't stay for his birthday."

"I will."

"I just don't want him to be angry because I didn't say goodbye."

"Don't worry about him. We'll be fine."

Cole took a breath and held it. "I pray to God that remains true." Now that he knew the truth about the money, his heart again softened toward her. He again dared to hope they had a future.

With the proof in his hands, he would end Hackett's reign of terror. After a short stay in jail and even quicker trial, Cole expected the outlaw gang to swing from a rope. Not only for the bank robbery, but the two men they had killed.

Then Cole would come back for Lenora. If she wanted things to remain as she'd outlined in that contract, fine. He would finish the small building across the corral and call it home for a spell.

Then do everything in my power to win her.

"You will be careful, won't you?" Lenora's jaw clenched.

"Always." Still he loitered, unable to make himself leave.

What if he didn't live to return? Could he kiss her goodbye, knowing it would break her heart? He refused to make promises he couldn't guarantee he'd keep.

Steeling himself, he grabbed the saddle horn and swung himself onto the sorrel.

"Cole." She drew closer, hand resting on the horse's shoulder. "Will I see you again?"

Her wistful expression nearly made him forget all about Jeb Hackett. For a moment, Cole felt as though the world screeched to a halt, and there was nothing in the universe but Lenora and him.

The next, he had dismounted and pulled her into his arms before he knew what was happening. With his hat pushed back, he kissed her with all the longing he felt.

Her lips trembled under his, but she yielded to his embrace. When he released her, she nearly staggered.

Before he abandoned his mission and stayed with her, he once again swung himself up into the saddle. "Lord willing, you will see me again. I promise."

With tears filling her eyes, she smiled. It was the loveliest sight he had beheld in a long time.

He leaned down, fingers caressing her cheek and delicate jawline. "I'll be back as soon as I can." He managed a smile as he straightened. "Besides, I promised Toby a present."

After a two-fingered salute, he backed Rowdy. A gentle squeeze to his sides and the horse moved from a trot to a fluid canter. When Cole reached the end of the road, before he disappeared down the hill, he reined in his sorrel and turned in the saddle.

She still stood where he'd left her.

Unable to resist showing off, he made Rowdy rear back on his hind legs. After a wave of his hat, he pressed on.

"Where can I find the sheriff?" Cole planted himself directly in the man's path to force him to answer.

Shrugging, the man hurried away.

This was Cole's third attempt to get information from the townsfolk. Everyone in Silver Peaks either dithered when he asked or outright avoided him. After he stopped again at the empty jailhouse, he walked up and down the street. He'd finally resorted to checking in the town's one and only saloon. Besides the bartender, three cowboys played cards at a corner table.

With his eye on them and his back to the wall, Cole rested an elbow on the counter. "Seen the sheriff?"

The barkeep polished one spot on the countertop, over and over. His gaze shot to the three patrons, then back. "Can't say as I have."

Cole sighed, taking care to keep his hands where the man could see them. "If someone started shooting in here, I'm sure he'd show up right quick."

Though the man's eyes narrowed, he continued to wipe the surface.

Cole gritted his teeth. "Tell him someone needs to see him at the jailhouse." Without waiting for a response, he headed back down the street.

Was this town so perfect they never had to lock up troublemakers? The answer seemed obvious—all the troublemakers worked for Hackett.

To the bartender's credit, Cole waited only fifteen minutes before a flustered looking man appeared. As he entered the building, he tucked in his shirt and slicked back his hair. After sizing up Cole, he scowled. "What d'ya want?"

"You the sheriff?"

"Who's asking?"

Cole pushed back his coat lapel to reveal his badge. "US Marshal Jesse Cole. I need you to gather six to ten able-bodied men for me to deputize so we can form a posse."

He straightened and gulped. "I'm Leland Mackay. Who are we after?"

Cole deliberated with himself and decided to state the crime first. "Men who may be guilty of bank robbery and murder. I not only have evidence but a witness."

"A witness? Here in Silver Peaks?"

"No, nearby." Cole watched the man's face as he spoke. "Lenora Pritchard." He deliberately left off her new married name.

Understanding dawned on the sheriff's face.

When he said nothing, Cole added, "A Cheyenne bank was robbed about six months ago. Two men were shot— and killed. One was a teller and the other a bystander."

Something subtly changed in the sheriff's demeanor. Brow furrowed and hands slowly unclenching, he seemed to stop breathing. Because he already knew about the robbery? Or suspected who the guilty parties were?

His Adam's apple bobbed as his gaze sidled away. "And who are you planning to arrest?"

"Jeb Hackett and his men. Charlie, Dandyman, Leftie and Horseface. Those are the only names I know them by. But that shouldn't be a problem."

"I see." That was all the sheriff said, apparently thinking over what he'd heard.

Cole waited, but the man didn't move.

Had he fallen asleep with his eyes open? He merely stared out the window, thick lips alternately pressing together or hanging open. That was the only indication that his mind was working besides the occasional blink.

Finally he looked at Cole and sank into his office chair. "Sorry, Marshal. I can't help you."

Had he heard right? "What?"

"I said I can't help you," the sheriff repeated, his voice decidedly louder. His gaze shot at Cole, then to the surface of his desk. "Nary a man in this county isn't beholden to Eli Hackett in one way or t'other. Nobody dares raise a hand against him or his son, Jeb."

Cole clenched his jaw. "Including you?"

Shoulders hunkering, he shifted in his chair.

"So you'd let criminals go free so you can protect your own hide?"

The sheriff's face hardened. "I guarantee it'd be just us two. Against how many? Jeb and his buddies—plus whoever Eli has nearby? It'd be suicide."

Cole leaned his knuckles on the desk. "So you're giving up before you lift a finger."

The sheriff's palm scrubbed his chin—like he missed a beard that once had been there. "You go find an army, and I'd be glad to help."

"Very well." Cole straightened. "I'll be sure to save you a spot in the back. Where you'll be safe." He turned on his heel.

As he stomped down the street, he contemplated his options. Next to none. He wouldn't put it past the sheriff to warn the Hacketts since it sounded like his job relied on their good graces. Even if Cole left immediately and traveled to Cheyenne, he wouldn't get back with a posse before the gang went to ground.

Could he count on soldiers from Fort Laramie? Technically, he couldn't order them to assist. However, asking seemed his best option. He couldn't stand by and do nothing.

Changing direction, he strode toward the telegraph office, a tiny building at the end of the street. Two people were inside. A gray-headed man with an imperial mustache and beard sat at a desk filled with telegraph equipment while the younger, sporting bright red hair, sorted through messages on a slotted shelf. The inside of the building was well kept and orderly. A small door led out the back.

The older man spoke. "May I help you, sir?"

"I'd like to send a telegram. Official government business." Cole revealed his badge.

His eyes widened. "Yessir. Would you care to dictate your message?"

Cole glanced at the younger man who paused in his task, shoulders stiffening. Because he was listening? "I'll write it out."

The man shoved a sheet of paper at Cole who quickly composed his message to the commanding officer at Fort Laramie. As an afterthought, he added a request for a response as soon as possible so he would know how to proceed.

As the older man read the message, the blood seemed to drain from his face. He peered at Cole. "You want this sent right away?"

"Yes."

He glanced over his shoulder at the younger man. "Red, why don't you run down to the mercantile and get yourself a soda water?"

The younger turned, a frown on his face. "What?"

"Just do it."

He glared at his employer, then slouched out the door.

"Just a safety precaution," the man explained. "Mind keeping an eye on him for a moment?"

Peering out the window, Cole watched the young man stride diagonally across the street toward the nearest mercantile. Hands in his pockets, he kicked a rock.

"He's on his way."

Behind him, the man tapped out the message. "There. It's done." The gray-headed man lifted his chin, mustache curling under a pressed lip.

"How long should I wait for a reply?"

His eyes shifted. "Don't know. Could take an hour."

Really? Cole gripped the door frame. He didn't relish hanging around the office that long. Frustration—along with its twin, tension—coiled inside him. The longer this process took, the more his nerves skittered on edge.

Something wasn't right. His gut tightened.

Making up his mind, he said, "I'll be back in half an hour." With that, he strode away.

The sun, high in the sky, baked the dusty, brown street. Most folks who'd been sitting under porches were now absent, hiding from the heat. Cole avoided the dark and cool saloon. Too many a lawman had been shot in the back as they'd lingered where outlaws hung out. Besides, he got the distinct impression it was one place the Hackett gang favored.

That left a couple mercantiles, including the one where he'd had a run-in with Mr. Richards. Cole chose the other place, the one the redhead had entered.

In the cool dimness, several patrons lingered. Their conversation abruptly halted the moment he stepped inside.

The proprietor nodded a greeting in his direction.

"I'll take what he's having." Cole indicated the telegraph worker, whose eyes widened. Like he had been found out?

Scared glances passed between him and the three other patrons—all male. No one said a word as the proprietor retrieved a soda water. "Red" muttered something about going back to work before slipping out the door.

Cole paid for the drink, then looked around as though considering what else to buy. The longer he loitered, the heavier the silence. Finally, one of the locals murmured something about the unseasonable hot weather. Another replied how a drought would affect the crops.

"Anything else?" The proprietor flattened his hands on the counter.

Cole took his time turning, like he suddenly realized

the man was talking to him. "Not that I can see. Unless you can tell me the time."

"Three twenty-three." A patron had his pocket watch out faster than a vulture could spot a carcass.

Because they wanted to get rid of him?

"Guess I'll be moving along." Cole finished his drink and set the empty bottle on the counter.

After stepping into the bright sunshine, he allowed his eyes to adjust. If anything, the street seemed even more deserted. The horses that had been by the saloon earlier were now missing. Only Rowdy stood, head lowered as he dozed, not far from the sheriff's office. The wind stirred the dust, creating a brown wave that raced a tumbleweed down the street's center.

Where was everyone?

A prickle of unease crawled across the back of his neck. He gave a low whistle to Rowdy. His horse's head jerked up, yanking the reins from the hitching post.

As his gelding clopped toward him, Cole watched his twitching ears. Though Rowdy focused on him, he could clearly see the horse sensed something farther down the street.

"What is it, boy?" He spoke in a low voice. As he patted his neck, he draped the reins over his sorrel's withers so that he wouldn't accidently step on them. Watching his horse's response, Cole pretended to adjust the cinch strap.

Yep, something—or someone—Rowdy didn't like was down the street, out of sight.

"Come on, boy." Cole crossed to the other side, walking beside his horse, opposite where danger might be. When he got to the hitching post not far from the telegraph office, he remained next to the gelding, again pretending to check the saddle.

In an alley diagonally from him sat a buckboard

wagon. Several barrels clustered against a building. Though Cole couldn't see anyone, he trusted his horse knew something he didn't. In another building, a curtain fluttered. From an open window above, he heard a woman talking, then a sharp "Hush."

Again, he draped the reins over the post, confident Rowdy wouldn't wander but could come if he whistled.

The telegraph office was a good thirty feet away. He would have to walk alongside one building and past a small alley before he reached the door. After pulling his hat snug, he sauntered toward his goal. His scalp tingled as he approached the alley.

Movement along the base of one building had Cole ducking before he realized it was merely a piece of paper, fluttering along the ground. At the same time, he heard the distinct click of a gun being cocked.

He dived as a crack resounded. Wood splintered nearby. A woman shrieked.

Another click as a hammer cocked. The sound distant.

In seconds, he rolled inside the telegraph building. Still low, he slammed the door as a bullet pierced the flimsy wood. A third shot shattered one pane of the window.

Cole drew his gun, then swiveled when a sound startled him.

"Don't shoot!" Red peeked from behind the desk, eyes wide and hands raised above his head. "I'm unarmed."

"Keep 'em where I can see them."

"Yessir." Red gulped convulsively. His hands remained in sight while his head lowered.

A glance told Cole he had no gun. But that didn't mean one wasn't nearby. Where was the gray-haired man? The back door was open a fraction. Because he'd fled?

Though no more shots came from across the street,

Cole remained crouched out of sight. "Where's your boss?"

"I—I don't know. He was gone when I came back from the mercantile."

"Is that usual?"

"No. He never leaves."

So, graybeard knew about the trap?

Cole moved closer to the young man, just in case his would-be assassins decided to storm the door. "What were you doing under the desk?"

He pointed. "A wire came loose. I was going to fix it."

"That happen before or after the shooting?"

"Before."

Cole studied him. "So my telegram wasn't sent?"

"Don't think so." He shook his head. "Nothing would have transmitted with that wire unhooked."

"Are you able to send a message?"

Red shrugged. "Yeah. But I usually don't."

"Do it. Only keep your head down so it doesn't get shot off." When the young man got in position, Cole had him relay his earlier message except he added, "Meet at the Pritchard ranch, thirteen miles due east from Silver Peaks. Matter of life and death."

Chapter Twenty

As Lenora stepped off the porch, she yelled for her son. Where had that boy gone? Probably skinning something or gutting fish with his new bowie knife. Hadn't she told him to stay close? The yard remained dismally quiet, the landscape glowing with a golden cast from the late-afternoon sun. No response echoed her one call. She shielded her eyes as she panned the area. Nothing. Despite the warmth, she shivered.

Over four hours had passed since Cole left. She'd given up pacing in the house and could no longer concentrate on her mending as she sat on the porch. A brief interval of working in the garden couldn't settle her nerves. The thrill from the kiss she and Cole had shared slowly faded, replaced by a growing unease.

Was he safe? Had he accomplished his mission?

She squeezed her eyes shut. "Lord, please watch over Cole. Please bring him back to us. To me."

When she opened her eyes, a flash from a nearby hill caught her attention. What was that? At first, she imagined it was the sun as it sent out brilliant beams of dying light. Then she thought it was Toby. No, it couldn't be. He would never wander that far without permission.

When she saw nothing else, she scanned the rocky hills. Another gleam, from farther away, sent a shaft of fear down her back.

Someone was signaling another person. With a mirror? It seemed obvious that the message was about her. And about the ranch. Did they know Cole was gone?

"Toby," she shrieked. "Toby, where are you?" She raised her voice. "Answer me this instant."

"Coming." His young voice reached her from somewhere behind the house.

She ran around the building. "Toby, get in here. Hurry."

From the distance, she could see he'd been fishing. He wore a happy smile, three or four fish dangling from a line in one hand, his pole in the other.

"Toby, run!"

He paused only a moment, his expression changing from the urgency in her tone. Immediately, he picked up his pace, Blister bounding alongside him.

When her son reached her, Lenora grabbed his shoulder. "Get inside the house. Take Blister. Hurry!"

While he and his dog bolted toward the front door, Lenora ran to the barn to retrieve her shotgun. She grabbed some of Cole's stored ammunition. It didn't take her long to return to the house.

Again, she thanked God that Jeb hadn't stolen the rifle and shotgun.

Panting hard, she slammed down the crossbar on the front door. In moments, she shuttered her bedroom window. "Toby, help me with these." She grabbed the panels beside the fireplace and put them into position over the two windows in the great room. They slid into the grooves Amos had crafted. Once they were secured, she called Toby into her bedroom. Blister followed, panting from the growing tension.

Together they pushed the heavy dresser off the rug until the trapdoor was fully exposed. They lifted the panel and retrieved ammunition from the small opening. She didn't have as much as she liked, but enough to let Jeb know she wouldn't surrender easily.

Afterward, she shut the door to her bedroom. With her rifle in one hand and the shotgun within reach, she pushed back one shutter to peek out the window. Nothing could be seen. That didn't mean Jeb and his men weren't out there. She left it open to keep watch.

"Toby, go check the latch on the door in the roof. Make certain it's secured."

"Yes'm." The quaver in her son's voice betrayed his fear.

She flashed him a tight smile. "Don't be frightened. We're perfectly safe in here. I'm just being cautious."

"Okay, Ma." He scrambled up the ladder while his dog barked and whimpered.

"Hush, Blister." Lenora's sharp voice silenced him instantly. She softened her tone. "It's okay, boy. Toby'll be right back."

"It's locked." Her son's voice called from above.

"Okay. Come down and stay low. Understand?"

"Yes'm." He soon squatted beside his dog, hand stroking his fur.

The room returned to silence except for the sound of Blister's panting. Lenora continued to check all the windows, wishing now she had one at the back of the house. What if Jeb or his men were approaching from that way?

The agonizing minutes passed.

"Ma, will we…?" A suppressed sob cut off Toby's whisper.

Lenora threw a glance at him. His young mouth trembled, eyes bright with fear as he sat on the floor by his dog.

"Come here." She held open one arm, inviting him into her embrace.

He rushed to her, burying his face against her shoulder as he knelt beside her.

"It'll be all right, son." Battling her own fears, she caressed his back. "Hackett wants to take us to his ranch, understand? Our lives aren't in danger. We're just not going without a fight."

When he lifted his face, she smoothed the tears off his skin with a gentle thumb.

"Are you sure, Ma?"

"Yes, I'm sure." She didn't speculate aloud that Jeb would wait to hurt her—hurt them both—after they were at his place, surrounded by a dozen men. Lenora would not allow herself to be taken. Once in his clutches, he would make certain she died a thousand deaths.

Better to die here—once—than there.

"My stomach hurts, Ma." Toby clutched his middle.

"You're probably hungry. Why don't you have the rest of your birthday cake?" She nodded in the direction where a piece sat on the table.

"But that's Cole's, remember? We were saving it for him."

"I know." She peered out the window as she spoke. "I'm sure he'll understand. And I can always make another."

He sniffed. "Ya think he's okay?"

She resisted offering him a flippant answer. "I'm not sure, Toby."

"Should we pray for him, Ma?"

She squeezed his shoulder. "That would be a wonderful idea. You start, but I'm going to pray with my eyes open so I can keep watch."

"Dear God," Toby began, head bowed, eyes closed.

"Please watch over Cole. Keep him safe. And us too. And Porky, Sheba, Nips and Rowdy. And please help Blister not to be so scared." His dog pressed against him, whimpering.

"And Lord, bring Cole safely back…" Lenora's voice died as the sound of thundering horse hooves reached her.

She straightened, listening.

Not one. But a half dozen? One seemed to be closer. Why? Or were they coming from opposite directions?

Her questions were soon answered by a horse flying into the yard. Footsteps stomped up the steps—two, three at a time. Though she expected it, the loud pounding on her door made her jump.

She leaped up, pointing her rifle at the door. "Get off my porch this instant or I *will* shoot."

Lenora and Toby are in danger.

The thought beat against Cole's brain in time to Rowdy's hooves striking the ground. He pushed his horse, knowing that every second counted. Though the miles flew under him, time dragged in agonizing slowness.

Please God, keep them safe.

After Cole had escaped through the back door of the telegraph office, he had whistled for his gelding. Amid a few more haphazard shots, he'd ridden out of town, beelining for the ranch. Whoever had betrayed him in town had likely informed Hackett or one of his men.

That meant the outlaw knew Cole was missing from the ranch, leaving Lenora and her son vulnerable.

I put them in danger. Dear Lord…

Just like he'd done with Andrew. If something happened to them, it would be his fault.

Hurry. Hurry. *Hurry.*

His plea kept in tempo with Rowdy's hooves. The sun slowly slid toward the horizon.

He was perhaps a mile from the ranch when he saw a dust cloud shimmering in the distance. Riders? They appeared to have the same goal—Lenora's ranch. Could he beat them there?

"Come on, boy," he shouted to Rowdy, hunkering down in the saddle. He gave the gelding more rein and squeezed his sides with his knees. "Come on, you can do it."

His faithful horse pushed harder.

They rode into the yard, perhaps minutes before the other group. While Rowdy was still moving, Cole grabbed his rifle and leaped off. A quick swipe of his saddlebags followed. Loathe to leave the horse unattended, he slapped Rowdy's rump to send him away from danger.

"Go, boy!" In three steps Cole bounded onto the porch and pounded on Lenora's door with his fist.

Her voice came from inside. "Get off my porch this instant or I *will* shoot."

"It's me. Cole. Open the door!"

After a ten-second eternity, the dull thump of the crossbar sounded as a group of men thundered into the yard. The door opened a fraction. Two or three shots fired from the Hackett gang. Cole ducked and shoved his shoulder against the moving panel, forcing himself into the house. Rolling, he avoided the bullets that sprayed against the wall.

Lenora shrieked while he kicked the door shut.

"Bar it." He was already on one knee and rising. After sliding open one shutter partway, he smashed out a windowpane and fired with his pistol. He heard a yell, the scream of a horse and men's shouts. Another volley of bullets came their way, shattering more glass. Turning his head to avoid the flying missiles, Cole ignored the sting as something sharp sliced across his jaw.

For the next several moments, pandemonium continued as the men outside apparently tried to organize themselves. Hackett yelled obscenities. A tornado of dust swirled in the yard. Little was visible beyond shadowy forms of both men and horses. Cole took careful aim and squeezed off a round. Another yell told him his shot connected.

When Lenora moved closer to him, he grabbed her arm to pull her down. "Stay away from the door." Several bullet holes revealed the wood had splintered. By the time he looked back outside, the dust was settling. No men were in sight.

Still squatting, Cole crab-walked to the other window facing west and opened one shutter a couple inches. His action produced a barrage of shots.

Ducking, he turned and pressed against the wall as he reloaded his pistol. "We're going to have to wait until dark. They see me before I see them."

Face pinched, Lenora nodded.

"Are you okay?"

"Yes." Her word came out a little breathlessly.

"How'd you know I was coming? And to bar yourself in the house?"

She shook her head. "I saw someone signal with a mirror along the ridge and knew something bad was about to happen."

"You were right."

A noise outside caught his ear. "Marshal Cole."

Lenora's gaze met his. Jeb Hackett was the speaker.

Cole scooted up the wall just enough to yell out the broken window. "What d'ya want?"

"Give yourself up, and I promise we'll leave Lenora and the boy alone."

She grabbed Cole's arm. Lips white, she shook her head with vigor.

He raised his voice. "Can't say we're interested. Got a better deal?" He moved away from one window and flattened himself against the thick wall near the other. There the sun wasn't shining in. Again, he peered out, hoping that while he and Hackett talked no one would blow his head off.

The men remained invisible. Though the house was built up off the ground, the nearby area had an abundance of hiding places. Several glances revealed shooters behind a water trough, boulders and a cluster of trees.

"I see at least ten men," he said in a lowered voice to Lenora.

Before she could respond, Hackett again yelled. "The only other deal I'm offering is you dying."

Cole pointed to the table and whispered to Lenora, "Clear that off. I'll turn it on its side to provide an additional barricade."

In a hunched position, Lenora did as he bid. He pushed the shutter all the way closed so no one could see inside. After holstering his gun, he toppled the table. "Toby, get behind that. Good." The youngster, with his arm around Blister, crawled behind the heavy wood. With them safe, he could concentrate on keeping the house secure. "You as well, Lenora."

She surprised him by shaking her head. "This is my fight, too."

He wanted to protest, to tell her that his life was nothing without her. But if he died, how much longer would she live? An hour? A day?

"Okay. Stay down. Please." He rechecked his gun to make certain it was fully loaded. "We'll wait until dark before we try to pick them off. Right now they can see us long before we see them."

She nodded. "Just tell me what to do."

"What's it gonna be, Cole?" Hackett hollered. "You coming out alive or we dragging out your corpses?"

He again positioned himself by one window. "A contingency of soldiers are on their way from Fort Laramie." At least he hoped that was true. What if Red at the telegraph office double-crossed him like his boss? For all Cole knew, he could have sent a biscuit recipe to President Chester Arthur.

"They're six hours from here. Think you'll last that long?"

So, Hackett didn't know for certain if soldiers were on their way. At least he didn't assert they were not. Perhaps the telegraph had gone through?

Cole wouldn't count on it.

How long could they hold out on their own? Three? Four days?

The outlaw wouldn't be that patient and would likely try to burn them out. Before that happened, Cole planned to use the trapdoor in the roof and pay the men a visit in the middle of the night. Hackett wouldn't know what hit him.

"Lenora," the outlaw called. "Convince that hired hand of yours to give yourselves up. I swear no harm will come to you or the boy."

Cole's gaze met hers as he spoke in a lowered voice. "You know how you can tell Hackett's lying?"

"Yes," she didn't hesitate to reply. "His lips are moving."

"Glad we're in agreement." With a grim smile, he nodded. "Keep him talking for a minute. Let them see the barrel of your rifle so they don't wander closer."

With her head safely lowered, she pressed her hand to the wall near the window. "Jeb? What will you do with Cole if he gives himself up?"

Cole came up with his own answer. *Not invite me to a game of Old Maid.*

Half listening to their conversation, he hurried to the other side of the room and braced his back against the wall. With his foot, he pushed the heavy stove toward the door. "Toby, stay low and come help."

The youngster did as he was told.

"Don't touch it." The metal was just hot enough to burn skin. "Use your foot like I am."

Together, they scooted the heavy iron across the floor to provide a bullet barrier to the front door. Though it was still a couple feet from the panel, Cole felt confident it would help. The stove would also add protection in case Hackett's men stormed the door.

From the outlaw's bullying tone, Cole could tell the man grew tired of bargaining.

By now, the sun had sunk below the horizon. He directed Lenora to take her rifle and position herself by the northern window. "Fire at anything that moves. But no wild shots. We have to make every one count."

"This is your last chance," the outlaw roared.

"I got a deal for you, Hackett." Cole peered out the window. When no one fired, he took an extra second to study where his next shots would go. "If you and your men go now, I'll let you live."

Not three seconds later, a rain of bullets riddled the house.

Chapter Twenty-One

How much longer can we last?

As the night grew darker, terror nagged Lenora. Though Jeb no longer directed his men to barrage them with fire, they still took occasional shots to remind them the threat remained. Several men had stormed the front door, but Cole had injured too many of them before they'd even gained the porch.

Now it was quiet. More or less.

She crawled across broken pottery and debris to join Toby behind the overturned table. "How are you doing?"

"Okay." His voice came out small. In the darkness, she couldn't see his face, but heard the fear in his tone.

I have to be brave. For his sake.

Truth was, she felt about at a breaking point.

"Here is some bread for you and Blister." She shoved part of a loaf at him, the only thing that she could find that might not be laced with glass.

"Are we gonna die, Ma?"

She fumbled for his shoulder. "Cole will do everything to make sure that doesn't happen."

"I've been praying." His sentence ended with a stuttering sniff as though he could no longer repress a sob.

Fighting tears, she pulled his head closer and kissed him on his mop of hair. "Me, too. Remember that God is greater than anyone in the world. That includes Jeb and his men."

Before she broke down and gave into her own fears, she crawled back toward Cole.

"How are you holding up?" His whisper came to her through the darkness.

She swallowed her terror. "Well enough."

"And Toby?"

"Good." When her voice quavered, she rammed confidence into the tone. "Under the circumstances."

How she wanted Cole to pull her close. Her heart was so full of what she wanted to tell him that it threatened to spill out. But what could she say?

In the small amount of light that came from the outside, she could barely make out his profile. His narrowed eyes never ceased surveying the area. His lips tightened, jaw inflexible.

I must not distract him.

He was keeping them alive and would continue to do so until his last breath. An invisible hand clutched her throat in awe. What had she done to earn such fierce loyalty? And from a man who barely knew her? Or was he merely doing his duty as a US marshal?

If only she didn't carry the terrible burden of a monstrous secret. Before they died, she wanted to tell him about it. To beg forgiveness for not revealing all she knew. Weeks ago, he could have taken the money to Cheyenne. But she had been too afraid that he would despise her for hiding it. That she would lose him forever.

"Cole?" she whispered. "I need to tell you something."

He twitched as though he saw movement in the darkness. "Something's happening."

She scrabbled toward the other window. A flame sprung into life in the distance.

"Don't waste ammo," Cole cautioned. "They're too far away."

In fascinated horror, she watched the torch bob across the horizon. "What are they doing?"

Jeb answered moments later by yelling, "You prepared to lose your barn, Lenora? Horses? Livestock?"

Cole joined her at the window.

In terror, she clawed his sleeve. "Will he kill your horses? The cattle?"

He yelled, "You'd be a fool to destroy it, Hackett. Why not just take everything after we're dead?"

In tense silence they watched the flame disappear behind the barn. A small orange glow sprang to life and grew. Horrified, Lenora watched the blaze crawl up the building and creep across the roof.

"Go check the other window," Cole ordered in a terse tone. "See what they're doing while we're distracted." In another moment, he lifted his rifle and fired. Twice.

A glance out the side revealed two men materializing out of the shadows and moving closer to the house.

"Cole!"

"Shoot them," he ordered, busy with what he saw out his window.

Lenora fumbled for her rifle, railing at herself for setting it aside. By the time she retrieved it, the men were under cover.

How foolish. They had been clearly visible for several seconds because of the inferno's light. Even so, she lifted the barrel and aimed. Before she took a shot, searing pain cut her.

She screamed.

In an instant, Cole was beside her. "Are you shot?" Desperation ripped through his tone.

"No, I…" She whimpered, pressing her hand to her neck. Wet warmth filled her palm.

"Lenora, where are you hit?"

"I'm okay. Just a graze. On my collarbone." She wasn't sure if a bullet or flying woodchips had struck her.

Cole rose and slammed his body against the wall. "Hackett! If you want Lenora alive, you'd best instruct your men to stop shooting at her."

His furious admonition had its desired effect. Even from a distance, she could hear Jeb berate his men.

The interior of the house lit up with an eerie orange glow as fire consumed the barn. Horses squealed in alarm while her son's sobs echoed inside the room.

"It's okay, Toby." Lenora suffocated the sobs that threatened. "The horses are all out in the pasture. None of them were in the barn."

Even so, the sound—like human screams—sent chills through her body.

She looked up, clearly seeing Cole standing in the room.

One moment, he was reaching to close the shutters and the next he spun with a cry and crumpled to the floor.

"Cole!" She shrieked his name.

No answer.

She crawled across the debris-filled floor. He groaned. By the time she reached him, he rolled to his side and struggled to sit up.

In the red glow, he appeared covered in blood. A dark stain spread across his shirt.

"I'm all right," he ground out. "Just…"

Lenora grabbed a towel and thrust in on the wet spot

so hard that he nearly toppled. "Where were you hit?" She heard herself babble a dozen questions, unable to stem her fear.

"Caught a bullet…here."

She felt his upper arm, her fingers sticky with warmth. Another wound on the back of his arm proved the bullet had passed through.

He cradled his elbow, groaning. "Bind it. Stop the bleeding."

With tears streaming down her face, she ripped the hem out of her apron. "This is my fault. *My* fault. I could've stopped this hours ago." As she bandaged his wound, she whispered, "I'm sorry, Cole. So, so sorry."

"For what?"

She shook her head, unable to admit the depths of her weakness.

Grunting in pain, he slumped back against the wall.

I need to end this. Now.

She bolted to the open window. "Jeb. I'm ready to make a deal. Do you hear me?"

"Hold your fire. Hold your fire." The phrase echoed until stillness again filled the night.

"Lenora, no." Cole's voice grew stronger.

She had to do what was necessary—what she should have done long ago. If she could save Cole's life, she was willing to sacrifice his love for her.

"I know where the money is, Jeb. You hear me?" She peered out the shattered window. "You were right. Amos stopped here after the robbery. I have the satchel."

"Don't." Glass scraped as Cole shifted his weight.

"What d'ya want for it, Lenora?" came Jeb's question.

"I want your word that you and your men will leave and never come back."

"Deal." His voice rang with excitement. "Where is it?"

"I want your word."

In the darkness, she heard his low chuckle. "Okay, I promise. Soon as I know, me and the boys will ride out."

"All right. The money is—"

The words died as something hit Lenora, knocking the air from her lungs. Cole rammed against her, stifling her voice. "No!" he rasped in her ear. "Don't you understand? As soon as he gets his hands on the money, we're all dead."

"If it's the only way to save us then—"

"It isn't. You said it yourself. If Hackett's talking, he's lying."

She gasped, trying to catch her breath. "What if he means what he says?"

"Listen to me." Cole's voice grew hard. "He wants you, but he wants the money more. They got away with over twenty thousand dollars. As soon as he gets his hands on it, he won't need us any longer. He might still try to lure you out, but Toby and I are useless to him."

She gulped air. In the fading orange light, she read anger—and disappointment—on Cole's face.

"I'm sorry," she said again, remorse eating at her. If only she could blot out the betrayal he must feel.

He fumbled for her hand, fingers crushing hers. "Promise me you won't tell him, Lenora."

She would do anything to gain his forgiveness. "I promise."

"I'm waiting." Jeb's voice rose outside.

"I have an idea." Cole breathed in her ear. "See if you can stall him."

"What are you going to do?"

"Use the barn's fire for us." He shuffled over to the loft's ladder. "Toby. Help me."

"What's your decision?" Anger built in Jeb's voice.

"I'm trying to remember exactly where it is. Give me a moment."

In the reddish glow, she could see Toby take the gun. With difficulty, Cole pulled himself up the ladder.

"Bring the rifle up here, Toby," he whispered.

Her son clambered up.

"How do I know you'll do as you say?" Lenora called.

"You don't." Hard amusement laced Jeb's voice. "I gave you my word. You have to trust me."

Two dull thumps sounded above in the loft as Cole apparently took off his boots.

"Come on, Lenora. Where is it?"

She toyed with telling him he burned half of it when he torched the barn, but discarded the idea. "Once you have it, you'll leave this territory?"

"What difference does it make?"

"Because I want to be as far from you as possible."

"Then *you* leave." Jeb's voice degenerated to muttering, like he was arguing with his men. "This is your last chance. I'm done talking. Tell me now or we'll do to your house what we did to your barn."

"Kill me and you'll never find the money."

"Fine. You can watch your son burn to death."

In the distance, another flame sprang to life, the carrier staying low. Lenora stifled a shriek of fear when it moved out of her line of vision.

They are going to start a fire at the back of the house.

Where was Cole? She pressed her hand to her mouth to keep from screaming a warning to him.

A crack of a rifle sounded from above. A man yelled. The torchbearer? Another shot was fired. And another.

Cole!

Men started yelling, apparently unable to detect where the bullets were coming from. To add to their confusion, Lenora also fired out the window. One man, who had risen for a moment, grabbed his leg and stumbled out of sight.

"He's on the roof," Jeb yelled. "Get him!"

Bullets flew at the house. But as Jeb's men rose to zero in on Cole, Lenora got them in her sights. She took careful aim and squeezed the trigger.

In the pandemonium, she heard Jeb cry out. "I'm hit, I'm hit!"

Another several minutes passed while men continued to shoot at the house. Gunfire slowly died away. Finally, Lenora could hear nothing but her panting breath. She finally realized that Toby stood across from her, shotgun in his hands. Had he been firing out the window too?

The pounding of horse hooves followed, then faded away. Were the men leaving?

She took care, peering out the window, but could see nothing, even though the smoldering barn still cast some light.

Lenora jumped at the sound of something falling hard behind her. Cole's rifle had crashed to the floor. A moment later, he slid down the ladder and landed heavily.

"Don't move." Lenora's soft voice pierced the agony in Cole's body.

As her gentle hands smoothed a cool, wet cloth over his face, he groaned.

He lay on the floor, head resting in her lap. Jagged glass and rubble dug into his back and thighs. "What happened?" He tried to rise.

"Lie still." None too gently, she pressed against his chest to keep him prone.

He hissed as he moved his injured arm.

"We're safe for now." Her voice quavered. "Please don't move."

Cole obeyed. "What happened?" The last thing he remembered was shooting from the roof.

"You fell when you climbed down from the loft." She ran her fingers through his hair. "It's a wonder you didn't break your neck."

He remembered now. After he'd landed, his head had hit something. Cole lifted his good arm and felt the goose egg on the side of his skull. Gingerly, he moved his ankle and growled at the pain. "I've got to get up and—"

"Jeb and his men are gone."

"We have to keep watch. Make sure they don't come back."

"Toby is keeping an eye out." She stroked Cole's forehead. "You can rest easy."

He let his head fall back. Truth be told, he would rather not move. Her gentle fingers caressed his skin.

So tender. So loving...

If only he could stay there forever.

Then he rallied himself. What was he thinking? They weren't out of danger yet.

Again, he fought the desire to remain in her arms. Again, he lost. Her touch was sweeter than any dream. Of their own accord, words escaped his parched lips. "Lenora, I…"

"Let's run away," she said as her fingertips moved across his cheek. "You and me and Toby. Somewhere far from here."

He fought to understand. "Where?"

"Anywhere. San Francisco. New York. Even Europe."

His mind had difficulty grasping what she was saying. "You mean leave your ranch?"

"Yes. Get away from the likes of Jeb and his father." She took a shaky breath, voice cracking. "I can't take it anymore. I can't take *them* anymore."

He didn't know how to answer. Hackett types were everywhere. Nowhere on earth was there a place where they would be away from men like them.

Then the absurdity of his own life struck Cole. How had he imagined he would track down all the outlaws in this country? The utter folly of his vow—spoken as a young man—reverberated through him.

As he looked up, he realized he could see details of Lenora's face. Was it morning already? Blackness smudged her skin. A gash ran across her collarbone, caked with dried blood. Lesser scrapes crisscrossed her face and neck. From flying shrapnel? Dried tears etched her cheeks.

"Just say yes, Cole. Please."

What had she asked him? He fought to focus as he sat up with difficulty. "What are you saying, Lenora?"

"I can't...can't do this anymore." Her mouth quivered. This? Getting shot at?

"After today, you won't have to." He reached around her shoulders, pulling her closer with his right arm and gently squeezing.

She leaned her head against him as they sat side by side. "Say you'll run away with me. We'll be able to live a good life with the money. Anywhere we want. Don't we deserve our share of happiness?"

He stiffened, mind clearing. "What're you...? You saying we should take the robbery money?"

"No one'll know."

"*I'll* know. And you would too." He withdrew his arm as anger flared over her continued betrayal. "Did keeping the money after Amos died bring you happiness?"

"I was *hiding* it, not…" She bit her lip. Self-recrimination froze her face and dried her tears.

"Is that so?" For a moment, he let the full import of the question sink in. "Two men died the day of the robbery. Even though returning the twenty thousand dollars won't bring them back from the grave, it's the right thing to do. That money's not mine. Or yours. And certainly not Jeb Hackett's."

Her face paled under the smudge of gunpowder.

Cole went on. "The lives of their wives and children will never be the same again. I wouldn't spend one dollar of that blood money."

Scorning his pain, he clutched the loft's ladder to pull himself to his feet. He fought a moment of dizziness. As he looked around, he realized the whole room lay in shambles. All of Lenora's bone china was smashed, pieces scattered across the floor. Dented tins and pots rested haphazardly around the room. Along with the door, the table and chairs were splintered. No doubt, not one windowpane remained intact.

Toby slumped against one wall, fast asleep. His hand rested on a dozing Blister.

Cole's own hands were covered in gunpowder. His shirt was torn, his left sleeve stiff with dried blood. Without thinking, he slapped his holster to make certain his gun was still there.

Lenora stood nearby, eyes filling with tears as she stared at him. "I'm sorry." She wiped one dirty hand across her cheek, smearing black. "Forgive me."

He wanted to tell her he understood. She'd just endured more than anyone should ever have to in a lifetime, not just fearing for her own life, but for her son's. And for the future of her ranch.

Cole had just opened his mouth to comfort her when the air filled with the sound of pounding hooves.

Chapter Twenty-Two

A squeak of terror escaped Lenora when she heard the horses. Was Jeb back? They had next to no ammunition. Before Cole had awakened, she ascertained they wouldn't last another hour.

"Wait." He held up his hand, listening. His expression relaxed. "My message got through."

"What message?"

"The one I sent to Fort Laramie. These must be the soldiers."

"How do you…?"

Without heeding her question, he limped to the door and yanked it open.

Toby jerked awake. "What's happening?"

"It's okay." Lenora held up her hand to stop his questions. "Stay here." She grabbed her rifle and followed Cole through the two-foot opening. By the time she stepped onto the porch, he was already down the steps. He favored one ankle, his wounded left arm hanging limply at his side.

As she saw who rode up the road, her heart sank. Not Jeb Hackett. Infinitely worse.

It was his father. Looking like an older version of his

son, Eli sported the same sneer, as though other humans were somehow lesser beings. Despite the fine sheen of dirt on his coat, he appeared impeccable. His face was clean-shaved, blond-white hair curling under his pristine hat.

Dust boiled up under the hooves of a dozen horses. Eli drew closer, the sheriff at his side with a company of men from town. She recognized Mr. Richards, the mercantile owner, as well as the blacksmith, hotel owner, telegraph man and several others. Not a rabble, but a group of respectable men from Silver Peaks.

Lenora's warning to Cole died in her throat as the men stopped fifteen feet before him. He would have no time to return to the safety of the house.

After the dust died down, Eli spoke to the sheriff. "That him?"

Leland Mackay nodded. "Yes. That's Cole."

"All right, men." Eli turned in his saddle. "You know what we're here for."

Cole seemed to assess the mob's intent in an instant. "I'm US Marshal Jesse Cole. And who're you?"

"Eli Hackett. And you killed my son." His upper teeth flashed as his lips tightened. "Around here, we string up murderers."

"Glad to hear it. Although you're six months late."

Eli frowned. "What?" He looked around as though the answer would be found in the men with him.

"You should've strung up your son six months ago after he murdered two men. Not only that, he robbed a Cheyenne bank."

"That's a lie."

"Is it? I have evidence to the contrary." Cole dug a crumpled bill from his pants pocket and held it up. "This newly minted five-dollar note had been delivered to that bank a day before the robbery. Most was taken. When Jeb was here recently, he gave this to Lenora. Proof that he was involved in the robbery. Or at least strong evidence. But I'll let a court of law decide that."

Eli drew himself up on his horse. "Irrelevant. You shot my son last night. He isn't going to make it through the day. Around here, that's murder. We're gonna make you pay."

"Since when are you the judge and executioner? Don't I get a trial?"

"We don't have time for this." Eli jerked his head in an arranged signal. "The law's the law."

A couple men moved forward.

"I'm a US marshal." Cole yanked his badge off his vest and held it up. "*I'm* the law here. Jeb Hackett and his men trespassed on Lenora's property."

"Don't you mean your property?" Eli snarled.

"They brought the fight here. Look at us. Look at Lenora and her son." Cole waved at them on the porch. "Since when do respectable, law-abiding men war on women and children? And on their own property? I'll tell you. They didn't want her testimony to prove that they were guilty of robbery and murder."

"She's just as guilty. Married to that lying thief Amos Pritchard."

Before Lenora could stop Toby, he jerked out of her hold. "My pa wasn't a thief."

Eli's lip curled. "Yes, he was."

Cole pinned his badge back on his shirt. "And how would you know that, Mr. Hackett, unless your son is too?"

A startled look crossed the older man's face.

"Listen to me. All of you." Cole's voice rang in the morning light. "As long as you don't stand up for what is right, men like Eli and Jeb Hackett will continue to steal what is most precious—starting with your souls. And when will it stop? Go ahead and lynch me. But my voice won't be the last you hear. Other lawmen will follow. And the price they exact will be nothing compared to what you're paying now by allowing this man to talk you into doing what is wrong. Don't you see what's happening? Already his brand of 'law' has seared your consciences."

With amazement, Lenora watched as indecision flowed like a river through the men. Sidelong glances passed between them. A couple backed their horses away from Eli.

His face purpled. "What are you doing? This man needs to pay for his crimes."

Instead of convincing them, Eli's words had the opposite effect. More pulled away. Some muttered excuses under their breath. Others merely departed without a word.

Eli's rant drove more away. In a matter of minutes, only he and the sheriff were left. Rage marring his face, he looked around as though in disbelief.

He turned to the sheriff. "Do something, Leland."

The lawman's shoulders hunched. "I—I can't, Eli. It's just us two against him. And you heard him. He's a US marshal."

"If you won't do something, I will." Eli reached for his rifle.

Cole drew his pistol, almost faster than Lenora could follow. However, a hollow click resounded in the hushed morning. Again, he pulled the trigger.

Eli let out a maniacal laugh and took careful aim at Cole. "You're a dead man, Marshal."

Without hesitation, Lenora lifted her rifle and squeezed the trigger.

With a scream, Eli flew backward, flailing for the saddle horn. As he righted himself, he clutched his arm.

Cole and the sheriff looked at her, expressions rippling with amazement.

None looked as surprised as Eli. Red blossomed across his shoulder and chest. "You shot me." He let out a string of curses.

Clutching the gun, Lenora met his glare. "Get off my land, Hackett." Her voice grew stronger. "Next time you—or any of your men—step foot on my property, I will shoot to kill."

The sheriff gaped at her a moment longer, then grabbed the reins of his companion's horse. "Let's get out of here."

Still shouting obscenities, Hackett allowed himself to be led away.

Cole remained standing in the yard, staring after them. The rifle clattered from Lenora's shaking hands. Only when Toby's arms slid about her did she realize she had burst into tears.

Lenora sat in what was left of her home, listening to the rhythmic shoveling that came from the backyard.

The soldiers had finally arrived from Fort Laramie. The first thing they had done was to tend to everyone's wounds, then they cleaned up her house. Now, a few men were digging up her husband's coffin. Even Toby had gone to watch.

Not her.

She remained seated, head lowered, bombarded again with the awful memories of *that* night.

"Take it," Amos rasped. In the dusk, his skin appeared ashen, a corner of his mouth crusted with dried blood.

After her husband's body had been found, Jeb Hackett

had made a big show of providing a proper burial for his friend. The undertaker had done his work in town, but Lenora hadn't gone to the viewing. Everyone apparently believed she couldn't bear the sight of her husband laid out in the beautiful coffin Jeb had purchased.

Not true. She did not need to view Amos's body because she had already seen death in his face.

The gravediggers had come to the ranch the next day and shoveled out a vast hole, but an impending blizzard had prevented them from burying Amos right away. In the middle of the night, Lenora had crawled into the pit and dug farther, deep enough to bury the satchel. She had pushed dirt over the money, confident that once Amos's coffin rested on it, no one would think to look there.

And no one had.

How foolish to believe that once the satchel was buried, she would be free from its temptation. *I am as guilty of keeping the money as Amos was in taking it.* She now realized that in the back of her mind she had trusted in it—a "just in case." And when things got rough, she had turned to it instead of God. Somehow she thought that the money—and even her own strength—could keep her and Toby safe.

The scripture that Cole had read on their wedding night came back to her. *"...only You, Lord, can make me dwell in safety."*

She could not guarantee her security. The money certainly could not. How stupid to trust in either.

"Dear Lord," she whispered, "forgive me..."

Humbled and repentant, she leaned forward to pray. In the quietness of her soul, she knew God forgave her, but what about Cole? Never would she forget the fierceness of his face and tone when he had verbally chastised her. She deserved the reprimand.

"Mrs. Cole?"

Lenora straightened and stared at the uniformed young man before her. Was he speaking to her? It took her a moment to realize *she* was Mrs. Cole. Still.

"Yes?" She smoothed back her hair.

"I wanted to tell you, ma'am, that we recovered the money." He touched his hat, almost like a salute.

"Thank you for letting me know."

Why was he smiling at her? Didn't he know she was a thief by association?

"The marshal told us what you did, ma'am." His face glowed. "That you'd hidden the money from the outlaws—to keep it safe. And that they'd tried to take it from you by force."

"You mean last night's shoot-out?"

"Yes, ma'am." Nothing but admiration beamed from his eyes.

Cole was covering for her? Apparently he had told them something that made it appear as though she was some sort of heroine. She rose and smoothed her apron.

"And I wanted to let you know that we'll put everything back the way it was. We're so sorry we had to disturb the graves." The young man was so sweet and seemed so young that she wanted to tousle his hair like she did Toby's.

Instead, she folded her hands. "You are all very kind. Thank you."

A brilliant smile broke out on his face. This time he did salute her and turn on his heel, military style, before marching away.

Lenora glanced around her home, again sighing. The officer in charge had insisted on leaving provisions since Cole would depart with the men. Not only that, they had reinforced the door and even nailed some fabric over the broken windows to keep out insects. Nothing could be done yet about the wall's chipped plaster or the destroyed items. All her beautiful bone china had been shattered in the gun battle.

But she could rejoice that *they* lived.

Cole had done what he'd promised—put an end to Jeb Hackett's reign of terror. Until he disbanded the gang, she knew he wouldn't rest.

Then he would move on, doing the great work that God had called him to do.

She prayed Cole would someday find it in his heart to forgive her for not revealing the truth about the money.

Bowing her head, she determined not to stand in the way of his noble task. "Give me the strength, Lord, to love him enough to let him go." She clasped her hands together. "No matter what happens, I trust in You for my future."

"Is this it, Marshal?" A uniformed man hoisted a satchel out of the deep hole.

Favoring his injured arm, Cole took only a moment to pry open the bag and peer inside. "Appears so. Good work."

While he had stood by, soldiers had dug up Amos Pritchard's grave, removed the coffin and uncovered the money.

Cole handed the bag to an officer. "Safeguard this until we can return it to Cheyenne."

"Yessir."

"Make sure you restore everything back here."

Without waiting, he limped toward the pasture to talk to the young man who skulked by the barn.

Toby fell into step beside him, not saying a word. Because he knew Cole was leaving?

Whistling for Nips, he grabbed his saddle off the ground. "Can I count on you to take care of Sheba and Rowdy while I'm away?"

The youngster nodded. When Cole said nothing more for a moment, he asked, "Are you really a marshal?"

"Yep."

"How come you didn't tell us?" His green eyes seemed to burn.

Cole took a deep breath before answering. "I had to keep it secret. At first. I planned to tell you the night of your birthday, but..."

"So you gotta leave?" Toby toed the grass. Because he wanted to hide his trembling chin?

"Yep."

"For how long?"

"Dunno." *That depends on Lenora.* With some awkwardness, he saddled and bridled his horse. The youngster helped since Cole favored his injured arm.

Out of the corner of his eye he watched Toby, who seemed ready to burst. "Did your ma talk to you? About the money?"

"Yeah." He rested his hand on the pinto's rump.

"And?"

His mouth worked a moment. "She told me it was wrong to bury the satchel. That she should've given it back right away."

Though Cole was pleased they'd had the conversation, he was puzzled by her declaring she could have returned the money—given the satchel's location and Hackett's watchful eye.

Toby threw his arms about him. "I don't want you to go." A suppressed sniff followed.

Cole patted his back. "You know I gotta finish this job. Make sure the money gets returned to its rightful place."

All the while he had chatted with the commander, he had been aware that Toby was nearby. Listening.

Though Cole had downplayed Lenora's wrongdoing, the youngster had no doubts about his father's part. And no matter how much Cole wanted to stay, the money was his responsibility.

Or was he running away because of his uncertainty about Lenora?

In the hours that had followed her confession about the money, a storm had beat upon his thoughts. She could have told him about it—a long time ago—that she knew where it was. But she hadn't. That lack of trust equated to a lack of love. Had he misunderstood all her tender gestures and soft glances? Had he merely imagined she had responded to his kiss?

Toby's shaky exhale drew his attention.

Cole put his hand on the youngster's shoulder. "I want you to take care of your ma for me. Can you do that?" He wanted to say so much more, but the tightness in his throat prevented him.

Mouth screwed with sorrow, Toby nodded.

Cole hesitated a moment, then held out his hand. With amazing composure, Toby shook it before turning and walking away.

As Cole surveyed the ranch, a peculiar shudder ran through him. As though he wouldn't see the place again. Something inside him tore, creating a wound that would never heal.

Returning to the house, he contemplated that the hardest task yet awaited.

Lenora stood inside the great room, back toward him as she seemed to study the chaos. For the longest time she didn't move. Had she truly not heard him stomp up the steps?

Cole spoke softly so he wouldn't frighten her. "Your home will probably never look as beautiful as when I first saw it."

Swiveling, she gasped as she pressed her hand against her breast.

"Didn't mean to scare you, ma'am." Funny how the first phrase he'd ever spoken to her seemed appropriate as he said his goodbyes.

"You'd think that after last night's shoot-out I'd be more alert."

"You should no longer have a reason to grab your rifle in fear." That was Cole's hope anyway. No Hackett would terrorize Lenora again.

She gulped as though seeking to speak in a normal tone. "Didn't you say that there would always be Hacketts in the world? No matter what, I need to learn to keep my gun nearby."

He stepped closer. "You shouldn't have to, Lenora. If I had my way..." He paused at the sound of stamping horses. Was the company of soldiers assembling already?

Her gaze strayed to the door. Because she too knew they had only minutes?

She straightened. "At least you've accomplished what you set out to do here." Her tone was matter-of-fact. Cool. "I'll forever be grateful for your help in getting the ranch back on its feet. With God's help, I feel confident I can make a go of this place."

I? Not we? The meaning blared with crystal clarity. Since Cole had done his duty, his services were no longer required.

He was about to speak when one of the soldiers came up the steps. "Begging your pardon, Marshal. The commander told me to inform you he is about ready to depart."

Out in the yard, bridles jingled and leather creaked.

"I'll be right there." After the soldier retreated, Cole turned back to her.

"Go. We'll be okay." She lifted her chin. "We'll be more than fine now."

Unable to believe his ears, he lingered. Had it all been a show on her part? As long as he had been useful, she had been kind. Now that he was no longer needed...dismissed.

So be it.

He squeezed the brim of his hat, prepared to march out of her life.

"Before you go…" She shoved one fist into the pocket of her apron. "I hope you can someday find it within yourself to forgive me."

What?

"For hiding the money." She rushed on as though he'd asked. "For not being brave enough to return it."

Was she worried he would betray her?

"You couldn't have." He sought to reassure her. "Not with Hackett watching your place night and day."

Her gaze again strayed to the door when a horse whinnied. "You'd better go. They're waiting."

It seemed they had nothing left to say to each other. In an instant, Cole decided to never return.

"I'm leaving Sheba and Rowdy." They would be the perfect birthday gift for Toby.

"Of course. This is still half your ranch. A bargain's a bargain."

With a jerk, he straightened. He managed to say in a cool voice, "Take care."

He was already down the stairs when her footsteps pattered behind him.

"Jesse."

It took him a moment to realize she was calling him. By his given name?

"Wait. Please." She fixed her gaze on him, hands clenched at her sides. Several times, she gulped air. "Thank you for all you've done for us. For *me*. I will never forget what you sacrificed. What you gave."

He stared up at her.

"I will love you as long as I live." Her beautiful lips trembled. "Even if I never see you again, I will never stop loving you."

Tears welled in her eyes as she appeared to struggle to keep from saying more. He opened his mouth, uncertain if he was about to speak or because he couldn't.

She loves me? And the next rapid-fire thought followed—*I can't leave.* The longing to hold her in his arms rushed on him with such force that he nearly staggered.

Behind him, a horse snorted and another pawed the ground in impatience. "Ten hut!" One of the soldiers called the company into order as the commander joined the group.

"Marshal Cole, we are ready to depart," someone called.

He glanced over his shoulder. "Yes. Thank you."

"Go." She nodded in encouragement, her voice again under control. "Finish what you came to do."

Finish...

Stark reality cooled the burgeoning recklessness that fired his heart. Cole *had* to finish the job he had promised to do—take down the Hackett gang. As long as one member roamed free, Lenora would not be safe. Cole had to ensure her future, even if he was never part of it.

Turning his back and walking away from her was the hardest thing he had ever done. As he mounted Nips, his gaze kept straying to her.

She lifted her hand in farewell while he gave one sharp

nod in acknowledgment. After moving to the front where the commander waited, Cole listened to the men fall into formation as they trod down the dusty road.

He couldn't help but cast multiple glances at the trio behind him—Blister barking his farewells, Toby smudging his tear-streaked face with the heel of one hand and Lenora stiffening with a calm, but grim semblance of a smile.

She loves me.

The wonder of that truth pounded in him with every clomp of his horse's hooves. Some day, Lord willing, he would return to her.

Turning in his saddle, he forced his thoughts to what lay ahead. After he returned the money to Cheyenne, he needed to hunt down the remaining members of the Hackett gang. If they were smart, they would have high-tailed it out of Wyoming Territory by now. Or holed up somewhere.

It didn't matter. For Lenora's sake, Cole would not rest until every one of them was dead or in jail. He wouldn't give up, even if...

The harsh truth stared him in the face. Cole clamped his teeth together so hard that his jaw hurt.

I won't give up, even if it takes the rest of my life.

Chapter Twenty-Three

"Tighten that rope," Lenora yelled when the calf threatened to break free. Though the heifer couldn't escape from the corral, she didn't relish the idea of chasing it. Like they had the last two.

Toby wrapped the rope around the saddle horn and wheeled Rowdy so that the line grew taut. He kept the bawling calf immobile long enough for her to brand it.

"Three down, fifteen to go," she muttered as she thought of the remaining cattle in the back pasture.

For several days, she and Toby had rounded up the unbranded stragglers. And late this morning, they began the task. Their routine was still inefficient, but they would have to improve if they hoped to make a go of the ranch. Before winter, Lenora planned to sell half the herd. Not just the steers. With God's help, she and Toby would be able to manage a smaller operation.

The sooner she learned to handle the difficult tasks, the better. Still, she couldn't help but remember how much easier this had been when Cole was there.

I can't think of him now.

In the two weeks since he had left, she had maintained a brave face during the day—for Toby's sake. But at night...

Would the ache for him ever lessen?

She squared her cramping shoulders. "Okay, let her up."

The heifer bolted to her feet. Breathing hard, Lenora leaned against the fence. The May sun sizzled down on them. She longed for her cool skirts, not these pants that seemed to hem in the heat. Maybe the early-morning hours would be better for this chore. Or evening. They'd started too late in the day.

After Toby opened the gate, he giggled as the calf scampered out, bucking in freedom. He climbed back onto his horse. "Ready for another one?"

He was good at roping, no doubt. And he liked to show off.

"No, I..." She pushed back the hat and swiped her forehead with her arm. "I think we're done for now."

"Aww." He made a disappointed face.

"Fine. You do the branding and I'll—" She broke off when Rowdy suddenly raised his head and whinnied, long and loud. His nostrils flared as his ears pointed toward the road. Even Blister, who had been snoozing in the shade, leaped up and stood at attention.

An answering neigh came from the distance.

After Lenora grabbed her rifle, she squinted and shielded her eyes. A lone rider came into view.

"It's Cole." Joy rang through Toby's voice. "Cole! Over here." He stood in the stirrups and waved his hat like crazy. Blister began barking in excitement.

The gun nearly dropped from her grip. Why was Cole here?

The next moment, she was scrubbing her hands on her pants and slapping dirt from her shirt.

He pulled up alongside the corral, gaze taking in everything before settling on her. How hard had he ridden? And from where? Nips's neck was wet with sweat. She could only stare while her son babbled nonstop. In less than a minute, it sounded as though he told Cole everything they'd done in the time he'd been gone.

"Good to see you, too." He grinned at Toby.

Lenora couldn't say a word, afraid that if she did, she would gush with questions like her son.

"Looks like you've quite the task." Cole nodded toward the cattle. "Mind if I help?"

A shiver ran through her. Hadn't he said those exact words when they'd first met?

Finally she found her tongue. "We just finished for the day."

"Y'sure?"

Her heart squeezed as he smiled and leaned his forearms on the saddle horn.

"I was—was about to make supper." She tried in vain to swallow the grit in her throat. "Do you have time to join us?"

As she waited for an answer, her heart felt like it sped up to an impossible speed.

"I'd like that." The dimple in his cheek showed. "Toby and I'll tidy up here while you head to the house. If you like."

She could only manage a nod before dashing from the corral.

First things first. In a frenzy, she scoured her face till it stung, then shook the dust from her hair. After peeling off dirty clothes, she slipped on a blouse and skirt. With shaking fingers she bound her hair with a ribbon.

Back in the kitchen, she discovered the stove was cold to the touch. Lenora shuffled pans, dropping a couple of them. What could she make? Nothing was ready. Not even coffee. She reached for the tin, but ended up knocking it from the shelf.

"Sounds like a tornado in here."

She wheeled at Cole's voice.

Leaning a hand on the doorjamb, he grinned. She was about to apologize for the lack of a decent meal when he strode in and dropped his saddlebags on a chair. With casual flair, he tossed his hat at the pegs by the door, chuckling when its landing stuck.

After she grabbed the coffee tin from the floor, she studied him. The gash on his cheek—the one she'd stitched—was well healed. Though his left arm seemed a bit stiff, he walked as though his injured ankle bothered him not a smidgen. His hair had been cut, and he'd had a close shave. Not only that, he wore a new shirt and pants.

"So what's the occasion?" She pointed to his clothing.

"I swore in the new sheriff of Silver Peaks this morning."

"Leland Mackay's gone?"

"Yep, as well as a few hangers-on. Seems the townsfolk are done with the Hacketts." He scratched his chin. "You know, they offered me the position first."

Of course Cole wouldn't take it. Becoming sheriff would only tie him down.

"So you stopped by the ranch…because you were in the area." She didn't ask, but spoke with mounting sadness. Her hope that he would stay faded. Did he only come to get his horses? Before moving on?

"I brought you something." Cole untied the flap on one of his saddlebags and retrieved a rectangular bundle, wrapped in paper.

"What's…?"

The question died when Cole unwrapped bills. Stacks of them. He arranged three neat piles on the table.

"Where'd you get all that money?"

"The Bank of Cheyenne." He raised one palm. "But I didn't rob it, if that's what you're wondering."

Why'd he bring it? Her heart sank at the obvious answer. He planned to pay her for his half of the ranch. After tying up this loose end, he would be free from all obligations to her.

She stared at the money. "That's way too much."

"It's only fifteen hundred dollars." He fingered the bills.

"Fifteen…?" She gaped. "This whole ranch isn't worth that much."

"What does the ranch…?" A frown wrinkled his forehead before understanding blossomed. "Ah. Seems we're talking at cross-purposes." He chuckled, mischief sparking in his eyes. "This ranch may not yet be worth this much, but it could be. Once we do some improvements."

"Improve…?" What was he talking about? "You know I can't afford that. As soon as I find buyers, I'm selling off half the cattle. Maybe more."

"No need to. We can manage what we have quite nicely."

More confused than ever, she pressed her fingertips to her temple. Her hand froze when she finally heard what he said. She gulped. "We?"

"Of course."

A squeak of disbelief escaped her. Her heart began to pound. "Aren't you just passing through? On your way… farther west?"

"Nope. My wandering days are done."

"But isn't that money for your half of the ranch?"

"I kinda forgot to explain." He tapped the bills. "This is your reward money."

She recoiled. "Reward? For what?"

"Not only for information leading to the arrest of the gang that robbed a Cheyenne bank, but the return of the bankroll." Cole fanned one bound stack of bills. "This is all yours."

"I don't deserve that." She backed away even more. "You of all people know I can't take one dollar."

"The bank disagrees. Since I knew you might decline, I accepted on your behalf." He set down the stack. "Before the US Marshals Service let me resign, they gave me two stipulations. Swear in the new sheriff and deliver the reward. Since those're done, I'm a free man."

She stared at him as he moved closer. "But—but what about hunting outlaws?"

"Not interested." His softened expression made her chest tighten. "After I formed a posse, we chased down the remainder of the Hackett gang. For the last two weeks, all I could think about was you. Returning to you as soon as I could."

"But you can't quit because of me. Stopping outlaws is your life's mission."

"Not anymore." He shook his head. "My only mission now is here."

She caught her breath, still unable to believe what he was saying.

"I want to be a father to Toby." He took her hands. "And a husband to you. If you'll have me."

His tender touch and gentle voice erased the last of her doubts.

"Oh, Jesse." She slipped her arms about his neck. His hands came around her waist, holding her so tightly she could barely breathe. But who needed air?

"That's the second time you've used my given name," he murmured.

"It is?" She pulled back to stare into his face.

"The first time, it proved to me that I was no longer just 'Cole' to you."

"When did I…?" Her mind remained blank.

"It was moments before you told me you loved me. Night and day, I haven't been able to get your words out of my mind. Or forget the look on your face. I came back for you, Lenora."

"Even after I tried to convince you to keep stolen money?" She balled her fists against his chest. "I'm an outlaw—worse than Amos."

"Not a problem." His blue eyes twinkled. "I know how to handle outlaws."

She smiled then, fingering the buttons on his shirt.

He cupped her jaw, stroking her cheek with his thumb. "I love you, Lenora Julia Cole. Will you let me be a true husband to you? And in more than just name?"

"Oh, Jesse," she breathed. "A thousand times, yes."

With that, he kissed her with a tenderness that made her heart quake. Again and again, his lips nuzzled hers. For a long time, he held her. But not nearly enough for a lifetime.

A creaking floorboard caught her ear.

Cole turned his head and chuckled. "You can come in now, Toby."

How long had her son been listening?

He stood in the doorway, a huge grin on his face. Blister sat beside him, his gaping mouth appearing to grin, as well.

Cole's grip tightened about her waist. "Is it okay that I kiss your ma?"

"Yessir." If possible, the young man's smile broadened.

"Good. 'Cause I plan to do it a lot. And I don't want you coming after me with your big ol' bowie knife."

Toby laughed, his voice cracking. His gaze flickered between them.

"C'mere, son." Cole held out one arm, beckoning for Toby to join them.

Once his arms came about them both, Cole tousled his hair.

"Do you know Toby prayed for you?" Lenora smoothed one hand over her husband's chest. "Long before you showed up on our ranch."

"I believe it." His face grew serious. "And since God brought me here, I'd be a fool not to stay."

"I'm glad the Lord answered Toby's prayers. And mine." When her voice broke, the two men she loved most in the world hugged her hard.

After her husband again sought her lips, Lenora kissed him back with all the love that sprang from a trusting heart.

* * * * *

*If you enjoyed THE MARSHAL'S MISSION, look for
RECLAIMING HIS PAST by Karen Kirst
A FAMILY FOR THE HOLIDAYS by Sherri Shackelford*

Dear Reader,

I hope you enjoyed reading *The Marshal's Mission* as much as I enjoyed writing it. I based this story on my great-grandfather's life—he was an undercover US Marshal. Then I found out that though he had been married to my great-grandmother, he wasn't directly related to me. What a woman—she outlived five husbands!

The West has always fascinated me. It was a pleasure to research the lives of the tough men and women who shaped our country.

I'd love to hear from you. Write to me at anna@anna zogg.com or PO Box 1642, West Jordan, UT 84088. Please visit my website at annazogg.com.

Anna

Get 2 Free Books,
Plus 2 Free Gifts—
just for trying the Reader Service!

Love Inspired HISTORICAL

Love Inspired HISTORICAL

*Elizabeth Dumont came to town to be a mail-order bride…
but arrived to find her would-be groom marrying someone
else! With nowhere to go, she's grateful for a temporary job
caring for foundling triplets, even if it means interacting
with her ex-sweetheart, pastor Brandon Stillwater.
But when Brandon offers a marriage of convenience that
will allow her to adopt the babies she's come to love, can
they let go of their painful past to build a future—and
a family—together?*

Read on for a sneak preview of
THE BRIDE'S MATCHMAKING TRIPLETS,
the sweetly satisfying conclusion of the series
**LONE STAR COWBOY LEAGUE:
MULTIPLE BLESSINGS.**

"What did you say?" she asked.

"I asked you to marry me. I can see that you genuinely
care for Jasper, Theo and Eli. Just as important, they care for
you. If we married, we could petition the Lone Star Cowboy
League to adopt them." His voice softened until she could
hear the yearning in it. "We could be a family."

A family. She could be mother to those three darling babies,
see them grow into the fine men she was sure they could be.
She could stay in Little Horn, deepen her friendships with
Louisa, Caroline, Fannie, Annie and Stella. She would finally
have a home to call her own. All she had to do was give up on
love. For he hadn't offered that.

She must have taken too long to answer, for his shoulders
slumped.

"Have I offended you?" he murmured, face so worn she
wanted to reach out and stroke the lines from beside his eyes.

"No, of course not." She brushed at her skirts, anything to keep her hands too busy to touch him. "It was very kind of you, Brandon, but we both know your heart wasn't in it."

His mouth quirked, more pain than smile now. "It seemed like the perfect plan for us both. I've come to care about the boys, but I'm not in a position to adopt them. And I was under the impression you wanted to stay in Little Horn."

She did. Outside her aunt's home, she had never felt so welcome anywhere, until those vicious rumors had started.

"And there are those rumors," he added as if he had heard her thoughts.

She fought a shiver. Rumors. Gossip. How easily they tainted a life. If people in Little Horn thought her of poor character, she might well find it impossible to secure a position in the area. And how would the people of Little Horn react if those rumors tarred their pastor with the same brush?

Heat flamed through her. "You're concerned about what people will say about us. You're worried for your reputation."

He colored. "My reputation will survive. I'm more concerned about yours."

She put her hands on her hips. "Oh, so now you agree that I'm some kind of fortune hunter?"

"No." He puffed out a breath. "Elizabeth, please. Consider my offer. You and the boys would have a secure home, a place in the community. I can protect you. But if marrying me is unthinkable, even under those terms, I'll understand."

David McKay had offered her a similar arrangement, and she'd accepted. But this was Brandon. Brandon, who had once claimed her heart.

Brandon, who had abandoned her when she needed him most.

Don't miss
THE BRIDE'S MATCHMAKING TRIPLETS
by Regina Scott, available June 2017 wherever
Love Inspired® Historical books and ebooks are sold.

www.LoveInspired.com

Turn your love of reading into rewards you'll love with
Harlequin My Rewards